DON'T MENTION THE MOON

Also by Richard Cohen

DOMESTIC TRANQUILITY

DON'T MENTION THE MOON

Richard Cohen

Seaview/Putnam
New York

Library of Congress Cataloging in Publication Data

Cohen, Richard, date.
  Don't mention the moon.

  I. Title.
PS3553.0426D65 1983   813'.54   82-19248
ISBN 0-399-31009-6

Printed in the United States of America

To Ann and John

CONTENTS

DON'T MENTION THE MOON

1. How I Found My Job

"Taste-tester for a manufacturer of artificial flavorings. Proofreader for the *Daily Racing Form.* Consumer hot-line operator for a maker of diapers and baby wipes. I suppose you meant to become a jack-of-all-trades?"

He fanned himself with my resumé and gave me a suave sneer. He was wondering how I could remain upright in my chair after receiving the sneer that had made him associate editor of a major magazine. But I wasn't undone, I kept my confident smile on, just the way they teach you in all those interview-preparation courses that thank God I had never sunk to taking. I wasn't fazed, because now that I'd seen him, a job under the associate editor wasn't quite what I wanted.

For two years, I'd been trying to find the first rung on my personal ladder in impersonal places. Any enticing but cryptic want ad could get me temporarily excited about doing my duty to the Gross National Product. "Okay, Rich," I'd say to myself, "time to become a responsible clotheshorse of society so Dad will finally say your name without shaking his head." I'd put on the brown corduroy suit I bought with his graduation check, and my forest-green tie with the little silver coats of arms that have turned tea-colored over the years. I'd leave on my rounds early, glad to feel like one of the morning marchers, with the breeze uncombing my hair and the newspaper blackening my fingers. I was alert with a sense of destination—should I use Sixth Avenue today or Fifth? Walking through midtown, I stood straight to look good for a thousand strangers. I recombed my hair in front of the slick black marble of

11

an office building lobby, and in the elevator I kept my chin aimed up at the inspection sticker, to impress any possible employers present. I entered the reception area and saw decoroso lighting and potted trees and haut-vinyl furniture, and around the bend a field of desks, with my contemporaries toiling and spinning. . . .

"I've got to give you a tryout," the associate editor said, "since Personnel sent you up here." Rereading my interview sheet, he shook his head.

The associate editor was a couple of years older than me. I was unshaven because I'd spent my blade money on a lottery ticket, as practice toward membership in the lottery-playing class. *He* was unshaven as a matter of style, to show that he was one of the fashionable late-nighters who are also dynamos in a meeting. He wore entrail-pink eyeglass frames with lenses eight times too big for his eyes. If his beige linen jacket could talk, its first words would have been "White wine." On his desk were dummy sheets of magazine articles, and on the frosted glass of his partition were magazine covers with a distinctive slanted typeface and a famous logo of an outstretched hand clutching a gold bar: "*Grab*—the Magazine for Successful People Only." I had bought the publication a few times myself, when I'd won a race or two at OTB and wanted to linger on a bench, eating a meatball hero among the secretaries and criminals in Bryant Park.

The job was simple. *Grab* gets hundreds of letters each week from readers asking advice, and can print only a few in its letters column, "The Grab Bag." For public relations' sake, they answer the remainder by personal letter. A coy little statement of this policy, at the top of the letters page, convinces millions of subscribers that *Grab* is a magazine that cares about them, and that *Grab*'s publisher would really love to see everyone on the highway drive the same brand of German sports car he does. A correspondent is kept on the staff solely to answer reader mail. His salary is a nominal— very nominal—promotional expense.

"Well, is there a chance for advancement?" I asked, because I knew you were supposed to ask that, and I wanted to act sincere enough to tell myself I had tried.

"We have a policy of in-house promotions," he said. "I didn't start at your desk myself . . ."

I knew he meant "For the correspondent's job we hire naïve or desperate people who'll either burn out or remain humbly content at the same job till it's time for their retirement party." But that didn't worry me. I figured that either I'd hate the job and leave fast or, if I liked it, I'd be the first "Grab Bag" correspondent to rise to editor-in-chief in six months.

So I said, "Sure, I'll answer the poor suckers' letters."

The associate editor was too success-conscious to say, "Go to the desk directly on the other side of my partition." He had to call in a secretary to escort me there. She wore the same style of glasses but one-upped her boss by having pink-tinted lenses. She gave me some letters to answer, and told me they were letters to answer; gave me a sheaf of *Grab* notepaper, and told me it was a sheaf of *Grab* notepaper; flicked on my electric typewriter, and told me that with my typing speed of seventy words per minute I wouldn't have much trouble typing out replies at the desired rate of ten per hour, including reading time.

The first letter in the stack said:

DEAR GRAB BAG,
 Recently I found evidence in my department head's checkbook that he is paying for treatment of a disease our company disapproves of. Naturally I don't want to add to his distress by openly humiliating him in front of our vice-president. It would be more tactful and display more managerial creativity if I took the vice-president's secretary to bed and told her the scandal while licking her ear. But there's a chance she's the source of the malady. How do you suggest I bounce-pass the info to the vice-president without hurting the secretary? And if I'm made the new department head, should I offer to pay for her blood test before our weekend in Aspen? Love your mag; keep bringing us those great "Climber of the Month" interviews.
                          Successfully yours,
                          BORN TO BE VEEP

The letter was hot, damp and lumpy. My palms were sweating onto the stationery, with the kind of awed admiration you might feel for an acrobatic trick performed by a member of another species. There are many kinds of talent in the world, but this guy had one of the rarest and most useful: the talent for getting other people fired. He was in the Midwest, but the shock waves of his great gift were shaking me out of my seat in New York.

It took me a minute and a half to write my reply.

DEAR BORN,

 Who are you kidding? Your letter came on company letterhead; the typing pool is already spreading the rumor and getting you your promotion. Meanwhile I'm staying in a friend's loft above a factory that makes cap visors, and when I went out this morning, I stepped over a derelict who was sleeping wrapped in a blanket of cardboard with rows of visor-shaped holes in it. What is most clear from your letter is that you want to go to bed with that secretary *because* you think she has V.D. Grab Bag recommends that you fulfill this desire as soon as possible and find out whether your info is correct. Whether your economic niche could be filled by someone with a healthy mind is a question for philosophers, not for popular magazines no matter how high-toned.

          Successfully yours,

I loved this work!

I was communicating with a human soul hundreds of miles away, with an honesty I might not show to a relative. Barriers had been broken. Staying within a preassigned format, I had said things the format had not been intended to contain. A man who would otherwise never have heard the truth had heard it. I had done a good job; now he alone had the choice of whether or not to reform.

"How are you doing?" the young woman asked as she came to collect my first product.

"Fine." I handed her the reply letter.

Five minutes later the associate editor came out from behind his partition and stared at me through fogged pink-framed glasses. He did nothing but stare at me for so long that I began to worry about his ability to cope—a quality he would need in order to maximize his career. At last he retreated behind his partition, where there was a phone to call Personnel on.

I knocked on his frosted-glass door and walked in. He opened his mouth to speak, but I beat him to it. I pointed my finger at him and said, "You're a young fool. You're throwing away your chance in life and you'll never get it back. You don't know what you're doing."

I left him there, amid paste-up sheets and grease-penciled photographs.

● ● ●

"The Voider Brush Company is only number two in this field," said the metropolitan sales manager, "so we have to try harder." He laughed and nodded as if he'd said something very original and clever. He picked up an olive-green sample case from the floor and shoved it toward me across his steel desk. From his shirt pocket he took a piece of paper folded into a square the size of his conscience. He gave me a "can I trust you?" look, and though he found the answer disappointing, he unfolded the paper because he had no choice. I felt sorry for people whose positions of authority, instead of freeing them, forced them to deal with people they didn't want to deal with.

He slid the paper across the desk, keeping his fingers on it to postpone relinquishing it. His voice quavered with superstitious zeal.

"On this sheet you will please find a list of the best customers of the Fuller Brush Company, which has been obtained by our Covert Operations Department after sustaining acceptable casualties. From now on you will carry burning in your heart our motto, in honor of these brave men: 'Beat Fuller!' You will knock on the door of a welfare mother with twins sucking at her breasts and seven larger children in the background fighting over a candy bar, and explain why it's more practical for her to spend her monthly check on our Deluxe Thoroughbred Currycomb than on giblets and collard

15

greens. You will persuade a blind woman that her bathroom décor will be severely jarring without our Pastel Rainbow hairbrush assortment. You will get the terminal cancer patient's signature for membership in our Brush of the Month Club. You will praise the child for stealing from her mother's purse to buy our All Grown Up cosmetic applicators. You will sell hairbrushes to the bald and shoe-polish kits to the double amputee. Every six months you will return to inform them that their old brushes have been superseded by new models." He stood up behind his desk, reached over, and grabbed my hair to shake me into enthusiasm. "Now go out there and sell brushes! You could use a good hairbrush yourself. Can I charge one to you at the employee discount?"

"No, thanks." I picked up the sample case and headed for the door.

"Probably have Fullers at home, you traitor," he shouted after me.

The Voider office was across the street from Penn Station; my sales territory was the Upper West Side. I was to start in a housing project in the no man's land south of Lincoln Center. A name and address had been circled in red on the spy document, with the notation "Zipporah Litovsky—a *very* good customer!"

Intent on comparing the address on my sheet with the numbers on the doorways, I bumped into someone and my sample case collided with another object. I saw a gray-faced kid maybe two years younger than me, with the messiest, sweatiest hair imaginable, wrinkled shiny black pants, a seersucker jacket that would fit him if he gained forty pounds and stood up straight, and a string tie with a steel clip in the shape of a guitar. He carried a sample case that looked exactly like mine, but brown.

"She's in that building." He pointed behind him. "Ground floor, to the right. She cleaned me out; I'm taking a week off."

He walked past, and I went where his finger had pointed.

I pressed a doorbell inlaid with the Hebrew letter *chai* in gold. The bell chimed the first six notes of "The Star-Spangled Banner." The door opened, but nobody appeared to have opened it—until I looked down to the level of my solar plexus and saw the top of Zipporah Litovsky's head.

She looked up and beamed at me as if I were the plastic surgeon of her dreams. Her face shone with the most pleasant expression possible on the face of the homeliest thirty-year-old woman on earth. Her eyes were the color of dirty carrots, and a purple scarf encircled her neck. Only her hair was attractive. Long and light brown, it grew straight back, catching the light as if it had been brushed a million strokes.

"Come in, there's tea brewing." She turned and retreated. I closed the door and followed her into a living room.

The room was filled with thousands of brushes.

Steel shelves lined all four walls. In the middle of the room, two oak bookcases stood parallel. At the sides of the bookcases were classroom chairs of pale laminated wood. A footstool with a ridged rubber top stood in one corner. High on one green wall was a round clock with a white face, plain black numerals and a red second hand. And taped to the front edges of the shelves were strips of paper with numbers like "600-670."

I walked along the wall shelves, fingering their contents. What memories this living room brought back! For two weeks one summer I had shelved books in my neighborhood branch library. The hours of standing behind the counter and seeing if I could read the notices on the bulletin board across the room; the days of trying to make small talk with a boss whose idea of a big-time hustle was to pocket people's overdue fines. The smell of old pages, cloth bindings, glue; the smell of the honorably minor mind between covers; the color of sunlight falling through an ocher shade and a smudged window onto oak tables spattered with magazines . . .

There was not a single book on Zipporah Litovsky's shelves, of course. They were crammed with brushes. The brushes were neatly stacked on their sides or backs, depending on their size. They were arranged by subject matter: hairbrushes and combs started in the 000s; household brooms, mops, dusters, in the 100s; artists' brushes in the 200s; a vast array of shoe brushes in the 300s. The bookcases in the middle of the room were filled with toothbrushes of every size, shape, material, color, and nationality, all brand-new in plastic cases leaning on metal brackets. Taped to the top strip of the bookcase was a white label that said: "Biography."

I turned to look at Zipporah. She was smiling as if she had no idea what impression she made on visitors.

Some people have the map of Ireland printed on their faces. On Zipporah Litovsky's face was the floor plan of the Bellevue Hospital psychiatric wing.

She stood on tiptoe, peeking down at my sample case from a shy distance. "What nice merchandise are you selling me? My husband'll kill me for buying so much brushes. But he's at work, he'll never know."

"May I have a glass of water?" I croaked.

"Not tea? Okay, there's some ice water in the fridge."

I took my sample case on a dash to the kitchen. On the kitchen counter, piled up to the cupboards, were rows of sponges wrapped in cellophane. I opened a cupboard: stacks of wrapped soaps and rows of unopened scouring-powder cans. Another cupboard: ranks of boxes of steel-wool pads, in mint condition except that the colors of the packages were fading.

I snubbed Zipporah's metal teapot, which sat on the unlit stove with two tea-bag strings hanging out. I opened her refrigerator. Standing on the top shelf, and lying flat on the lower shelves, were twenty-seven quart bottles with grapefruit-juice lids, filled with water, and one bottle half full of grapefruit juice. The refrigerator door was empty except for a little jar of vitamins, a little jar of capers, and half a lemon in Saran Wrap.

I had noticed a silver ring on Zipporah's finger, but I didn't believe she was married. A husband would not tolerate those refrigerator contents.

I seized a water bottle, and, as I'd hoped, it was real and solid and cold in my hand. Not bothering to search for a glass, I twisted the cap off and drank down a pint. My hand and gullet, at least, were freezing their way back to the real world.

When I returned to the living room, Zipporah was pulling dollar bills from her purse one after another. Her face was bent within sniffing distance of the purse as she drew out clothy old bills. With her elbows at her sides, she held up a hunk of money and did a shimmy, jiggling and giggling. "I know I'm a bad girl," she sing-songed, "but I can't resist temptation."

I took a step forward, spellbound by the money. My knees shook when I thought of what a sucker I had been presented with, how easily I could hurt her and make her like it, as if I were a car company or a food-additive manufacturer. I took another step forward—and my hands opened, and the sample case dropped to the floor. It fell onto its side, the latch opened, and brushes—I have no idea what kind were in my case, I had never examined it—raced over themselves like refugees in their haste to touch the carpet of their great protector.

I ran out the door, but I know that when Zipporah picked up the brushes she felt awful that she hadn't paid me.

My only regret was that I hadn't seen how her bedroom and bathroom were stocked.

• • •

The way I sank onto the stool and grabbed the counter for support, the owners of the Greek coffee shop must have worried I was going to collapse on their premises and sue. Before the waiter had budged from the far end of the counter (he was doing a ventriloquist act for the waitress, flapping the styrofoam lid of a take-out coffee cup up and down) I was shouting out an order for a grilled cheese sandwich and a seltzer.

"And a tuna sandwich," I added. "And a jelly donut . . . and a tossed salad . . . and a jelly donut, did I already say that? And tea with lemon," I finished, in Zipporah's honor. I hoped my abrupt departure hadn't offended her. I ordered more than I could eat and almost more than I could pay for, simply because I had to speak, touch, chew, I had to participate in a sane exchange of money for goods. Three plates, a bowl, a glass, and a cup and saucer arrived at my counter space. Seltzer bubbles tweaked my eye.

"I'll never make it in this town," I said out loud, blinking, and

19

seeing myself in the mirror behind the counter. A pot of clear water and one of coffee steamed on the two burners. Above, in black magic marker, a row of signs listed the prices of Greek specialties. Should I become a counterman? Would I reach that point someday? Flip those burgers all day long, pick up dimes as you wipe the counter with a wet rag. A liberal-arts education is a wonderful asset.

"Maybe I should leave town, break the umbilical cord. Work on a ship or a farm, or drive a truck. If I stay around here I'll end up doing messenger work."

The front door of the coffee shop opened and a man came in. He was short and tan, with curly blown-dry black hair, and he wore a white polyester suit with blue piping. He wore the collar of his white shirt outside his jacket collar, like an Israeli, or a swinging single, or an Israeli swinging single. He sat down two stools away on my left.

"Messenger work is the pits, I know," he said.

Over the next approximately five seconds, I took a bite of tuna salad, a gulp of tea, a bite of grilled cheese, a sip of seltzer, a bite of jelly donut, and another gulp of tea. "What—is this place miked?" He'd been outside when I was talking.

"I'm here to offer you a job," he said, with a slight foreign accent.

I would have asked him, "How do you know I want a job?" But if he was psychic, he was inaccurately so, for I no longer wanted one, at least not today. I just wanted to eat coffee-shop food, pay the bill, and walk back to my friend's loft in Chelsea. Nevertheless a sense of economic and filial duty made me ask what the job was.

"Being and watching," he said.

I picked up the tuna sandwich and tried to concentrate on finishing it. I thought, Is he armed? Will the waiter help me restrain him if he pulls a gun?

"Your job is to exist as a free human being, unbound to any regimen; just to watch the world. Watch the people, the pigeons, the sunlight on Park Avenue—whatever you come across. See and enjoy. Your job, unlike everyone else's, is *not* to be a ventriloquist's

20

dummy. Do only what you want, speak only for your own interests. Be as idle as you please, and join any activity you like. Getting up any hour of the morning you want to, lingering to follow through a thought, strolling half the city to find the right sandwich—from now on, consider that your occupation."

It did occur to me that he was telling the truth. But if he was, I *especially* wanted to protest my recent experiences. "Being and watching. Very nice, that's what I always wanted to do." I stood up, and picked up the check that the waiter had slipped under my saucer. The big talker next to me didn't offer to pay my bill.

"The pay's good," he said, "but it comes sporadically and unpredictably."

I walked toward the exit. I noticed that there were four red vinyl booths with wooden backs on each side of the aisle. A forty-year-old red-haired man was talking to a brunette with pierced ears in a booth on my right; a poster of Crete hung on the wall, and an empty bottle of retsina, mantled with white candle drippings, stood in a wall nook.

"So are you taking the job?" he called.

"Yeah, sure." I pushed open the glass door and walked out. I had decided not to look back, but at the last moment I did, and saw him pull a folded cardboard menu from between the steel tongs of its holder.

Thank God for sarcasm! I'm not the type to have refused him with a point-blank curse. I had said, "Yeah, sure," and it occurred to me that if he wanted to be literal-minded he could consider that an acceptance. And I was already fulfilling the job duties—I had no choice. If I had seriously accepted his offer, I would be walking down the same street in the same way; in fact, I'd probably feel more constrained about it. By not believing him, I was free to do whatever I liked—which was exactly what he wanted.

I'm already doing it, I said to myself.

Stop! Don't fall for a lunatic's con game!

But how was I supposed to stop being and watching?

If I had been a religious believer, I probably would have considered the guy a heretic. But having been raised without faith, I've

21

always been willing to entertain any possibility; and I don't mind that prophets usually seem like nuts.

I walked down Ninth Avenue under sunlight. It was early June, and my corduroy suit hung heavy. The sidewalk was narrowed by the awnings and boxes outside food stores. Gray-eyed carp and bass and bluefish lay on beds of ice in crates. Mangoes, papayas, watermelons with one specimen split down the red middle, cantaloupes, boxes of berries, heaps of greens tied with red rubber bands, frying peppers curled like witches' fingers—these were the Korean and Portuguese and Italian markets. I passed Filipino markets with crusted dried fish in the windows; a rib-and-fish luncheonette that smelled like fried oysters; a storefront theater with a yellow-and-black poster in the window; a café where two paunchy Italians sat wearing straw fedoras with blue bands, gripping tiny coffee cups in fat hands; and I walked under an elevated road leading to the huge bus terminal. I looked at every face and had time to see it.

An ambulance flashed and sirened, and plowed through the avenue. The cars in front of it inched aside; a taxi swung into the cleared lane behind it, and sped through the street in its wake. Garbage men in dark-green tee shirts, their groaning truck blocking one lane, paused to look at the ambulance before picking up and swinging their shiny baskets. I heard roller-skate wheels behind me. I turned, and felt the wind when a tall black man with red knee pads swerved around me, shouting, "Go, medics!" A dog wailed as if the siren had burst his eardrums. A radio gave the stock market report undeterred: "On the most active list today . . ." A silver-haired teenager in little black shorts moved her lips at a man in a dark-blue suit, and at a distance it sounded like "Honey, honey."

The air smelled of bus fumes, incinerator smoke, rotten vegetables and fruit, human sweat, chewing gum, the river, garage dampness, cooking, pastry baking, dry cleaners' solvent, brick dust from an empty lot, wood and poster paste from a fence, dog shit, newspaper ink, cigars—and underneath all of it was the smell of air. Under all that, I smelled a current of air as pure as in the Rockies, blowing in from the water and down from the sky. It hadn't been destroyed, it was only harder to sense.

22

I felt my heels and soles hit the pavement in sequence and lift off it in sequence with each step. My toes curled and splayed inside their shoes; the arches and balls flexed and stretched; the nylon socks wrapped my skin and leg hairs tight and itchy. My heart sped when I walked and slowed when I stopped at corners; my face muscles changed when my eye met other eyes.

While all this was going on, I thought, Being and watching, being and watching, being and watching, being and watching, being and watching . . . And another part of my brain was wondering how everything could look so much better than before when everything looked exactly the same as before. And another part of my brain was marveling at how many parts of my brain were working at once. And another part of my brain was repeating that famous sentence, repeated so often in the past by certain older relatives of mine, "Rich, don't be a fool, Rich, don't be a fool, Rich, don't be a fool. . . ."

At Thirty-fourth Street I looked up to the second floor above a doughnut shop, and in a green window a shade darker than a garbage man's tee shirt I saw a sign: "Employment Service—Domestic and Overseas Jobs Available All Kinds—Hotels, Resorts, Restaurants, Laundry, Transportation, Ships—Waiters, Busboys, Drivers, Laborers—We Place Thousands Every Year—Union and Non-Union Jobs Available—Up One Flight to the Job of Your Life." The shadow of a building cut the green window diagonally.

I stopped, put my hands into my pockets, and read the sign over and over. A brown door with a small chicken-wired window led to a staircase which led to the employment office.

I felt as if someone was pushing me in the back—pushing me toward the door. I wanted to run upstairs and sign myself onto the raunchiest freighter or into the vulgarest Catskill hotel—anything to escape my responsibility.

How could I fulfill this assignment, how could I survive? Then I told myself, the guy in the restaurant didn't look starving, did he?

I had a hundred-dollar bill, crisis money, rolled into an empty fountain pen in my inside jacket pocket. Hadn't I always dreamed of breaking into that bill? What good was it doing me, rolled inside a fountain pen? Who had misled me into thinking that a crisis was something bad?

The light turned green. All the way to my friend's loft, I didn't hit a single red one.

2. How I Lost My Vocation

One of my eyes is my own; the other my parents bought for me.

That reminds me, I haven't really introduced myself yet. I'm naturally polite, but I'm always forgetting the formal courtesies, because of my upbringing. I was raised in the middle class, but my father was the first one in his lineage to go to a university, or to speak English as a child, and I will now do my impression of my parents trying to teach me etiquette:

Pater: "Hey! Pipsqueak! What are you standing up for?"

Mater: "What's the matter with you, can't you see he's leaving the table?"

Pater: "I see he's leaving the table. I'd like to know where the fuck he got the idea he can leave the table without asking to be excused."

Mater (on a rising note of ridicule): "Asking to be excused! What is this, *Father Knows Best?* Is this another one of your dictatorial whims?"

Pater (stubbornly insisting on being ridiculous): "Father does know best. I've worked my ass off to give this brat advantages; the least he can do is ask—"

Me: "May I be excused?"

Pater: "You goddamn well may not! We're talking about *you*, sonny, and you'll stay in that fucking chair—"

Mater: "What a mouth!"

Pater (scowling and folding his arms, Iagolike): "All right, I won't say another word. Let his mother teach him manners."

Mother (to me): "If you want to leave, leave. No one's stopping you."

Me: "I realize I ought to learn some manners, you know, but I don't know if this is the right way—"

Pater: "Don't you tell me what the right way is! We teach you, sonny, you don't teach us. Get the fuck out of this dining room if you don't like it."

Me: "Okay, but first—*may* I be excused?"

Pater: "Make fun of me, you little stinker, I'll make it so you won't need orthodontia."

My brother Joe: "Don't pay any attention to him, Dad."

Mater (to me): "Go, go. Why do you always have to get your father angry?"

On better days we wouldn't say anything at all; we'd just sneak off from the table one by one. Even my mother would leave the table before realizing she had to go right back and clear away the dishes. The first time I ever slept at a girl friend's house—the summer after freshman year—her mother said, "Good morning" to me at breakfast, and I assumed she was parodying a TV mother in order to tease and shame me. To this day, when someone greets me with "How are you?" instead of "Hi" or "Yo, what's happening?" I feel the confused, uncouth gratitude and irritation that a peasant feels when the lord of the manor trots by the field to chat about crops. You're asking "How are you?" of a person who was raised to tell new acquaintances that his sinuses are clogged or that a blister on his right heel is hurting his every step. I've learned by now not to say that sort of thing—it only took me two lost chances at intercourse—so when someone asks, "How are you?" I now smile and say, "Fine."

So—that introduction already—my name is Rich Redstone, I'm twenty-three years old, I'm six feet tall but only a hundred and fifty pounds, the bones stick out of my wrists and sometimes jab women when I'm only trying to drape an arm around them, I have very black hair and very pale skin and hazel eyes that are mostly light green, as pretty as the sky on some other planet. My hazel coloring was my mother's greatest delight for a long time—my poor mother. There's a little more green in my right eye, which is made of protoplasm. My left eye is made of glass, and it's a tiny bit browner, as

26

if the people in the optical factory thought a duller shade of hazel would be more real. No one can notice this difference unless I've told them or have let them come within kissing distance. It makes excellent seductive conversation, I assure you, and the occasional person who is squeamishly repelled isn't for me anyway.

How I lost my eye is, it was July Fourth, 1974—I was thirteen—and I went up to the parapeted roof of a Tudor-style apartment building to shoot fireworks with my friends, and my friend Sterling—Sterling Silverstein—kept trying to light the fuse of a six-inch rocket, but it wouldn't light, not because there was anything wrong with the fuse but because, in fact, that fuse had too much self-respect to allow itself to be lit by a klutz like Sterling. And I told Sterling this, vehemently, as I shoved him away from the launching area, squatted down for the book of matches, lit the fuse—I think I was still explaining to Sterling about the high standards of this very snobby and exclusive rocket, when I caught the rocket with my left eye. Luckily Sterling was not too much of a klutz to know how to get me to the emergency room.

Somewhere in their hearts my parents were excited and entertained by my accident; I could tell by the self-blaming way my mother shrieked and the uncharacteristically stoical way my father flared his nostrils. Summoning them to the hospital in pajamas they could just as well have changed out of, I had given them a priceless opportunity to act. My mother did want to go on the stage, back in the fifties, and spent a summer performing *South Pacific* at a Pocono resort with a leading man who actually went on to Broadway and Hollywood. (She made my father see every show he was in, and every movie twice.)

My parents raised me to be a boy. They praised me whenever I did anything athletic, rambunctious, or bossy, and they pretended that because I was smart I didn't have to try in school. That manly attitude was, I think, my father's main acquisition from the war in Korea, where his rank was master typist or steno sergeant first class—I forget exactly which. My father always told me I'd be a lawyer like him, but he never taught me anything that would steer me into law school. He never brought a law book home from his office to show me, though he did for Joe, and I never asked him what a lawyer did or how you became one. For a while, we both assumed I'd become one because I was his son and rambunctiously male. I figured that since I was doomed to be a lawyer anyway I might as well stay away from all scholarly activity until the awful time came.

Joe is Dad's partner now—they do real estate and wills and divorces in Queens, where they all still live—and when I was in college the two of them never stopped telling me that if I tried I could get into an Ivy League law school and do great and surpass them. I got the feeling they hoped I wouldn't do it. Fine, I *didn't* want to do it, and the only thing I disliked about ducking it was that I'd fulfilled their most secret hope.

When I lost my eye, it soured me on the schoolboy life of thoughtless roughhousing, and made me realize I had gifts—like my brain—which I could lose before I knew enough to try to keep them. But at thirteen, fourteen, fifteen, there's a limit to how sensible you're going to be. My new wisdom didn't prevent me from popping my eye out for the class's amusement when things got especially torpid in chemistry. And my strategy for developing my brain—since studying was taboo—was to lie around listening to rock 'n' roll and reading science fiction. With pathetic slowness I found my inner resources, while my parents knocked on my bedroom door asking permission to come in and yell at me.

You can function fine with one eye, and it's easy to pretend that the loss doesn't bother me. Most of the time I'm jaunty about it, and during one phase I made a habit of prowling through the girls' wing of my dorm at night wearing a black eye patch. Imagine the effect on young women who knew me by day as a normal tall, skinny guy taking notes in anthro class, and discovered me at night to be a very friendly variety of pirate. But being a cyclops does get me down at times. It's the first thing I think about every morning, when I rub ointment inside my empty eyelids and then pop the eye in after its overnight rest. (The patch is only for effect and decorum; I don't wear it when I'm sleeping alone.) In order not to be bitter, I tell myself I'm superior to people with two eyes who see less in the world than I do. The whole situation has brought out the brooding and profoundistic side of me which was completely hidden for my first thirteen years. Come to think of it, for the first couple of months after the accident I was really in shock, and didn't want to speak to anyone except Sterling. That was the first of several interludes of not knowing what to do with myself.

I went to the State University at Paumanok, majored in English because it was the lazy man's choice—and, to my shock, got interested in reading good books. Bang! I decided to become a professor of literature. Not because I "loved literature" like some sort of feeb, but because books were apparently among the few sensible things the human race had produced, and it would be sensible to get paid for enjoying them.

Most of my teachers *were* feebs, but one guy inspired me—Professor Jon-Paul Blatt. I wanted to become him, but taller. He was forty years old, but he dressed like a student, in jeans and plaid shirts, and he always wore a long, long buckskin vest with six-inch fringes. He was only five-four, so the tails of the vest swung low against his pants legs, exciting the female students when he stood with his toes wiggling over the edge of the auditorium stage, flinging his arms and rising on the balls of his feet to shout things like "Myth of death and rebirth!" at the back rows. I planned to get up on the same platform someday with an equivalent gimmick— maybe a cowboy hat or, if I felt shameless, my eye patch. Anything to get them to like reading.

Blatt was the most enthusiastic teacher on campus; his course in American novels was always one of the first to close. His voice altered the force of gravity in his classroom: you grew light, you fully expected the auditorium to float upward to a heaven of well-coordinated metaphors and consistent symbolic themes. After the hour, his students didn't stroll away from class—they floated, like balloons filled with Blatt-helium, breezing in groups of two or three, in blue or red or green goose-down jackets, over the heads of econ. and soc. majors. Blatt's fame was proof that literature worked: anything that could transform that gnome (we could all imagine what kind of misfit he'd been as a child) into a charismatic sex symbol, with a forthcoming series on public TV, was self-evidently magical.

One evening I sat down with my classmate Lois in a campus bar, a few hours after we'd been through the love bath of Blatt's lecture on *The Sound and the Fury*. It was traditionally the consummating lecture of the term: his best performance, and the last class before exams. The excitement in two hundred racing, leaking, scratching, finger-staining pens when Blatt preached Faulkner! *The Sound and the Fury* was the great American novel, he cried, waving a paperback copy of it that flapped open to the beat of his words, showing marginal notes in three colors to the kids in the front rows. The technical audacity of Faulkner—Blatt bounced on tiptoe as we wondered whether he would fall off the edge of the stage; the borrowing that becomes originality—Blatt's long hair fell into his eyes when he got really worked up; the microscopic description of an idiot's thoughts—Blatt's buckskin fringes flapped like hawks' wings; the profoundly patriarchal "metaphaw" of Time—Blatt's voice was high and nasal and he couldn't pronounce *r* . . .

Hours later, we were still catching our breaths as we sipped beer from steins with two-inch bottoms, and our feet slid searching for each other on the sawdust under the booth.

"What a teacher," I said to Lois.

She was a thrust-jawed, thin, blond book-worshiper who gnashed her teeth from side to side when she talked. "His perceptions are so acute," she said, touching my shoe with her shoe. "His phrasing is so cogent." Her fingertips kissed mine.

"I intend to become a literature professor." I stretched my legs toward hers. "I don't care how bad the economy is: I'll make it. But I wonder where he got that vest."

"Ask him; he's always open to students," she said, in the kind of hush in which she might have said, "Ask the Wizard." The arch of her foot climbed onto my instep. "I talked to him in his office—it's like getting a private lecture." Her shoulders shuddered with delighted memory. She leaned forward and took my wrist. With one finger I stroked the sinews on the back of her hairless hand.

"I'm not as fast a talker as he is," I said. "So I'll have to work very hard on some of the other skills of teaching." I looked into her bright-blue contact lenses. "Like—"

Suddenly she gave a little gasp and covered her mouth with her hand. "That's him behind you," she whispered.

I turned left, toward my blind spot, and a vision struck my eye. Diagonally behind me and across the aisle I saw the leather-vested back of someone short sitting on a barstool. An arm waved upward; brown fringes surfaced and fell like flying fish. We couldn't make out his words, but the tones of his voice made us feel the way a child feels when it hears its parents' voices from his bed and knows they're home.

"Let's go say hello," I said. "I want to thank him for what he's taught me."

Lois nodded so hard I worried her teeth might unclench—a groundless worry. She stood, and took my hands in hers. Her contacts wiggled on her eyes in excitement. "Do it. Express what you feel."

I wanted to kiss her on the rat bite. But I knew she would hold out for a few more hours of socializing, and in the meantime I felt uplifted, ennobled . . .

We approached. Blatt's copy of *The Sound and the Fury* was on the bar—you could tell his copy anywhere, so worn it looked about to fall apart, but indestructibly bound together by insights. I got misty just looking at the yellowing white cover with blue letters. Good old Blatt, I thought. He picked the book up. He thumb-riffled it from back to front like a deck of cards.

"I hate this fucking book," he said.

I staggered backward. I clutched Lois' hand as if we were children marooned on a desert island. And the rest of the customers laughed at Blatt.

He was drinking beer straight from a pitcher, and I'm sure that that pitcher wasn't his first. It was a quarter full, and lined with what an English professor might call an "intricate web" of foam. He picked it up, guzzled the dregs from the spout, and in midgulp dropped the pitcher onto the bar.

"That pulp imitation Joyce," he said, as if blaming Faulkner for

31

making the pitcher slip. He opened the book. "Listen to this prose: 'The day dawned bleak and chill.' Let me tell you, the great American novel will not feature pulpily portentous weather reports. And if you believe that swill about Quentin killing himself because of incestuous desires, there's a nice bridge in Brooklyn I'd like to sell you."

He swept the paperback off the bar, onto the floor; and when I picked it up, he laughed in my face and said, "One of my student missionaries! Devoted to the holy trinity of Faulkner, Fitzgerald and Hemingway—the Three Stooges of American literature, with Hemingway as Moe."

People from the other end of the bar came closer to hear him. They were all students; half of them must have taken his course; some might have been closed out of it and borne him a grudge; all of them had heard of him, and now they laughed in a crowd around him, to hear him disgrace himself. He was giving an anti-lecture, a literary satanic mass; and I held the old brown-edged, marked-up, yellowing copy of the book, my hands sweating with dismay, while he slandered great writers.

"Beware of Hank James, the Beacon Hill Counterfeiter, on the Most Wanted list for passing imitation hundred-dollar truths. And Conrad the Hypnotist—guaranteed to induce sleep in even the toughest cases. If you can find a single credible incident in 'The Secret Sharer,' I'll buy drinks for everyone here."

Everyone in the bar cheered, except us.

"Brethren!" He lifted his arms, with fringes flapping. "Literature is just TV for smart people!"

"That's not true!" I said. "You showed us how literature is a whole different way of seeing the world—"

"Brethren, what say ye to that?"

People booed, called me a wimp, and laughed in their drinks; and I held *The Sound and the Fury* tighter so I wouldn't attack Blatt by the throat and get myself expelled. I hated him for ruining himself, for being so reckless with his own honor.

"Student missionary," he said to me, "if you think you can learn anything about life from books, you ought to be locked up in the library compiling a critical bibliography of *Pilgrim's Progress* for your own protection."

I was becoming the butt of the joke for the whole bar. But that didn't bother me at all; I didn't care what those people thought of me. All I cared about was what I thought of Jon-Paul Blatt, my hero.

"Brethren, I want to testify in front of you all," he said, "and for this poor deluded soul's benefit, that when a teacher tells you a piece of literature contains *ideas*, he's lying to you. The ideas writers put into books are only to make the story go. And when a tweedy English professor tells you that fiction is more important than football, he's just trying to get more money for his department. Sports is recreation for the body, and literature is recreation for the brain. And when he talks about the *tools* of criticism or the *techniques* of analysis, he's just trying to compete with the science departments for budget allocations."

"Okay, everybody has to gripe about his job," I said. I put the book on the bar again. He swept it onto the floor again, and almost fell himself. I didn't pick it up this time.

"Brethren!" he said. "Imagine Henry James and Ernest Hemingway in bed. They are direct opposites in style and subject matter; together they make one whole human being. Henry would be the perfect wife for Ernest, except that he's afraid of guns. Henry says, 'Ernest darling, do you think that someday we will be held up as models of greatness by that penetrating critic Jon-Paul Blatt? He's such a—' "

"Such a prick," I said, loud.

And Blatt said, "Well, now you've learned the real lesson of my course." He lurched away from the barstool, staggered toward me and grabbed my shoulders for support. Part of me wanted to jerk away so he'd fall. But I stood very still, so he'd get a better grip; and I held his arm steady. I touched those legendary brown buckskin fringes; man, what an honor it would once have been.

"That's the lesson of my course." He did a left-face to re-address the patrons, and I took a little step to keep supporting him. "You see the noble results of a life devoted to the pursuit of beauty and the study of man's finest words. What's your name?" he asked me.

"Redstone."

"Redstone, you're the only person in my class who has shown evidence of learning my deepest lesson. I'm giving you an A."

"I don't want your motherfucking A, Professor. I've already got an A average on your papers, but you can shove it."

Someone cheered me! It felt so good, I could feel the temptation of becoming a glibby like Blatt and enthralling an audience of kids.

Then Lois came up behind me, took me around in a side hug, and whispered in my ear, "You're brilliant! Now he won't dare give you lower than an A."

I shook my head and stamped my foot like a child, I was so frustrated. "Lois, let's get out of here."

"Not till I get my turn," she said; and she followed her chin to the barstool on which Blatt was once again leaning. "Professor, you've touched upon some seminal insights in this discussion. You're speaking to the concept of the heart of darkness, which both Faulkner and Conrad knew so well; but, not content with merely analyzing it for us, you've raised your analysis itself to the level of drama. The lecture as catharsis—returning to the origins of Greek tragedy as a religious rite containing moral instruction. The idea resonates; it could provide a hueristic framework for the justification of criticism as art." She put her hand on his, ostensibly to balance him against the bar. With her other hand she touched his elbow, and stopped him from falling sideways like an umbrella. "I'd really like to talk to you about it sometime when you're free. I see possibilities for a colloquium, or a bag lunch . . ."

Blatt gave a very loud, bull-moose snort, to show how much of a stud he was by how much snot he could clear from his nose at once. He straightened up and placed his hand on Lois' so that three of their hands made a Lois-on-Blatt sandwich.

I took her by the waist and whispered in her ear, "This guy is really lecherous, isn't he?" But she didn't turn around and look at

34

me. I was getting nervous about her. She and Blatt were looking into each other's eyes.

"Buy you a beer," he told her.

Then I did something I had no right to do. I pulled her away, said, "Not while I'm here, you won't!" and started dragging her toward the door. "If you want to talk critical bullshit in bed with someone," I told her, "you can do it with me.".

I had just guaranteed, of course, that she wouldn't go to bed with me. But I'd also made her ashamed to hang around and sleep with Blatt, so it was worth it. I liked her, and I even admired the way she could talk jargon. I couldn't, and I worried about how it would hurt my academic career. But Lois loved words like "heuristic" and "seminal," and she would do anything to ensure a career of using them. I myself am a different kind of fool, and even though I'm usually all-accepting I tend to push people when I think it'll be good for them. It loses me jobs and friends. But I thought Lois could become a good scholar if she stayed away from us library rats.

Because she wanted me to, I succeeded in getting her out of the bar. As soon as I'd brought her safely to the sidewalk, she lashed into me with the haughtiness of a true intellectual.

"You men really know how to protect your turf. If a woman tries to compete with you, pick her up and toss her out. I'm sorry I had to use the despicable weapons of seduction, but I wanted Professor Blatt to know *me*, too, and you had no right to stop me just because you felt bested."

"Sorry." I was laughing. "Sorry, sorry, sorry!" I lifted my hands and laughed, digging my own grave. I liked her enthusiasm extremely much. She was so fine, it was almost an honor to apologize to her. When she walked away from me, I smiled to see the forcefulness in her angry stride, in khaki slacks and cordovan loafers, with her blue blazer swinging like a professor's training uniform, and blond hair bouncing away from me in time with my heartbeat. Not only did she never speak to me again, but she told one or two of her friends to avoid me, too. I became a statistic of sexism.

35

In Blatt's course I never wrote the final paper. I'd been planning a stylistic comparison of Hemingway, Fitzgerald and Faulkner, but when I tried to come up with a first sentence this is what it was:

"Moe, Larry, and Curly all wrote words, but Curly wrote longer ones because he spent a long time sipping his bourbon, and Moe wrote short ones because he had to keep going to the bathroom to piss out the wine."

And I wasn't even drunk when I wrote that. I perversely told myself I was trying to please the teacher.

I got an "Incomplete" in the course and ruined my chances of getting into a good grad school. I stopped hanging around the English department, for fear I'd see Blatt. I didn't even want to see his name on his office door.

3. The Shock of Recognition

And that, more or less, is how I got to be walking down Ninth, Eighth, Seventh and Sixth Avenues on a sunny June afternoon, planning what to do with the hundred-dollar bill rolled into my fountain pen. I've left out a few of my other spiritual crises, like the summer I started loading parcels onto trucks but came down with mononucleosis after a week. The real name of the illness was misemployment. I know very few people who are completely free of it. It hits the person who wants to be a movie cameraman but spends ten hours a day driving a cab; the one who wants to edit a fine magazine but ends up laying out photos for a journal of the pet-food industry; the one who *does* work for the fine magazine but can't afford to rent an apartment without a roommate. And the person who has a great job with a Big Eight accounting firm but would rather be teaching kindergarten or hauling up lobster traps, but is so addicted to the exposed brick walls and spiral staircase in his duplex that he can't quit. And the person who has a great job with a Big Eight accounting firm and *doesn't* know what he'd rather be doing, but knows he doesn't want to be doing this. He's glad only because his Big Eight salary lets him stock as many brands of unblended Highland malt whiskey as his cupboards can hold, like an upper-middle-class Zipporah Litovsky. Each night he gulps a different whiskey, as if, once he pinpointed the right Scotch distillery and the perfect smoky essence, he could also pinpoint the moment twenty-five years ago when he was barred from knowing his own wishes.

And me?

I was walking through Chelsea with my head full of a fantasy I'd heard from a guy wearing discount-outlet apparel. And the stupider and more insane his offer sounded to me, the grander I felt, the faster I walked down the streets until it seemed I was hitting an intersection every ten seconds with only a couple of feet of side-walk between, and the more incorrigibly I smiled and made eye contact with everyone, even the type of people who might very well stab anyone with the effrontery to look at them.

My friend Laurie's loft was in a narrow gray-brick-and-soot factory building on Fifteenth Street, between Fifth and Sixth. There was the cap-visor factory on the first floor, a ribbon factory on the second and third, a color printing firm on the fourth, and Laurie on the fifth. Laurie wasn't an artist; she was an international banker with a master's degree. In order to get permission to live in a loft zoned for artists, she had submitted a portfolio of a dozen photographs of the lofts or apartments of people she envied, painted over with monsters crawling out from under the couches and intergalactic pools of vomit seeping down the walls. She had entitled the portfolio "Twelve of My Brain Cells." Laurie had always been known for her artistic flair. In third grade she had done a famous red-blue-and-yellow painting, on newsprint, of her mother pretending to have a heart attack when her father refused to buy her a mink stole. The hypothetical stole floated in a blue-outlined balloon just out of reach of her mother's skinny pink arm. The stole was dark blue with dark-red stripes. But when she grew up, Laurie never even considered becoming a professional artist: she had strict personal standards. She believed that no one should enter a career that risked tongue clicks on the part of parents, siblings, in-laws, cousins, and, especially, neighbors who had moved away years ago but still found out the local gossip.

Laurie had let me live with her for the past month while I looked for work in Manhattan. We ate dinner together; she lent me money; we cried to each other when we felt like crying; I used her shampoo and she used my styptic pencil; but Larry Feinglass was her lover, and he was arriving this evening.

Laurie Weinglass and Larry Feinglass were the most well-matched couple anyone had ever met. I used to play Candyland and Old Maid with them, and I can vouch that they started holding hands in third grade. They played doctor together in elementary school, they fucked in junior high, in high school they made a pact of chastity that brought them closer than lovers, and in college they shared an apartment that smelled like a fertility altar. They were both five feet six and a little pudgy; both had collar-length blond hair and pink round cheeks; both wore pastel cashmere sweaters and khaki pants and spotless white jogging shoes. In college, instead of having separate wardrobes, they bought one double-size wardrobe and shared everything except underwear. They both had alto voices and talked in smiling nasal drawls that could have been packaged and sold as Essence de Queens. They both loved strawberry ice cream, they were both left-handed, and they both wore silver I.D. bracelets on their right wrists. Larry's bracelet said "Larry," and Laurie's bracelet said "Laurie." Once, in sophomore year, I was looking out my dorm window and saw Laurie walking up the street. I got sexually aroused by the sight of her slightly bulging pink sweater, blunt blond hair, and wide-assed wiggle. I sighed, and smiled as she walked closer, and envied Larry his happiness with her. I was too much of a friend to express sexual desire to her, so I felt sordid, looking at her in a sexual way when she didn't know it. But—you know how it is in college—I hadn't slept with a woman for a couple of weeks, so I kept looking, my penis rose, I kept my eyes on her chest while she walked closer . . .

It was Larry. Pink sweater and all.

I ran from the window, and even though no one could see it I covered my erection with a copy of *Tender Is the Night*. I didn't speak to Larry for a week, and I never told him why.

The real difference between Laurie and Larry was not their gender but their attitude toward school. They both did well enough at Paumanok to get into Columbia's graduate school of business, but, once there, Larry coasted, I don't know why. But one night he called me on the phone (I was still living with my parents), and, laughing drunkenly, he told me he loved his courses in corporate taxation and management of personnel more than anything in the world. I didn't realize at the time that it was the night before a test; and Larry's bragging (that's what I first thought it was) made me angry about my own situation; so I was brusque and didn't ask him what was really wrong. Stupid!—but not as stupid as I might have been. If I'd been in form, I would have counseled him to quit business school, on the theory that everyone should be like me.

Laurie graduated second in her class in business school. Larry came out second from the bottom. Even at opposite poles, they were alike. Laurie became hot stuff for a big firm, and Larry couldn't get any decent job on the East Coast at all. Eventually a good bank did recruit him because he was an Ivy League man; but it was in San Diego. It was so far away, and they both worked so hard, that they could see each other only a couple of times a year.

Anxiety makes me hungry—almost everything makes me hungry, in fact: anxiety, happiness, horniness, or despair, I'm always thinking of pizza, donuts, French fries, hamburgers, all levels of Chinese food including eggrolls, and especially barbecued spareribs; I stay skinny only because of my manic metabolism. I was pacing the loft with a glass of pre-dinner milk when Laurie and Larry walked in together. Their arms were around each other; squeezing through the doorway at the same time on two sides of a jointly carried canvas suitcase, they each got one sleeve dirty on the doorjamb. They were both wearing summerweight beige linen suits. Laurie's had a skirt; Larry's had pants. I ran up, wrapped my arms around both of them, and kissed Laurie on the cheek. She smelled of strawberry, and there was pink cream on the corners of both their mouths.

"Test Solution Number Thirty-six!" I said, flooded with nostalgia for my days as a professional taster. I started getting misty. "It's so great to see you together. I'm regaining my belief in love."

"We met right on the corner of Sixteenth Street," Larry said in his perennial summer camper's voice. It was a high, cheerfully whining singsong, as if he was always ready to burst out with a chorus of "A Hundred Bottles of Beer on the Wall."

"We didn't even plan where we met," Laurie said. "Larry's cab was stopped at the corner, and he saw me walk by, so he got out. Then we went for an ice-cream cone."

She meant *an* ice-cream cone, because they always bought one two-scoop cone and shared it, to avoid the calories of a second wafer cone.

Looking from one to the other, I sighed happily. Whenever I saw them united, I was glad they were united, but equally glad to see that they weren't really as identical as memory made them. Larry was a quarter-inch taller; his eyes were blue-gray, while Laurie's were bright blue; he stood with his left shoulder sagging, while Laurie always stood straight; he had lines in the corners of his eyes from smiling too much, but Laurie's skin was very smooth; he had cut his hair short, and she was growing hers over her collar. Larry had a California tan, and white shoes; Laurie had a Manhattan paste-face and brown shoes.

And above all, Laurie seemed dignified and self-possessed, while Larry seemed uncoordinated and apologetic and too ingratiating.

The fact was, he copied her. He modeled himself after her, with partial success. She had given him the idea of going to business school. What would he have become if he hadn't been her shadow since third grade? Probably even his body would have grown differently.

But I meant it when I said it was great to see them together; because love is great to see.

Larry took his jacket off, and from his suitcase he took a bunch of three-hole Xerox papers with his handwriting on them. "Here's my diary for the month," he said.

"I'll get mine." Laurie ran to her bedroom nook and came back with a bunch of Xerox papers of her own.

"Exchanging diaries!" I shook my head in admiration. "Just like Tolstoy and his wife. But you guys are better, you don't get mad at what you read. You just write in the margin, 'Yes, I've experienced the same thing many times.'"

They didn't hear me kidding them, because they were staring down at the pages while they sat cross-legged facing each other on Laurie's black-hemmed straw mats. Usually they sent each other their monthly diary extracts by mail; this time Larry was able to be a personal courier. Each of them was compiling a double diary in which the experiences of the two alternated, as if they had happened not three thousand miles away but only a sheet of paper away.

They looked up. Laurie slapped Larry's knee and laughed. "This fool hasn't slept with anyone else yet."

Larry slapped Laurie's knee and laughed. "This fool hasn't, either."

"Well, why don't you?" she asked. "Sexual frustration isn't gonna help anything."

He blushed through his tan. "Why don't you?"

"Maybe one of you has," I joked, "but you didn't put it in your diary."

They looked at me, then at each other.

"Not that I know anything about it," I said, hastily trying to extract my foot from my mouth. "I'm pretty sure Laurie hasn't. I'm just saying what if. No relationship between two people can ever be totally honest." Larry's crow's feet twitched. Redstone, you've done it again. Infatuated with my own idea, I breezed on, wounding their trust in each other. "It's a rule of life: when it's in your interest to conceal something from someone, you do."

They looked at each other, then at me, as if I was the atheist at a revival meeting.

"If one of us slept with someone else," Laurie told me without moving her mouth, "we would definitely put it in the diary and let each other read it."

"Absolutely," Larry sang out.

"I made this clear to Larry at the beginning," she said. "It's cheaper to make a long-distance call across the country than to take someone out to dinner, but if he really wants to, if his male hormones start interfering with his productivity at the office, if bankers have more leisure time in California than in New York, if he wants to learn firsthand what it's like in the meat market . . ." She lifted her head and threw a proud glance. "I insist only that he tell me. So we can discuss it and learn from it. Our love is based on telling each other what we do, not what *to* do."

Larry bent his head, smiling, and ran a finger back and forth along a floor plank. "Anyway, I have no such plans at the present."

I sighed. "Mated bliss. You guys may live far from each other, but you know how many of your friends envy you? I keep thinking, when am I gonna meet the person who does for me what you two do for each other?"

"You don't lack attractiveness, you lack capital," Laurie said. "A love life needs financing like everything else."

Larry looked at her in mock amazement. "You mean this kid doesn't have a job yet?"

"I was very busy looking for one today," I said. And I told them about my glorious experiences at *Grab* and Voider.

"That's a good day!" Laurie said. "Now you've got an idea what you don't want to do. Starting Monday, when you look for jobs you'll be more efficient."

"I'm gonna take some time off from interviews. In fact"—I tried to reach the proper tone of quiet laughter—"I was sort of offered a job."

Laurie clapped her hands. "A job! So what are you hiding it for? What is it?"

"Being and watching," I said.

Laurie and Larry merely looked puzzled. I, I was the one who was horrified at what I was saying. Why was I doing it? Did I want them to pity me? Did I feel guilty for questioning their fidelity? Five minutes earlier I had laid down the rule that people conceal what it's in their interest to conceal; now look what I was disclosing.

I didn't tell them everything, not the spooky parts—but the spooky parts were my only justification. Laurie obviously got the impression that I had been sitting at a lunch counter griping about my luck, that a hobo overhearing me had told me to become a hobo, and that I planned to take his advice.

"What are we gonna do with him?" she asked Larry. "He wants to just exist—that's his idea of a job. Exist and—what was the other? Observe."

"Not exist and observe," I said. "Be and watch."

"Oh, fancy language!"

"I didn't say I believed the guy," I said sadly. "I was just speculating: what if people could sustain themselves just by being them-

43

selves? What if they didn't have to sell half their time in order to buy the other half?"

My questions had made me want to brood, and I walked away to the middle window and stuck my head out into the cindery breeze. The sun was stepping back from the city like a parent tiptoeing out of its child's bedroom. The buildings looked purple and bronze, and the first few couples were walking past the factory buildings and the parked trucks to the discotheques. Did they look as if they wouldn't know what to do with more free time?

When I stuck my head back into the loft, my friends were looking at me with too much solemn curiosity. So I smiled, and that made Laurie say, "See, he's just saying things to try to worry us."

"I don't know," I said. "I've really been thinking about this. It seems to me that the only people today who are getting any fun out of their careers are women. If a woman today seeks a business career, it's for independence; if a man today seeks a business career, it's because he's afraid not to. He's afraid to do anything that wouldn't impress women at a cocktail party. He's afraid to live up to the ideals of love, freedom, harmony with nature—all those wimpy sixties ideals which everyone gave up on before we even had a chance. They're absolutely the right ideals."

Laurie shook her head slowly and vigorously, as if it was an exercise to strengthen her powers of smirking. Then she started analyzing me to Larry. "Listen, I've told him before, the idea that he's doing what he wants by being irresponsible is totally ridiculous. What he really wants is to be a senior partner at a Wall Street law firm. He's just ashamed to admit it and afraid to compete. Everyone wants material success. There isn't anything else *to* want. This is the world; this is where we are; and it's material."

"There isn't anything else," Larry told me, with the confident smile of someone who knew.

• • •

A few hours later I was lying in my sleeping bag on Laurie's cool, sloping floor. My friends had gone out to dinner and to listen to jazz. Laurie's refrigerator hummed in the corner behind my head.

Street light came in through the five vertical windows and made five white slabs on the floor. Propping myself on my elbow, I could see the silhouettes of hanging plants, and the Japanese folding screen that hid the king-size bed in the corner near the windows. The white cranes and maroon riverbanks and black river on the screen were invisible. Laurie's photos on the wall were all in darkness. So was the erotic Japanese print, above Laurie's bed, to which she'd taped little advertising photos of Big Macs and Coke bottles in appropriate places. Also invisible was my empty left eye socket, which is, believe me, a truly disgusting sight. Every night when I'm putting ointment on my left eyelid, I look in the mirror and grin, even though I could do it without looking. It's healthy to take a hard look at what you're really like, and I'm lucky I have this simple physical way of showing it to myself.

The front door opened; the metal pole of the police lock went *thlick!* By reflex I reached for the eye patch lying on the floor near my head, and slipped it into place. Four shoes clopped into the loft.

"Don't say anything about me, I'm still up."

But they didn't answer me. Their silhouettes passed in front of the windows from right to left, and then they were behind the screen, murmuring and hugging. It was as if a warm breeze had suddenly come through: a breeze that kept you up instead of letting you sleep. A breeze you hadn't ordered: somebody else's weather, which made you restless.

I laughed—quietly, so I wouldn't disturb them. I'd listened to them fuck on camping trips, in dorm rooms, behind the door of my parents' bedroom at parties; I'd glimpsed them feeling each other up in youth center stairwells and at junior-high-school dances. It never bothered me before because I'd usually had someone of my own. The first semester of college, they'd been so hot to break their one-year chastity vow that they hadn't slackened their pace when their roommates entered with their own lovers. One night during freshman orientation, we were in a group of fourteen kids who all decided to bring our blankets onto the lawn behind the dormitory, just because no one was gonna tell us not to. We didn't even know who was making love and who wasn't; but we were proud to be sexual. We must have been really young, to be so unashamed.

Now I felt bad for spoiling their privacy, and wished I could get up and leave without embarrassing them. I felt as if I couldn't get up and go to the bathroom without ruining their night. That was an exaggeration, because they were very tolerant and didn't object to my being there; but I had decided to object for them. And of course, now that I'd decided it was wrong to intrude, my hearing got very sharp. I heard every roll of their bodies, every sag of their mattress. If I didn't, I imagined I did, and pictured all the hot wet naked sweaty things they were doing.

I tried to tell myself that they were a pair of mutually dependent neurotics who used lust to make up for the lack of higher impulses, and who were dragging themselves deeper into emotional slavery. I tried to think of other things. I tried to think of what I'd do once I got my own place to live in. I'd make dozens of new friends and invite them over all the time; I'd keep away from my old friends even if they liked me, because I'd want a completely new life; old friends were a bore, you never really knew each other that well, only well enough to get away with condescending to each other. Somewhere I'd find a whole island full of people who knew that all you had to do to be happy was be; why, instead, was I living at the Future Bank Presidents' Club?

In the dark, when no one was watching me, when I was off guard and my limbs were languid, when the darkness was too warm and I itched from sweat, I examined myself and succumbed, I succumbed to the most humiliating and debilitating of sins—

Self-pity!

I felt sorry for myself!

Ninety feet away, the mattress thumped, the box spring creaked, the lovers whispered . . .

There was a cough; then: "No!" Then stillness. A car whooshed by outside.

"Rich?"

After a beat, I recognized it as Larry's squeak. If only he had trained his voice to be authoritatively deep the way Laurie had. If you weren't looking, it was hard to tell which one was talking.

"Mind if I go over there to get a beer from the refrigerator?" he asked.

Before I could answer, I heard his bare feet running on the wood, and felt him go past. The kitchen equipment was against the rear wall; he opened the refrigerator, and in its light I could see why he had suddenly wanted a beer. He was naked in all his limpness.

"Malteds are supposed to be better for that," I said.

"Well, at least I'm *with* someone."

Snotty in his hour of stress! He slammed the refrigerator door, chugged the beer, tossed it into the wastebasket under the sink, and trotted back to Laurie.

A few minutes later a voice whined, "That doesn't work, either."

"Well, what do you want from me?" the other voice said impatiently.

"I'll get another beer. I just have to loosen up. The flight tired me out."

Larry walked by me, got another beer, and drank it standing near my sleeping bag.

"Sorry you have to hear all this, Rich," Laurie called out.

That's okay, I thought. It's my job.

"What do you do about these unique accidents?" Larry asked me, too loud.

"Sorry, I've never had one."

I couldn't help saying that.

His second beer can clinked against the first in the wastebasket. I watched his bare feet pace in front of the kitchen equipment. In the voice of someone urging himself on, he muttered, "The dollar is getting stronger, the dollar is getting stronger . . ."

"The stock market is rising," I said. "The economy is straightening out. The gross national product is going up, up, up. Corporate profits are swelling."

"Thanks for all your help," he sneer-whispered as he walked back. "You have no way of knowing this, but having responsibility for a lot of money does create stress."

47

After he got back to Laurie's corner of the loft, there were more mattress sounds and more whispers. Soon a voice called, "Rich, mind if we put on the TV?"

"Not at all." I sighed silently. I was afraid it was my fault. Were they finally old enough to be inhibited in front of a third person? But they were too nice to tell me so, the poor kids.

Blue light filled the bed alcove.

"Go get some beer and potato chips."

Larry padded back my way and let forth the refrigerator light. Aluminum cans slid squeaking along aluminum shelves.

"Rich, wanna watch TV with us?" Laurie asked from the far end.

"No, thanks. I have to try to sleep."

But I couldn't sleep, and with my left cheek against the floor I could see the blue flickering from the little TV. I saw their reflections sideways in the black windows. They sat naked on the mattress against the wall, tilting beer cans against their lips, and dipping into a bag of potato chips wedged between them. I could see only their tops clearly. I could see that the differences between them, while physically small, were emotionally quite significant.

"I know why it happened," Larry said. "I've been sexually deprived for months, and now I'm trying to deprive *you*, to get even."

Laurie was silent. Then she said, "You sound disgustingly proud of yourself."

Oh, please don't say anything cruel to him! I begged her in my thoughts—like begging, Please don't die! of a loved one who has just died. I wanted to get up from my sleeping bag and yell at them, order them to be kind to each other. It would have been just like me to do it, but I knew that the only right thing was to go to sleep and let them be by themselves. I would try to fall asleep, and even if I couldn't, they would think I had, so they wouldn't be embarrassed tomorrow.

"The real reason for this problem," Laurie said, "is that my job threatens you, Mr. Sexual Equality." And despite her cutting words, her voice was tender, as only a long, true lover's could be, who had lived through everything with him. "The way to get over

48

it is to become a big success. Not to envy me and have me pat you on the head."

"I don't care about success anymore," he said. "I just want to live with you again. I'll quit my job and come back here—"

"You will not! If we let love keep us from what we really want, it'll turn to hate."

"Or you could come out to the Coast to work—"

"Lar-ry," she warned. Despair was tempting him to cross the line—to time-travel into the dreaded past, to imply that the woman's career came second. We all knew that only New York was a big enough financial center for Laurie.

"We'll work something out," she said.

"We say that a lot. It's getting to be like saying, 'I'll get back to you.'"

I turned my face to the floor and rested it on my arm. I thought, Larry, you've got to move back to New York! Become a bank teller, a counterman, anything, just come back!

"If you want to sleep with other people, do it," she reassured him. "I know how hard it's been for *me* to control it. After months of just phone calls and writing, I was looking forward to finally touching you. . . ."

Then, thank God, I heard the blankets shift and the mattress rock. I heard the sweet moan that comes from two mouths closed over each other. The TV was still on, the lovers hadn't even bothered to switch it off; it was keeping me up, and I shut my eyes tight, but I was so happy for them I didn't care. "Swim all month long without worry," said a woman on the TV. Laurie and Larry giggled, then one of them turned off the TV, and the loft was peaceful and dark.

I told myself to breathe slowly and evenly. It's a good way to force yourself to sleep when you're agitated and distracted. And childishly, on the edge of sleep, I said to myself, I did it! I got them to make love!

Then I heard a groan of disgust. The potato-chip bag rattled across the floor as if someone had kicked it. I heard sheets flapping; fingernails scraping thin cotton . . .

"I guess not," someone said.

49

And I fell asleep—but only after I stopped myself from cursing out loud, and after I stopped punching my forehead and grimacing.

When I woke up—why did I wake up? was it light or dark? light *and* dark? oh yes, the refrigerator door was open, but it was still deep night—I was still half in a dream. There was a building across the street, and the ground floor was SUCCESS, and the second floor was LOVE, and the third floor was FREEDOM. I smiled at all of them—I wanted all of them, and it was hard to choose—then with a shock I saw that there was a fourth floor. Someone was operating the elevator, but he wouldn't take me to the fourth floor until I named what was on it. I said, On the fourth floor is WHAT I WANT. It's only for me. It won't be there till I get there. I don't know its real name, but the first time I hear it I'll know it. It's not on earth but it's in a loft. . . .

In the craziness of night-waking, I remembered the other world from a few seconds before, and wondered what the refrigerator was doing open. I shut my eyes against the light-pain. I didn't hear any food being taken out. The refrigerator door shut. A false snack alarm, how often I've had them myself! You feel so bad, no food is good enough, though food is what you want. You want a food that isn't in the refrigerator. No food you can think of will do.

Feet padded up to me and I sensed a body crouch down to the floor.

"Rich, you awake?"

I rolled onto my side, and opened my eyes in the darkness. A hand encircled my right wrist, and I started to panic. The cool links of someone's silver I.D. bracelet slid against my thumb. Someone stretched out beside me. A hand slowly and quietly pulled down the sleeping bag's zipper; the hand reached in and took me by the waist; a leg covered my leg; a mouth covered my mouth with the tastes of beer, salt, and strawberry solution number thirty-six; I smelled cologne rising from a lightly sweating neck; I feared the sleeping bag would split a seam.

Two legs slipped between mine; the weight of an abdomen pressed onto mine. A foot nuzzled mine; a knee kicked mine; a hand

50

stroked mine; a pelvis bumped mine; a nose rubbed mine; a pair of lips chewed mine; a tongue tapped mine; a row of teeth knocked against mine. I rolled out from under, and drew away for air. We distended the sleeping bag like twins kicking inside their mother. I reached for an arm; I groped for a flank; I searched for a sign . . .

It had been ten years since I'd been so thrilled to feel a vulva.

4. I Have Always Depended on the Kindness of Strange People

Larry must not have heard us, because for the rest of the weekend he and Laurie held hands and shared ice cream more rompishly than I'd seen them in years. I made sure to go out alone at night, and I came home late and drunk so I wouldn't know whether they'd done anything. The next day, I cheerfully refused to accompany them in hailing Larry a cab for the airport. I waited on Laurie's bed, with the sun on it and the lights off, and reminisced. When I heard the elevator come up to our floor, I hurried to the kitchen end of the loft and got myself a Coke and a hunk of cheddar cheese. Laurie found me standing there with one food item in each hand.

"You louse," she said, shaking her head and smiling.

"Why, because I eat up all your food?"

"Because you make me sleep with you."

I had made her sleep with me by lying fifty feet away in the darkness, silent, while she was in bed with someone else! Whenever Laurie did something dubious, it was because someone made her; when she did something others would reward her for, it was because she was self-reliant. Well, we both felt sinful and confused and afraid and happy; we didn't know how close to come to each other, or whether we had to treat each other differently; so we had to talk to each other in moralistic snippets and pseudo-misinterpretations.

"Larry's still your true romance," I said.

"You don't think *that's* changed, do you?"

"No—that's what I just said."

"I don't even want to hear you suggest it."

"I'm not suggesting it."

"Well, I'm just telling you, *don't*." She turned away from me and moaned, "Larry, what should I do? He'd probably tell me to go ahead and sleep with you—if I had to do it with someone, it might as well have been a friend. Larry, why are you so kindhearted and far away?" She scowled at my cheddar and cola. "What's this, some kind of Redstone aphrodisiac?"

"Now that you mention it, protein and caffeine are both very useful . . ."

She took both my hands, raised and inspected my culinary attributes, and shook her head. Then she took a sip of the cola and a bite of the orange cheese. Then she got a cola and a piece of orange cheese of her own, and walked with them toward her bed.

"Protein and caffeine," she scoffed. "Thank God his practice is better than his theory."

I watched her blue-jeaned ass in a way I'd previously tried not to; and I said to myself, You'll be making love five minutes from now, but you can never tell her you love her. She's Larry's. You are not a heel, you don't steal your friends' lovers. You're just a convenient substitute. Poor Larry would probably forgive us if he knew, and that's why it's especially wrong to fall too deep.

But I have a handicap. Not my eye—I mean the fact that I'm a romantic. In principle, I think sex can be a simple physical recreation; but whenever I actually sleep with a woman, I start falling in love with her and planning to make noble sacrifices for her. When I lie next to her, our hearts quieting down after sex, I start choosing, and sometimes saying out loud, the names of our future children. I know how improper it is. In Laurie's case, especially, I couldn't dream of using the word "love" out loud. She'd throw me out. We knew we were a mismatch. Sitting on the edge of the bed, she was probably worrying I'd use the word "love." In our days of friendship I had told her about crushes I'd had on women I knew only slightly. She knew about my naïve idealism. I should have walked up to her and said, "We won't do it again. We'll be like before. It was inevitable, it was an interesting lesson, but the main lesson was that we weren't changed by it. So that's all."

Instead, I walked up to her, mumbling to myself, "Hope, Constance, Grace . . ."

Those were going to be the names of our daughters.

She set her cola and cheese down beside the bed, sat over the edge with her legs apart, and smiled in the most unillusioned, unmisty, and suddenly unworried way. Her round cheeks didn't blush. Her blunt blond hair didn't bounce with joy against her collar. But the folds in the crotch of her jeans flexed.

She held her arms out, to guide me to a seat beside her. She patted the mattress and said, "All this time, you've been missing the convenience of a personal banker."

I knew that I'd have to move out of her loft to save her virtue . . . one of these days. . . .

• • •

In the morning, I put on my blue-and-white seersucker jacket, which I'd gotten back from the cleaners with its eternal grayness still present at the cuffs and around the top button. I put on the forest-green tie with tea-stained coats of arms—my only tie—chino slacks, and my buckskin shoes. When Laurie finally looked up from her breakfast of wheat germ and the *Times*, she stared at me in alarm.

"I'm going to see Brassberg about a job," I said.

"But you hate Brassberg!"

"Yes, but why should that stop me from using him? That's what you've been telling me for a month."

The way she shook her head and gulped another spoonful, you could swear she was disappointed I was taking her advice. "So you decided not to exist and observe anymore."

"I can be and watch just as well at an office, collecting a salary. Didn't you tell me that too? I realized you were right; aren't you glad?"

She pursed her lips and looked around for an answer. She found it in the *Times*. "Of course," she said, reading. "I'm sure you'll find a wonderful job."

She must have understood that once I made enough money, I'd

54

have to leave her. And yet by seeking a job I was also trying to win her approval. After all, in sleeping with an unemployed man she was breaking a sacred principle.

There's nothing like a set of directly opposite reasons, to get you to do what you don't really want to do. An hour later, I was sitting in the office of Brassberg Personnel. It was in one of those tombstone-gray skyscrapers on Fifth Avenue in the Forties—buildings that used to be swank, but now on the ground floors there were rug stores and radio stores where prices were arrived at by an inspired reading of the customer's face. Brassberg Personnel was on the second-floor mezzanine, because Brassberg liked his applicants to climb the stairs and get breathless enough to take any job.

In the main room, the phones and typewriters were going so loud it was as if they too were trying to sound eager in order to get hired. There were four young employment agents at desks; and along the back wall sat young men and women in interview clothes. They chewed their nails; combed their hair; filled out application forms; practiced their touch-typing on the clipboards. They stared at the tops of the walls and took deep breaths; and they reread clippings from the *Times* want ads as if reading their own obituaries. Whenever one employment agent visited another's desk, he made sure to crack a joke and laugh and not look at any of the applicants. And whenever the receptionist called a name, everyone looked up startled.

"Mr. Redstone!"

I got up, walked down the corridor, and knocked on a walnutlike door that had a plaque saying, "Mr. Selwyn Brassberg." A familiar sullen baritone said something so muffled you had to guess from the circumstances that it was "Come in." Then it said, "Come in" clearly as I entered and saw him rub the saliva off his thumb onto his green desk blotter.

It was Selwyn Brassberg, the fat boy and thumbsucker of my childhood peer group.

On the wall behind him was an orange-and-black Princeton banner; on his desk was a Princeton tiger's-head paperweight. Also on the desk were five cups of coffee at various stages of emptiness; five white plastic cup-covers, nonchalantly strewn; and two cups of prune yogurt with spoons propped inside.

"Redstone, you're dressed disgracefully as usual," he said, sticking his hand out.

"How you doing, Selly?" I shook his hand and gave him a grin. I loathed and feared him, but he was an old, dear friend. We'd spent our childhoods insulting each other, and even though he was born six months after me he'd always been the *oldest* child I'd known. At three, his mother had taught him to nag his father into taking the civil-service test. In kindergarten, he had ordered the teacher to distribute the rhythm sticks more equitably among the class. In first grade he'd sweet-talked extra paint jars from the supply office, and ordered extra milk and cookies for himself as a commission. In second grade one day, I said I wanted to be an astronaut when I grew up, and another kid said a cowboy, another a fireman, and Selly said, "When I grow up I want to be a self-starter." For elementary-school graduation he got his first checkbook and I was one of the jeering and backslapping schoolmates for whom he wrote his first overdraft, for two mushroom pizzas and four Cokes. In junior high he came down with Ivy League fever, started wearing Princeton orange and black, and circulated a petition demanding that the school provide speech therapy for all students with detectable New York accents. In the high-school cafeteria he started a riot one day by grabbing the microphone and demanding the division of the sophomore class into eating clubs.

"You already know how I am," he told me, picking up one coffee cup after another and putting it down. "I'm successful." He lifted his right hand, thumb extended. He hesitated and looked at me apprehensively. "What the hell, you know all my secrets," he said, and shoved the thumb into his mouth. He puffed on it like a pipe, and a trickle of spit flowed down the slope toward his index finger.

"I have what everyone wants, Redstone," he said. Then he turned white, and the thumb fell. "Excuse me." He pedaled his leather swivel chair backward toward a white door. Painfully he lifted himself by the door handle. He clutched his bladder and turned to me. "The ultimate status symbol: a private bathroom." Then he waved toward a magazine on his "In" tray. "Page sixty-eight. Read it while I'm busy." He groaned, and tottered behind the door.

The magazine was the latest issue of *Grab*. I'd seen the cover when I had my job tryout: a young couple in gold sweatsuits and white headbands, grinning carnivorously at each other from opposite sides of a huge dollar bill, which they were pulling apart to symbolize their divorce settlement. But I hadn't noticed the second headline down the left margin: "Success of the Month—Twenty-Three-Year-Old Personnel Whiz."

It's one thing to scorn a magazine and what it stands for. It's quite another to be unawed by people who have *articles* written about them. My heart beat fast as I flipped to page 68. In the upper corner of the page there was a picture of Selwyn at his desk, looking just as I'd seen him: fat, rumpled, wearing an oversized Brooks Brothers suit, and grinning with an uncanny combination of sheepishness and pomposity. The only difference was that instead of his thumb he was chewing the eraser tip of a pencil. The caption under the picture said: "Selwyn Brassberg's gutsy motto: 'You're not giving your all till you can feel your pancreas shrivel into ashes.'"

The bathroom door opened; Selly walked to his desk by pushing his swivel chair from behind. With one hand he pressed the small of his back. With each step he gave a little shake of his leg.

"Just a touch of the old prostatitis," he said, sitting down with a grunt. His intercom uttered two chimes. He pressed a button, and the receptionist said through the speaker:

"Coffee, Mr. Brassberg?"

Selly shut his eyes tight and sucked in a breath. He murmured to me, "You want coffee?"

"No."

He opened his eyes and pressed the "Talk" button. "Two, regular, two sugars." He looked at me with lowered, guilty eyes. "I ordered one for you just in case." Then he took a gulp from the nearest coffee cup on his desk. He wiped his mouth with his thumb and said, "My internist says I have the body of a sixty-year-old chairman of the board. He wanted to tell me I'm getting an ulcer, but I soon disabused him of that—the ulcer as status symbol went out with black-and-white TV. My orthopedist wants me to go in for a disc operation—that's the posh ailment. So, Redstone." He looked at my tie, and pretended to try to hide a sniff of pity. "Today's the day I've been waiting for all my life. The day you come begging to me to save you from being a washout. I tell you, they laughed at me when I refused to go to any college after Princeton turned me down. But I knew that I didn't have four years to waste at an inferior institution. Live fast, that's my motto. Here I am, twenty-three, and I already have to eat stewed prunes for breakfast. I was developing a marketable persona when you and the other kids were trading baseball cards. True, I missed out on many of the formative experiences of our generation. I never passed out from wine and Quaaludes at a Springsteen concert. I never gave myself a tattoo with a razor blade and Bic pen ink. But I tell you, when I'm interviewing an unemployed Ph.D., trying to help the poor simpleton by asking what he can possibly do on this earth, and, overcome by enthusiasm, my thumb enters my mouth—I assure you, the overeducated wonk doesn't laugh. He all but offers to wipe my saliva up with his hanky. So, Redstone, what shall we do to rescue you?"

His picture was in a magazine, I said to myself. Maybe he knows the right way to live after all.

When you see a person's photograph in a magazine, and then you look up and see the same person in the flesh, it's as if you're seeing a supernatural spirit incarnate. Even if you've known him for years, it's as if this were the first time you'd ever seen him. Even if you think he's a jackass, you say to yourself, "Everyone has heard of this jackass! He must have planned to be a jackass, for this very reason!" Even people who have been in magazines themselves, and know themselves to be twerps, are impressed when they see their colleagues, whom they also know to be twerps, in magazines. And even geniuses can't be sure they're geniuses until they've been put into magazines by morons.

My picture had never been in a magazine.

58

But only part of me was intimidated by Selly: the boy-from-Queens part, the part that was deluded into thinking that other people's desires were worthier than my own.

I laughed in his face. "Selly, we've been rivals all our lives, we've always had contempt for each other's goals. But I've achieved some things even you might envy."

I stopped, and shut my mouth.

"Yes?" he sneered.

Discretion warned me not to tell him. But I had to tell him; I had to one-up him, it would gall me for weeks if I didn't.

"I'm fucking Laurie Weinglass from morning to night. And I've been contacted for a mission that could put me out of your reach forever. I've done things you don't have to wear a suit to do."

He smiled pityingly. He stretched out his right arm and tugged the gray gabardine cuff. "Brooks has my measurements on file, old boy. When I want a suit, I tell my receptionist the fabric and color, she calls the store, and I get my suit, fitted in the classic Brooks Brothers style, without having to shop for it. And they know I like the right sleeve a quarter-inch shorter for thumb clearance. One's tailor knows everything. That's achievement, Redstone. Now"—he pulled his Rolodex file toward him, over the saturated blotter, and twirled the cards—"let's see what openings we have for a college graduate, good intellect, wobbly grip on reality but not completely unsalvageable."

"How is it that I have a wobbly grip on reality, when you're the one who doesn't hear what the other person says?"

And he didn't. He twirled his Rolodex cards as if I hadn't said a word; and that was how I knew I'd one-upped him. He'd probably wished he could sleep with Laurie, at times. I laughed out loud—and he didn't respond to that either. It can be liberating to talk to a self-involved person: you can say whatever you want, he won't care.

He lifted his head, biting his thumb excitedly. "Advertising is the field for you! I have an entry-level opening in a Top Twenty agency. Very nice people, in fact they're the ones who came up with that super-successful campaign for Destructo Chemical: 'Nice

People Making a Nice World Nicer.' They're also doing the presidential campaign for that Utah state assemblyman, Jason A. Fleece. The one with the fresh approach everyone's raving about. Sings his speeches while he plays country guitar. Could you do a jingle on nuclear proliferation by this afternoon? It impresses them if you come with samples."

"I saw one of his commercials once. He's a lousy guitarist. Also he's a warmongering bigoted fascist dinosaur."

"But he's such a nice guy you'd never know it!" Selly leaned toward me with eager expectation; leaned back in disappointment. "Okay, I see you're making it hard for old Selly. No fascists, I'll have to write that on your form." He twirled all his Rolodex cards, shook his head, and clicked his tongue. He pushed the file away and opened his side desk drawer to get a manila folder. "You come up with some pretty rigid restrictions. But there are more jobs in heaven and earth, Redstone, than are dreamt of in those time-wasting philosophy courses you took in college. How about becoming a trainee for a nomenclatural consultant?"

"A who?"

"A small but growing company that specializes in inventing names and titles. Authors hire them to think up funny names for characters, titles for books—even chapter titles at a bulk rate. They developed the title for that new bestseller about the Communist detective: *The Scarlet Dick*. They aid parents seeking unique names for babies; artists seeking titles for paintings; entrepreneurs with names for restaurants or boutiques; shipbuilders with names for ships; real-estate people with names for apartment buildings, suburban tracts, shopping malls." He leaned forward. "Have you ever looked at the world, Redstone?"

"I've given it a passing glance now and then."

"Well, have you ever noticed that everything, whether associated with the Ivy League or not, has a name? And nothing can simply exist without being named? It seems to be an obsession of some sort. Universal social climbing. Well, *someone* has to name them all, and it's too hard for most people—or it will be, if this company promotes itself correctly."

"Oh, let them name their own things, Selly! I don't want to take that away from them!"

"What lack of vision," he said sadly. "This company was called in as emergency consultant to that brilliant young author—"

There was a rap on the door. The receptionist walked in with a cardboard tray and two coffees. She picked each cup up with a two-fingered grip and placed it down on the blotter.

"Coffee?" Selly asked me.

"No, thanks."

"Can I have yours, then?"

"Please don't. Think of your prostate."

"I would rather my prostate thought of me for a change. See, Redstone, that's the trouble with you: you're always willing to accept things as they are. Coffee gives me energy; coffee has made me a success. Has my prostate? Do I start interviewing at eight in the morning because my prostate wants me to? No, my prostate would rather be lying in bed. My prostate doesn't care if I make two hundred thousand a year, or two thousand. My prostate doesn't care if my suits have four cuff buttons or only three. My prostate just wants to lounge around oozing its secretions in the most hedonistic manner. Well, I don't believe in pampering, and that includes my own organs. If they can't take the pace, they can get out. And I'll tell you, if I had a miniature coffee cup keeping warm on a miniature hot plate at the base of my urethra, instead of a prostate, my sex life would be a lot more active, too. Now—let's see what's the job for you." He flipped the pages in the manila folder, dabbing his lip with his finger. Then he slammed his palm onto the page. "Okay, here it is! I'll get you hired as a novelist."

I was certain he was lying, or else he'd finally gone crazy. "Novelists aren't hired," I said. "Besides, I couldn't write a novel. I've sometimes wished I could, but I don't have the discipline."

"These people will discipline you." He held the job description sheet up and read it without showing it to me. With one hand he grabbed a coffee cup and gulped all its contents down. "They have a steady demand for fiction, will provide an immediate audience for everything you write, and will pay you a living wage for writing.

These conditions would make you the envy of Herman Melville or Edgar Allan Poe. Normally they require someone with previous publication, but they've experienced some turnover recently. Their description says: 'We prefer an applicant who is capable of being in uncertainties, mysteries, doubts, without any irritable reaching after fact or reason; however, he or she *must* be an English major.' "

I had trouble speaking for a second—because I was awed and honored. "That's Keats's definition of a poet: someone who's capable of being in uncertainties, doubts and mysteries, without being upset et cetera. Professor Blatt used to quote it a lot. He said it defined what was most celestial in human beings. And you think *I'm* qualified?"

"Well, shit, you're an English major, aren't you? You have part of the qualifications; you can fake the rest. That's what job-seeking is all—"

Suddenly his face turned ivory. "Stay here." He pedaled his swivel chair backward, as fast as he could, to the bathroom door.

A minute later, he emerged, even whiter. He sank into his chair, and pedaled himself forward listlessly to the desk. His hands trembled.

"I have bleeding," he said. "That goddamn coffee—why don't they ever warn you of the dangers?"

The pouches on his face quivered. His right hand trembled at his chest and tried to rise. He tried to lift his thumb toward his mouth—he couldn't, the hand shook, the thumb wagged back and forth in front of his mouth, and when his mouth lunged for it, it dipped away.

"Redstone, if you would," he said. I must have hesitated a moment, in horror at his deterioration. He snapped at me, "Redstone! Be so kind!"

"Kind!" I scrambled out of my seat, around to his side of the desk. "You don't need kindness; you need someone to dump your coffee onto your head and throw you out of business!"

But his hand was shaking so much that his jacket sleeve had ridden up to his elbow, and short-term kindness was necessary. I took his wrist and held it steady. I pulled his hand upward until his thumb bounced against his lips. Then his rooting instinct took over: his lips puckered and searched. But his thumb kept wagging, stumbling, bumping from one side of his lips to the other like a blind dog seeking its master. It jiggled at the entrance of his mouth and started to slide off his lower lip. Finally I clamped his fist in both my hands, to stop the shaking. He got a tooth-hold on the tip of his tongue, and pulled it in the rest of the way by sheer suction.

His cheeks went in and out, frantically at first, then more calmly. His face pinkened; his panting slowed.

"You thaved my life," he lisped through his thumb. "Here." He dipped his head toward the desk blotter, and took his thumb out of his mouth just long enough to write three lines on a memo slip. He immediately put his thumb back into his mouth and puffed hungrily. The slip of paper dangled in his other fingers.

"Go to this address," he said as a bubble popped in the corner of his mouth. "By the time you get there, I'll have talked to them. Don't hesitate—this is your chance."

"Selly," I said, "you've always done favors for people who made fun of you. You're too good to burn yourself out in this sleazy place."

But he was picking up the telephone receiver in his free hand, not hearing me at all. That was Selly. So I reached over and plucked the memo away, and headed for the door. Looking back, I saw him leaning with his face against the telephone console, pushing buttons with his pinky while puffing on his thumb.

"Hello?" he said into the phone. He looked up and saw me go; he wagged at me with his four free fingers. "Redstone! Tell the girl: two coffees with sugar."

"No!" I yelled, and ran out, holding the name and address, wet with saliva, of the place where they'd make me into a novelist.

5. One Hundred Years
of Exaggeration

The address was on Fortieth Street, across from the main library and Bryant Park. Well, it's gotta be a porn factory, I said to myself as I rode up in the elevator. You're gonna write sex scenes between eight-year-old girls and their gerbils for ninety-eight cents a page before taxes. But it's just an experiment, just a phenomenon you will discover and observe. It's part of your city. Your real job is not to do the work, but merely to find it.

I got out at the sixteenth floor. At the end of the hall there was a black door with three locks, and a gold stencil on the door said: YER PRESS.

I rang the bell; a gray eye blinked at me through the peephole; then the eye ducked down, and the three locks opened. The first lock sounded like an arrow thwacking into its target; the second lock sounded like the trapdoor of a gallows; and the third lock sounded like a coffin sliding down a gangplank. The door opened an inch; I had to push it the rest of the way. The door-opener was an old man wearing a wrinkled white shirt, torn at the underarms, and with a blue pack of French cigarettes showing through the pocket.

I had nothing to lose. "Rich Redstone reporting with some hot ideas about gerbils," I said.

The old man just muttered something I couldn't understand, and shuffled away into a room behind an unmarked door.

"Thanks for the welcome," I said, and looked in all directions a bit helplessly. I was in a square waiting room whose white walls were decorated with the jackets of dozens of books I had never

64

heard of. There was a receptionist's desk, but no sign of a receptionist: no scattered papers or clips, no personal effects. There was another closed door, and it said: MS. FLIME. I cleared my throat and was about to knock on the unmarked door the old man had gone through, when from behind the marked one I heard:

"Ugly witch!"

It was a female voice, shrieking. Then a different female voice: "Homely sow!"

I turned in my tracks. I walked up to the Ms. Flime door and put my ear to it. Then the other door opened and the old man came out. He looked at me with very slight curiosity; then he leaned an ear to the Ms. Flime door, and laughed mutteringly to himself.

We both heard:

"Grotesque harpy!"

"Misshapen troll!"

"Repulsive animal!"

"Nauseous deformity!"

"If we weren't in business together I'd leave for Florida!"

"If we weren't in business together *I'd* leave for Florida!"

"A motorcycle ran over your face!"

"You got your nose caught in a pants presser!"

"They're passing a law that you can't go out in the daytime!"

"I'm getting an injunction to make you wear a paper bag over your head!"

"If I dreamed about you I'd wake up screaming!"

"If I dreamed about you I'd have a heart attack in my sleep!"

"Help, help, she's looking at me!"

"Ow, help, I'm turning to stone!"

"Freak!"

"Mutant!"

"Sport!"

"Abnormality!"

Smack!

Smack!

My head snapped back when I heard flesh striking flesh. I said to myself, Maybe there's someone in there that I have to rescue. My usual romantic fantasy surged up in my mind; I saw myself break-ing down the door with my shoulder, running in with my shoulder aching, and grabbing a letter opener out of the hand of a once-beautiful woman who was about to commit a desperate crime. I would find a plastic surgeon to repair the disfiguring scars on her face, then we would go live on a Pacific island, all alone, because she was used to hiding anyway. . . .

What I actually did was, I knocked on the door. Voices hissed; heels clacked; the door opened.

Two red-haired, fiftyish ladies stepped out. One was wearing a tan pantsuit, holding a brown cane, and smoking a long brown cigarette. The other was wearing a flounced white dress with a cornflower print, two flesh-pink hearing aids, and pink lipstick. Their backs were straight, their chins were lifted, their nostrils worked hard. Each of them had the red imprint of a hand on her left cheek; but the one in the dress had a dime-size birthmark in the middle of the red imprint, and the one in the pantsuit didn't. And that was remarkable, because they were identical twins.

I looked from one to the other. Mysteries, doubts, and confusions flooded over me, just the way the ladies probably wanted them to; but I swam with it. "Sorry to interrupt your game," I said to them, "but I have an appointment—I was sent by Brassberg Personnel."

The one in the dress clapped her hands together with joy.

"So you're the dear boy Selwyn Brassberg recommended so highly!" she trilled. "I'm Ardella Flime. Delighted to meet you." She gave me a limp hand to shake, and when I shook it the bones seemed to squish out of the way like minnows.

"Ardith Flime," the one in the pants grunted. "Brassberg better be right." She gave my hand a single shake, and it hurt so much I had to keep myself from rubbing it.

"Come into my office for an interview," they said simultaneous-ly. Whose office? I wondered. I didn't want to offend one of my two future bosses by choosing the other. But when they led me through the Ms. Flime door, I saw that they shared one wide room, with a desk and a window at each end. Ardella sat down at the slender Lucite desk on the left; Ardith sat down at the massive mahogany desk on the right. Their backs faced each other. There was an oval Persian rug on the floor in front of Ardella's desk, and a white bearskin rug in front of Ardith's. Above Ardella's desk hung a watercolor of lilies and bamboo in the Chinese style. Above Ardith's desk hung a reproduction of Munch's "The Scream."

Ardith invited me to sit by her desk; then Ardella invited me to sit by hers. They glanced at each other. Ardith raised her cane head-high.

"Why don't I just stand in the middle of the room for the interview?" I said; and Ardella clapped her hands and said, "He'll fit in perfectly!"

So I stood precisely halfway between the two desks, and whenever I shifted my weight onto one foot, the sister on the opposite side would glare at me. And this is what I learned about the job:

Yer Press was a company that produced books on private commission. Their books weren't found in bookstores, weren't reviewed in newspapers or magazines, weren't bought by libraries; they were unknown to the literary world, even the readers of one Yer Press book had rarely read any of the others. Each Yer Press book was specially created to please the customer who had ordered it, who had specified many of the characters and events, and who was sent the entire limited edition in a half-dozen cardboard boxes. Unlike the reader of a regular book, the Yer Press customer was perfectly sure he would get the entertainment he desired—if he didn't like something in the manuscript, he could have it rewritten. The cost of publication was fifty thousand dollars. Most of the customers, of course, were rich people, and mostly their taste ran to pulp fiction in fine bindings. Though there was a lot of variety, the typical patron was a husband who commissioned a romantic novel in which his wife was the heroine. He gave it to his wife as a present for her birthday or anniversary, saying, "Here, you've read so many of the damn things I had someone write one especially for you." Laughing with delight and surprise as she opened the box and saw her own name in the title, the wife gave him the strongest, most sincere kiss she'd given him in twenty years, and asked, "Who did you possibly get to write about *me?*"

67

Rich Redstone, that's who.

Where the old man had disappeared to was the writers' room. Here, in Ardella's phrase, was the "room of one's own" where the Yer Press novelist typed out his assignment at a brisk and confident pace; also answered letters from customers satisfied and dissatisfied; also sent out advertising flyers to rich people on mailing lists; also, as I'd seen, went out to open the front door.

I soon got the impression that the Flimes believed in keeping a very stripped-down and versatile staff. There was a receptionist's desk, as I said, but Ardella as much as admitted that it was just to make the place look official.

"You can't keep a receptionist these days," Ardith added, snarling. "They want the world."

"Why pay someone to just sit and file her nails and look in the mirror?" Ardella said, touching her birthmark.

"And," I said, playing along, "answering the door would give a writer much-needed experience of life."

They both nodded, and, without even looking at each other, both told me simultaneously that I'd made a very mature and thoughtful comment. I could see that I had found their wavelength. Clearly, the Flimes loved dollars so much that they wanted to take in as many as they could for their very own, the way some other pair of middle-aged sisters might have loved to take in stray dogs.

Ardella was the softheaded one, and Ardith was the hard-nosed one. Ardella's voice was like a flute that had been thrown down the stairs; Ardith's voice was like a clarinet that had been used to spank children. Ardella fluttered her hands when she asked me questions; Ardith flicked her index finger like a switchblade. Ardella hummed to herself, looked out the window, and turned down her hearing aids when her sister spoke; when *her* sister spoke, Ardith coughed, rattled her desk drawers, and pounded her cane on the floor. Ardella's red hair flipped away from her neck; Ardith's red hair clung to her head in a bun. Ardella laughed "Hee!" and Ardith laughed "Ha!" Ardella called me Rich and Ardith called me Redstone.

"We've always been completely opposite," Ardith told me, looking away from Ardella.

"We've always worked each in our own domain, not interfering with the other," Ardella said.

And they told me how Yer Press had been founded. Both of them had always aspired to be completely different kinds of writers. When they had worn entirely different pajamas as children, Ardella had written nice, pretty fairy tales and Ardith had written scary ones. When they'd sat next to each other in high school, Ardella had written optimistic compositions about the woods and the flowers, and Ardith had written grim compositions about world problems. When they'd worn different-colored letter sweaters in their room at the same college sorority, Ardella had written short stories about coeds falling in love with their teachers, and Ardith had written short stories about teachers taking their coeds on booby-trapped field trips. In their first New York apartment, they had worn very different garments indeed—a fluffy-collared pink housecoat for Ardella, a pair of chino slacks and a bra for Ardith—when they sat at separate identical typewriters, on opposite sides of the dining table, while Ardella's fingers trilled out a plantation romance and Ardith's jabbed out a hard-boiled mystery. And their habiliments surely could not have been mistaken for each other's when, at the exact same moment on a spring day in 1955, both of them looked up simultaneously from their typewriters and said in unison, "If rich people would commission us to write just for them, we'd make more money than Hemingway."

Yer Press was born. Ardella wrote an ad to be placed in *Town and Country;* Ardith wrote an ad to be placed in the *Wall Street Journal.* Their first commission was the biography of a linoleum tycoon on the occasion of his retirement; their second, a girl-and-horse novel for the ten-year-old daughter of a Mafioso.

"And it was all because of a little . . ." I said.

They leaned forward threateningly.

"All because of . . ." I said.

They glowered at me belligerently.

"All because of a little—talent and hard work," I said, because although I like to challenge people, I'm not suicidal. But I said to myself, All because of a little birthmark! It was the one difference between them, and it had blossomed into a lifelong, symbiotic hate. Why? Had one parent disliked the birthmark and the other parent liked it? Did Ardith think that Ardella's birthmark was the secret of beauty; and did Ardella think that Ardith's non-birthmark was the secret of beauty? Did each sister hang around the other in order to gloat at how she was wasting the secret of beauty? And by now, did the world look completely different to you depending on whether or not you had a dime-size birthmark on your left cheek? Maybe so, after fifty years of exaggerating its importance—or, since there were two of them, twice times fifty years: a total of a hundred years of exaggeration!

But there was at least one similarity in their world-view: both Flimes offered me the same low salary. Which I accepted happily, because just looking at the birthmark on Ardella's cheek and the non-birthmark on Ardith's cheek made me happy. The red hand imprints on their cheeks had almost faded, but each sister still gave a sniff of contemptuous amusement when she unavoidably looked at the other. It must have been unavoidably, perhaps a neck reflex or a desire to make sure nothing was being stolen. Most of the time they ostentatiously looked in opposite directions.

• • •

The Flimes had just finished telling me how efficiently they divided their labor—how Ardith handled the business end, the direct mail, the contract negotiations, while Ardella supervised the literary work, how their tastes were so different that they never had to worry about stepping onto each other's turf—when they both insisted on showing me around the office together, because neither would trust the other to do it alone.

"Welcome to the writers' room," Ardella said when she opened the unmarked door. "You'll have that pretty little desk in the—"

"In the right-hand corner," Ardith interrupted.

"In the *left*-hand corner," Ardella said.

There were four desks in the white-cinderblock room, which was precisely enough desks for two employees. The room stank— or, as a writer would say, "The room was fetid"—from cigarette smoke. Standing in the narrow aisle, with a hand on each of his desks, was my only co-worker, the old man. He glared at me through cold gray eyes, and chewed something. There were nut particles on his wavy purple lips. I looked at him more closely than I'd had a chance to before.

There was something odd about him: he looked as if he belonged on a book-jacket photo. Not the decrepit shirt, of course, and not the shrunkenness of old age. But if he stood straighter, if his hair was darker, he might have the scared, arrogant glint of a weathered writer. Yes, I *had* seen his face on book jackets. Even now he stood with the tense pseudo-indifference of someone waiting to be recognized. He took the blue pack from his pocket and hung a cigarette between his lips. It shook at me with old-mannish contempt.

"This—" Ardith said.

"This," Ardella said, pushing past her sister, toward him, "This," she said, wringing her hands in joy, "This, of course, is *&?#."

I gasped in awe. Yes, it was *&?#, the legendary erotic novelist who had changed his name to a series of punctuation marks to celebrate the obscenity of all language. This was the man whose books had been hidden at the back of the shelf in my parents' bedroom closet—behind the soft-core porn, behind the hard-core porn, behind everything. When my parents went shopping, I climbed a stepladder, stretched my arm past the toolbox and the vacuum-cleaner bags, and almost sent the pine shelf toppling under my weight. It was my first memory of serious literature. He'd spent most of his career in Europe, having been spurned by his native land till he was too old to care; but he figured in American literary history as a brave symbol of our cherished right to be filthy and perverted. If I remembered my newsmagazines correctly, he was such a nonconformist that when his books were finally accepted by an American publisher he disgustedly swore off writing, joined a Madison Avenue ad agency, and became a copywriter specializing in housewife-and-repairman commercials. He hadn't published anything since his ground-breaking children's classic, *A Bikini for Butch.* I'd thought he was dead. But there he was, almost eighty years old, with patches of white hair and patches of red flaky skin

71

on his head, a torn, wrinkled white shirt on his back, Mexican hua-
raches on his sockless feet—and stinking up the whole room, where
I was supposed to work, with his highbrow French cigarettes.

"I *am* glad to meet you," I said, because Professor Blatt would be
eating his heart out.

*&?# stared at me with the kind of absolute loathing and disre-
spect that is the privilege of an elder. He grumbled something, like
curses I couldn't make out; then he rasped, "Ain't glad to meet
you."

You know, when he said that, I almost started to cry. My eye
stung and watered; it was an automatic reaction. There are some
people that you don't care whether they like you or not, and others,
as soon as you meet them, you ache for them to like you.

"What's the matter, your books aren't making enough money,
you have to work here?" I said, admiring him at the same time.

"Kid," he said, "if I had any dough left I'd be as big a jackass as
you. When I had it, I spent it all on—"

"*&?#ie, don't be crude!" Ardella piped.

"Of course, dear lady," he said with a wavy-lipped leer. Then he
grumbled some inaudibles, sat down and shoved his chair toward
his typewriter, and typed as fast as hate, with long, mottled, lumpy
fingers.

When Ardella called him by his diminutive, I got my first
glimpse of their relationship. She always indulged him, and that
made him bristle. He mocked her with leering courtliness, and that
made her fawn over him even more, since she was a devoted reader
of his. In public she sweet-talked him as if trying to make people
think they were lovers; but I once heard the Flimes scream, "Virgin!" at each other during one of their fights.

Once, I asked *&?# why the sisters *really* hated each other; was it
really just because of that silly birthmark? He only cackled, and
said, "Spotted One doesn't like Unspotted One." He felt protective
of the two crazy sisters; he may have hated them, but he was grate-
ful to them. Not only had they given him a job after he was
bounced from the ad agency, but he was so hard up that they let
him sleep in the office. I found that out when I snooped around, one

72

lunchtime, when the Flimes were out eating at separate tables at the same restaurant. In their office closet I saw a green sleeping bag—same color as mine, but older and with a hole in the nylon—and a beaten-up cane suitcase, and five wrinkled white shirts, each with holes in the armpits. That explained why, when I left the office at five o'clock each day, he was calling up a deli to have a salad plate delivered. Like most old men, he had trouble sleeping at night, and when he was up at four in the morning he'd turn the lights on and bang out a few pages of his current assignment. That made up for the hours during the regular working day when he rested his head on his typewriter and napped.

"But with your reputation," I said, "couldn't you get an easier job, like at a college or something?"

He just cackled again, and turned away from me to bang at his typewriter, with his white hair shining under the fluorescent lights and the red flakes falling from his scalp. It took me a long time to realize that he simply loved to write, and that if he couldn't write his good stuff anymore he would write pulp. The crabbier he acted, the more he loved what he was doing.

Since I was young and energetic and not ruined yet, he hated me. Fortunately, he liked to talk to people he hated. During breaks, he'd sit chewing dried fruit and nuts from his cupped palm—or licking the palm when the fruit and nuts were gone and he was too abstracted to get more from the bag in his desk—and stare nostalgically through a brown photo of a nude female writer, taped to the wall. And I'd start off:

"Tell me about the great old days of bohemia . . ."

He belched, licked his empty palm, chewed air, stood up slowly, hitched his pants, farted wetly, and said, "I'm goin' to the bathroom to void my inner life."

As he walked out, I heard fruit and nuts slogging in his stomach.

When he came back, with his belt loosened a notch, he gave a cackling sigh of nostalgia and said, "In the great old days of bohemia, we were so poor we had to scrape our own ink together from the insides of condoms and sanitary napkins."

73

He sat down, and gazed at the photo on his wall, shaking his head and clicking his tongue. "Look at those udders," he said under his breath. Then: "Kid, don't confuse a person's image with what he really is. I'm not my image. Why can't Americans understand that? In Europe I ain't treated like a dirty old man. In Europe I'm a fucking *sage*."

He lit one of his French cigarettes; it smelled like the perfume of a Frenchwoman electrocuted in her bath. He coughed and spat after the first puff. Ashes and phlegm dotted his collar. "Handkerchief!" he croaked. "For the sake of the muses, kid, gimme something to mop my collar. Gimme a handkerchief and I'll tell you the deepest secret of art."

He was half standing, leaning out of his chair and extending a shaky, wriggling hand toward me. A drop of saliva trickled down his chin whiskers. I took a clean white handkerchief out of my pocket, and instead of just giving it to him I stood up and dabbed the trickle off his chin first. But he grabbed the hanky away angrily—maybe he thought I was weird—and wiped his mouth and collar with hard, circular wipes.

Then he put my handkerchief into his pocket.

He turned toward the front of his desk, shoved close, and started typing.

Oh, what the hell, I thought. Let him keep the handkerchief.

He stopped typing for a moment, swiveled to face me, and said, "The secret of art is the same as the secret of life. Steal whatever you can get away with."

A minute later, when I was looking at my own work, my filthy handkerchief came flying at me from my blind side, and hit me damply on the side of my hair. It landed on my shoulder; I picked it up between the tips of two fingers, held it out at arm's distance, and dropped it to the floor.

"Thanks," I said.

6. What I Learned

*&?# was working on *Song of Mildred,* a book commissioned for the sixtieth birthday of a Scarsdale matron. Mildred was the Scarsdale matron's name; it was also the name of the heroine, who was quite a few years younger and—according to the text—"lacking the wisdom that comes only with the years." The heroine spent most of the novel drinking low-calorie mead, traipsing down stone staircases in long silk gowns created by the very finest medieval designers, and being wooed by genuflecting knights: Sir Murray, the advocate; Sir Morris, the keeper of the king's accounts; and, of course, Sir Milton, the court physician. The subject and the characters had been approved by the real Mildred's husband, a lampstore tycoon, and of course the castle in *Song of Mildred* was strikingly lit—"though lacking the visibility that would come only with later improvements in illumination."

I looked over *&?#'s shoulder as he typed an important stretch of dialogue:

> "What ho, fair queen? They say the dread Black Knight armeth himself to invade the neighborhood of our castle. I'll mount my faithful horse Cad-du-Lac and do battle with the villain by main strength."
>
> "Dear brave knight, be careful! The court physician saith the pressure of your heart's blood riseth treacherously. Forsooth, go not thyself, but raise a committee of knights to drive yon swarth intruder from our zone."
>
> "Never! By main strength, say I, for with the Northern Kingdom Exercise Program have I prepared for this joust."

"I know," I said. "The Black Knight turns out to be a well-spoken, law-abiding gentleman who just wants to find a peaceful greensward to build his manor on."

"Nix." *&?# shook his head as he typed. "Lamp tycoon wants him run out of Camelot."

I held my stomach in disgust. Learning about the literary life wasn't always pleasant. But I would have hung over his shoulder to learn more, except that he lit one of his cigarettes for the specific purpose of getting me away.

"I'll type my crap, you type yours," he told me. His cigarette smoke smelled like a burning stable. It drove me across the room, to work on my own assignment.

I was doing a book called *The Liberator of His People*. It was the freely construed life story of a South American *presidente*, who had ordered a large printing to make sure he had enough copies for his colonels, his mistresses, his legitimate and illegitimate children, and the entire diplomatic corps in his capital city. I didn't have to invent any of the scenes: he had invented it all already, and recorded it on a tape from which I was to extrapolate. I closed my eyes, took a deep breath, and said out loud, "Come, Shlockia, Muse of hackwork. Sing through me of the adventures of El Presidente . . ."

*&?# started having a coughing fit; he cursed me, threw his burning cigarette at my head. It missed, but I hunched over my typewriter, and as he lit another cigarette to stink up the room even further I began to type the great liberator's biography:

> The powerful Zis sedan, so solidly built by our Soviet friends that it put the jalopies of Detroit to shame, rounded the mountainside curve on two wheels, with a screech of brakes and a smell of burning rubber. Through the dust clouds behind it, the bullets supplied by the North American imperialists cracked into the mountainside, setting loose a rockslide from which El Presidente and his loyal comrades escaped by inches. A boulder the size of an imperialist's head crashed onto the fender, which was made of good socialist chrome that could easily withstand the shock. A CIA-smuggled M-16 bullet shattered the side-view mirror but inflicted no injuries.

Around the curve, the road descended the mountainside toward the peaceful village, then named for some fraudulent saint but later renamed for Fidel Castro. Swift as the progress of modernization under El Presidente's leadership, the Zis sped toward the market clearing. Goats, chickens, women with baskets on their heads, scattered before the oncoming grille of that splendid example of Soviet engineering; but the driver, a true man of the people, steered a harmless course between the stalls. Suddenly, from the corner of his eye, El Presidente spotted an undernourished boy weeping in the shadow of a hut, fingering a bowl of cornmeal which the tyrant's tax collectors had reduced to a few pale grains.

"Stop the car!" El Presidente ordered. "We must feed that child!"

"But, Comrade Excellency," said his steadfast driver, Comrade Pedro, availing himself of the freedom of discussion that is our ever-present goal in this regime, "the right-wing dogs nip at our very heels. Cowardly as they are, they have so many Yankee weapons they could undermine the people's revolution!"

"That boy *is* the revolution! I have seen an injustice in our land, and I must set it right! If we trust our mission of serving the people, the plutocratic cowards will never catch up to us."

And indeed, the pursuers' Cadillac, which had cost thousands of bowls of cornmeal for thousands of the oligarchy's victims, blew a tire as it swerved past the rockslide—a tire sabotaged by an oppressed black worker's spontaneous act of guerrilla defiance on one of the infamous assembly lines of the slave state of Michigan.

I was afire with the joy of writing masterpieces of dreck. But the faster I typed, and the more extravagantly I described his heroics, the sorrier I felt for the poor vicious dictator. I imagined that someday he'd be deposed, and if he survived he would kill the endless evenings of his Moscow exile by turning the pages of my book. It would replace his memory, his own knowledge of what had happened to him. When his hair was gray and he dressed up in his general's uniform to receive a Moscow University history student in his one-room flat, he'd flip through my book to refresh his facts before starting the interview. He'd think, Yes, that is how I stopped to buy food for a hungry village boy at the risk of my own life! The ends of his fingers would scarcely feel the paper, because of circulatory problems and the inadequate Soviet heating: but through the paper he could practically feel again the boy's knotted, lice-ridden hair. Poor El Presidente, depending on me for solace in his last years. He had always placed too much trust in his subordinates, hadn't he? He would begin to think he really had stopped for the village boy instead of driving straight through and running over a dog in the marketplace. He would forget that he'd made up the story of the village boy on a drunken fishing trip to impress some American journalists aboard his yacht. I imagined him lying in a Russian hospital with pneumonia, on the last day of his life: he looks at the antiquated glass intravenous bottle and the lack of fancy new monitoring equipment, and curses himself for not siding with the West. But he's comforted in his last breath by the memory of feeding a hungry village boy. El Presidente, why couldn't your life have been truer to your lies?

By the time the pursuers' Cadillac blew a tire, I was out of breath; I had to stop typing, because I didn't know precisely what noble words El Presidente would say next. I turned to my left so I could see *&?# with my good eye, maybe ask his advice or get inspiration by just looking at him. His head was on his typewriter, and he was snoring.

I'm sitting next to a literary legend, I thought. And I've learned from him, and copied him just like he told me to, and now I'm as good at this as he is. Who knows what else I'll learn, if I don't watch out?

The phone on our wall rang, and when I answered it I heard the familiarly leaky woodwind voice of a Flime.

"Rich, dear," Ardella fluted, "how are you coming along with that sweet El Presidente's biography?"

"Fine—"

I heard a click, like someone joining on an extension. "Redstone,"

Ardith honked, "how are you doing on that Presidente number?"

"I think I did some good descriptions—"

"I didn't ask you if it was good or bad," she snapped. "I asked you how you were *doing*. How many *pages* have you written? Quality is for dilettantes. Pros only care about filling up the pages."

Every English professor in the country gave a scream and fell to the ground.

It would have been easy for me to tell myself, She's cracked, and what she's talking about has nothing to do with real writing anyway. But I decided to hold back the easy judgment. I said to myself, You've started playing her game, so keep playing it until you've at least mastered the rules. And you can't write if you're holding your nose.

You can learn something from anyone, even a shmuck. A shmuck once told me that, and he was right.

So I said, "I've got thirty-five pages."

"Now you're talking. Get in here and give us a read."

"We'd be pleased," Ardella added, "if you'd drop over and let us peruse what you've done so far, from a stylistic standpoint as well."

"Yes, ma'ams," I said. "Should I make a Xerox copy so you can both read it?"

"Are you trying to tell us our business?" they both shouted at once. If you hinted that their hostile attachment to each other might be a bit eccentric and inefficient, they would suddenly act with perfectly efficient harmony for the purpose of threatening to fire you. So forget it, I told myself, and I took the one copy of the chapter into their office.

When I entered, Ardith and Ardella were sitting with their backs to each other: Ardella with her feet tucked in against the swivel legs of her chair, and Ardith with her feet up on the desk. Ardella was filing her nails on a pink emery board, fingernails extended. Ardith was filing her nails on a steel nail file, fingers curled.

I stopped in the middle of the room.

"Thirty-five big ones," I announced.

I looked to the left at Ardella. I looked to the right at Ardith.

Ardella swiveled toward the center of the room. "I'll be delighted to look at it."

Ardith dropped her legs off her desk and swiveled. "I'll take a gander at that."

Both of them stood, Ardith leaning on her cane. Both strode toward me; both stretched an arm toward the papers in my hand; both muttered snarls at each other. I held the papers away from my body like a matador's cape and stepped back. Ardella grabbed the left side of the sheaf; Ardith grabbed the right; I let go; I took another step back. "Give me!" Ardella said; "Give me!" Ardith said; Ardella kicked at Ardith's shin and missed; Ardith swung her cane at Ardella's head and missed; each of them tried to pull the papers away from the other; the sheaf tore down the middle.

Each Flime held one side of each page.

"Look what you've done, you menace," they told each other simultaneously. "I'll go read this and see if it's any good."

So they sat at their desks, presenting their backs to each other once more. Ardella read the left side of every page, with two fingers pressed gently to her slightly parted lips. Ardith flipped through the right sides, frowning, and twirling a finger in her ear.

They stood up. Ardith hobbled toward me with her cane. Ardella turned the notched pink dial of her hearing aid.

"It's thirty-five, all right," Ardith said, shaking my right hand.

"It's inspired!" Ardella said, shaking my left. "It reminds me so of the early work of dear *&?#! You're fitting in perfectly here!"

"Thanks for the compliment," I said in despair. "Ms. Flime, Ms. Flime, can I ask you a question, though? I mean, I'm glad you like my work, but don't you think you ought to give it a more complete reading before you accept it?"

I turned my head from left to right and saw both sisters look extremely puzzled.

"What do you mean?" Ardella said. "Do you have a problem accepting praise?"

"You're not the only one in New York who can fill up pages," Ardith said. "If you have any complaints, you can look for another job."

"Is he trying to insult us?" Ardella asked Ardith.

"Is he telling us how to run our business?" Ardith asked Ardella.

They both edged closer to me.

"You only read half of each page," I said.

"You insolent—!"

"You insubordinate—!"

Ardella raised her pink emery board. Ardith raised her steel nail file. "Get him, Ardie!" Ardella shrieked. "Get him, Ardie!" Ardith growled. They both charged, and while I was turned to look at the faster Ardella, Ardith smacked me in the ankle with her cane. I howled—I hopped—I felt like I'd been hit with a golf club. I grabbed my ankle with one hand and grabbed Ardith for balance with the other. But she raised her nail file and jabbed it at my right eye . . .

My only eye!

I gasped, and ducked, and the nail file went past my ear . . .

And Ardella, who was grabbing me from behind, screamed in pain. A dark speck fell from her left cheek. It looked like a dead fly.

Ardella stood with her hand pressed to her left cheek. She was crying. She lifted her hand away and looked at it. There was no blood on her cheek. There was no birthmark either. She now looked exactly like Ardith, but wearing a pink dress.

I let out a joyous yell. "This is wonderful! You're free! All your lives the birthmark's set you apart, and now you don't have it anymore!"

I went and gave Ardith a slap on the back. I went and gave Ardella a respectful little kiss on her bare left cheek. I felt like the liberator of the Flimes.

"You'd better leave the room for your own sake, Rich dear," Ardella said moistly.

"Get the hell out of here on the double, Redstone," Ardith growled.

"No," I said. "This is the best day of your lives; I'm gonna make you see that. Look"—I scrambled toward the surgically removed brown speck on the floor, between the Persian rug and the bearskin—"this was the source of all your hate for each other." And I was thinking, Yes, it's wonderful, people don't have to hate each other after all, the things separating them are tiny things easily removed, a small effort will clear up many years of misunderstanding. I bent down, and flicked that damn dead flylike speck across the floor with my fingernail . . .

I frowned. It hadn't felt right. The texture was funny.

I scrambled fast toward the speck. I pressed the tip of my index finger onto it, and felt it adhere to my damp fingerprints. I picked it up, and peeled it off my finger.

It was a dot of brown vinyl with a gummed white back.

Ardella walked up to me, sniffling, and offered her left cheek.

"Please," I said. "Try to live without it. You might enjoy it."

She tapped her cheek with her finger, and smiled sadly. A tear dropped from her eye, and she lifted her finger to let the tear cross the bare spot where the birthmark had been.

"I shouldn't," I said. But I did—I dabbed her cheek dry with the cuff of my sleeve, lifted the dot on my fingertip, and pressed it back on. She gasped with joy, and hugged me.

When I took took my finger away, the birthmark stayed on her cheek.

"You're fired!" Ardith shouted at me.

"I'm giving you a raise," Ardella said, resting her spinsterly left cheek on my collarbone.

7. My Contribution to the Literature of Wrestling

I had vowed to find my own apartment once I saved up enough money.

But it was amazing how little money I managed to save from my salary. I mean, I had to start sharing Laurie's household expenses, plus pay back the portion of my expenses that she'd lent me. I tried to earn a little extra by betting on the horses, but after I started working at Yer Press my congenital luck seemed to desert me and I lost every race. Plus I had to start buying house plants for Laurie, because the loft was a little bare and I wanted to thank her for her kindness.

I bought a potted tree which cost me half a week's wages. I bought a hanging plant in a macrame basket. I bought begonias, philodendrons, coleuses—and I'm the kind of person who can't remember which house plant is which. I had my wardrobe to maintain, too. I bought six pairs of socks that grew holes in their big toes as quickly as every pair of socks I've ever owned. I bought a linen jacket that lost a button the next week. I bought a couple of white shirts that acquired ring around the collar. I bought a new tie, green with yellow and black stripes.

One day, I was standing between my two desks, dipping a tea bag into a mug of hot water. I was in a creative trance, trying to think of some metaphoric touches to enhance the summing-up in the last chapter of El Presidente's biography, when *&?# barged in from the bathroom, faster than he'd ever walked in my presence before, and shook my elbow from behind.

"From France!" he said. "Look, kid, from France!"

No tea spilled from the mug. However, my right hand had had to carry the mug downward in order to keep it balanced, and the tea bag was now dangling in midair in my left hand. It swung against my new tie like the clapper of a bell—bong, bong, bong, stain, stain, stain.

I turned around and sneered at *&?#. "From France?"

He rubbed the end of my tie with his inky fingers as if that was a perfectly efficacious cleaning method. "I'll pay the cleaning bill," he laughed raspily. Then he smacked the wet tail of my tie with a comic book that was in his hand.

"Look!" he said. "They love me in France." And he began flipping open the pages.

It was a French comic book for adults. In the pictures, a group of affluent-looking men with open-necked shirts, and beautiful women with long, slim legs and globular breasts, were undressing at a picnic table piled with wine bottles and cheeses. Under the table reclined a shoeless woman with a long braid of hair, which hung down the vast opening at the back of her dress. She poised herself, knees up, to plant her pursed, edible-looking lips on the thin lips of a half-naked man who was gripping her by the buttocks. Perpendicular to the couple, a huge jagged crack was opening in the earth and starting to swallow up the table.

"*Alors,*" said the woman, looking deep into the man's eyes as the couple plummeted into the crack, "*c'est vraiment comme l'oeuvre de *&?#, n'est-ce pas?*"

*&?# lit one of his cigarettes and, in his excitement, blew it in my face. I coughed, and by way of apology he waved the smoke away— which isn't much good when an eighty-year-old man does it.

"Thanks for showing me your triumph," I said, inspecting my tie. I would have cursed him out, in the friendly way we'd gotten used to over time, but I said to myself, God, he's excited to be mentioned in a comic book.

That afternoon I gave my tie to a dry cleaner, and paid the bill myself. It came back still tea-stained, but with a thread unraveling from its underside. I demanded a free recleaning, and it came back still tea-stained, but with a second thread unraveling. It was a real Rich Redstone tie.

84

I've often wondered what it is about me that prevents me from earning a living as a male model. Clothes rebel against me. I myself like clothes, I'm fond of my wardrobe, I like ties and jackets and sweaters, but for some uncanny reason a day's wearing by me makes a garment look a season old. If I were to buy the most expensive suit in Brooks Brothers, probably a seam would rip while I was shaking hands on the first interview I wore it to. That's the way I am, it has nothing to do with the quality of the clothes, and it's exasperating, because I know there are people who refuse to see my good qualities after they've seen my clothes. And because I feel bad about it in myself, it upsets me when I see anyone else who's also dressed like a slob. What are you doing to yourself? I want to ask him.

I agitated *&?# about his shirts every day until he finally explained that he had ripped the underarms on purpose as an antiperspirant measure. Tearing cloth was healthier than spraying your pits with aluminum, he said. It made me realize that a genuinely logical truth is usually too ridiculous to argue with.

My weeks at Yer Press went by. The summer heat got horrendous, then less horrendous, but when the weather cooled off, *&?# started smoking more to make up for it. As he filled our little white room with stench, he would brag about how respected he was in Europe, and how stupid the readers in America were.

"In Amsterdam"—puff, puff—"they wait by the piers for the ships to dock with my books. In Copenhagen"—cough, cough—"the college students stay up all night reading my stories out loud."

After a while I learned not to listen to that kind of thing too hard. I leaned closer to my typewriter and rapped out my work. Taking a few seconds now and then to stretch backward, sigh at the ceiling, and wipe my hair grandiosely off my forehead, I typed:

And so, dear countrymen, this biography of El Presidente is at an end. But the story of El Presidente is not. For he is still with us, always lovingly watching over us like a father watching over his sleeping babes to make sure nothing wakes them up. Guard us in our sleep, El Presidente, and keep the night-

mare of imperialism from us! Thank you, El Presidente, and
may you live a zillion years!

I threw up my hands, like a liberated peasant celebrating El Presidente's birthday, and jumped up from my seat, and whooped.

"Finished El Presidente! I finished my first book! The zillion
years crack is too sarcastic, but maybe they probably won't
notice!"

I leaped up and down the cramped aisle; then I slammed the
entire wad of paper against the face of the typewriter. I had to type a
new title page, but it was worth it. *&?# told me not to be so happy,
since I hadn't seen what my *next* assignment would be.

"It can't be any worse or better," I said, and slapped him on the
back, and ran out to the Flimes' office to show them my work.

I paced the writing room for two hours, until they called me
in.

Ardith caned her way toward me and shook my hand. "It's
great," she said through the side of her mouth. "Two hundred and
fifty-six pages: exactly what we contracted for. I don't know how
you did it. I've been counting the pages backward and forward all
afternoon, and every time I recount them it's as if I'm learning
something new. Congratulations, you've really learned your
craft."

Ardella minced up to me, dabbing the corners of her eyes with a
lilac-bordered white handkerchief. "Rich dear, I read and loved
every word of it. What a life El Presidente has led! When I reread
the scene with the village boy, I cried. It all rings so true!"

I gave two little bows. "Thanks a lot for your appreciative
insights into my work. It's an honor to serve such a knowledgeable
audience."

Ardith snorted, and hobbled back to her desk to make a phone
call. Ardella squeezed my arm with readerly gratitude, and walked
to her desk dabbing her eyes, in the kind of transport of belief that
should have made any novelist throw his typewriter away in shame.
She pressed the palm of her left hand up under her chin and fluttered her fingers against her birthmark: a habitual gesture to make
sure it was still in place.

Then I noticed the man sitting in the visitor's chair at Ardella's desk. He was in his late thirties, with thin legs, and skinny hairy fingers clasped over one knee. He cracked his knuckles, looked up at the walls, and pivoted in the swivel chair on one heel. He had a black beard with a few white hairs in it, and wore a dark-blue knit suit that was too big for him, too heavy for the weather, too wide in the lapels, and dandruffy on the collar. He wore a navy-blue yarmulke fastened to his scalp with a bobby pin.

"You'll do a rather different project now, Rich dear." Ardella patted her cheeks with four fingers. "This gentleman—"

Ardith's voice interrupted, talking loudly over the telephone. "Hello, Señor Presidente? Ardith Flime at Yer Press. Your book's finished and it's a winner. Two hundred and fifty-six pages on the nose."

The man with the yarmulke looked around at me and raised his eyebrows, and I gave him my best "I don't know what's going on here" smile.

Ardella put a finger to her lips. "Ardith dear," she cooed. But Ardith turned her back and talked louder.

"You want two hundred and *sixty*-six? Well, that's a tall order, señor. We contracted for two fifty-six."

"Sister dear," Ardella said, advancing over the Persian rug and the parquet tiles to the bearskin. "Will you please conduct your half of the business in a tone that doesn't interfere with my half?"

"Look, Señor Pres," Ardith barked over the phone. "If you want ten more pages you'll cough up an extra grand."

"Ardie sweet, what are you saying to that nice Presidente? Ten pages isn't a matter for gouging. You want to lose the whole fee, you dear emptyheaded thing?"

"Keep out of my half of the room!" Ardith snapped. "Listen, El Commie," she said into the phone, "in this country we keep our bargains."

"Mother taught us never to shout." Ardella clamped onto Ardith's wrist.

Ardith broke free with a fling of her arm, and the beige telephone receiver flew out of her hand, banged against her desk, and kept banging as it hung from its curlicue cord. Inside the mouthpiece, someone asked questions that sounded like "Peepa peepa pee-pa peepa peepa *peepa?*"

"You are ruining this company!" Ardella screamed.

"*You* are ruining this company!" Ardith snarled.

"It was my idea and I should never have included you!"

"It was *my* idea and I should never have included *you!*"

Ardith hopped on her good foot and tackled Ardella, and they wrestled. They rolled over each other from Persian rug to bearskin and back. The visitor looked at them in astonishment, and I took pity on him—and on the Flimes, who seemed about to lose a customer—and I sat down behind Ardella's lucite desk to do some rational business. I stuck my hand out to the visitor.

"I'm the writer who'll be working on your project. Why don't you tell me about it so I can get a feel for the subject matter?"

He wasn't looking at me; he was blinking at the tussling Flimes. Ardith had Ardella prone, and was sitting on top of her and bending her leg back. Then Ardella jabbed Ardith in the guts, bucked, rolled out from under her . . .

"Well, let's introduce ourselves," I tried again. "My name's Rich Redstone."

"Baruch Litovsky," he said.

I stood up so suddenly that I scared both the visitor and myself.

"Cut it out!" I screamed—not at him, at the Flimes.

They parted from each other like the two halves of the Red Sea. Lying side by side, virginal chests thumping, they looked as identical as a hot dog with mustard and a hot dog with ketchup. They stared at me with bewilderment and fear. They flicked their wrists at each other, and their fists knocked together in midair. Then Ardith reached out with her thumbnail . . .

And flicked Ardella's birthmark off . . .

And picked it up from the floor . . .

And pressed it onto her own left cheek.

It seemed to infuse new life into Ardith's legs. She sprang up, and without the slightest trace of a limp she walked into the private bathroom on Ardella's side of the room.

Ardella dried her eyes, snorted, and rose slowly. Supporting herself on pieces of furniture, she hobbled to the private bathroom on Ardith's side of the room.

I rubbed my eye—not my good eye, my bad one. I closed it and rubbed it as if rubbing a crystal ball, and felt it slide in its socket like a ball bearing. I had the feeling that I was seeing all this through the glass of my blind eye. That was the only possible explanation. I was seeing the glass world that people with two eyes never get to see.

"Don't worry," I babbled. "Ardith stole the birthmark, that's all. Ardith stole it." Imagine, this was supposed to reassure the visitor that I was the rational and stable one in the office. "What'll Ardith do with a birthmark? She's not supposed to have one. It's all Ardella has. It's from way back in childhood. Ardella has a birthmark and Ardith doesn't, that's so they can hate each other . . ." Suddenly I noticed Litovsky blinking apprehensively at me, and I completely agreed with him; except that I was also saying to myself, Yes, this is fine, this is the confusion and mystery I was looking for.

I took a long, deep breath, and sat down. "Please go on. Your name is Litovsky?"

"Baruch Litovsky. I'm a very successful man in remnants. Cotton, wool, velvet—the strips of material left over after they cut the pieces to size. We buy them from textile mills and sell them to paper mills, stuffed-animal manufacturers . . . Well." He sighed. "It's not me I'm here about, it's my wife—"

"Zipporah," I said, at exactly the same instant he did. He looked at me strangely, and I smiled as if to say that I was merely fast at echoing people. But I was remembering her purple kerchief and beautiful hair, and the carrot-colored eyes at the level of my solar plexus. I thought, He married *her*? The poor slob—well, what do you expect? Look at him, dandruff on a navy-blue suit, where could he find an attractive woman? My hands were sweating all over the arms of Ardella's chair.

"My wife is crazy," he said. "For five years I've tried everything: doctors, rabbis, more rabbis, more doctors, a hypnotist, an acupuncturist. The most I got from it was, one rabbi talked her into endowing six stained-glass windows with pictures of Brushes from the Bible; and a psychiatrist let her stock his office with cigars and cigar cutters. She filled our house up with junk, and when I tried to throw it out she took herself and the junk to a cheap apartment. I started sleeping in the factory, the only place I have peace. Our house is standing empty. This, coming to you, it's the last chance. I saw your ad in the *Wall Street Journal*. I say to myself, Could this be the way to get through to her? Show her a book about her craziness, and it might shock her into acting sane. Therapy, done by sensitive people of letters."

He stopped, and craned his neck worriedly at the Flimes' bathroom doors.

"It's okay, they don't write the book," I said. "Please tell me more; I want to help you and Zipporah. I'm sure I'm especially suited to write on this subject. I'm eager to learn more about her—tell me, please."

He shook his head dubiously; but then he said, "Well, I've thrown away more than fifty thousand on her already. Why not another fifty? Money is nothing if it doesn't cure."

The two bathroom doors opened simultaneously, and the two Flime sisters came out. But Ardith, with the birthmark on her cheek, had changed into a frilly white dress with a pink carnation print; she'd let her hair down to her shoulders, and she'd put on two pink hearing aids. Ardella now wore a brown pantsuit, had no birthmark, wore her hair up in a bun, and carried a cane.

Ardith walked to Ardella's desk, without limping. She flicked her hands to shoo me out of the chair. She cleared her throat, as if testing her voice, and laughed flutily. "Don't try to displace the boss, Rich dear."

"Ardith?" I said. "Ardella?"

The other sister—the one who had started out as Ardella but now wore a pantsuit—limped over to Ardith's desk and turned her back to us. "That goddamn Presidente," she growled.

"Ardella?" I said. "Ardith?" I looked back and forth from Flime to Flime; and now I understood why *&?# never called them by their names, but only "Spotted One" or "Unspotted One." "Which one are you?" I asked both at once. "How often do you do this? Is

90

this the first time, or do you do it every day, or every year? Does either of you remember which is which?"

I looked to Litovsky for help, but not knowing the Flimes to begin with, he was oblivious of the change that had just occurred. He was exclusively involved in narrating his own troubles.

"She seemed okay when I married her. Then she met another man. Who, I don't know. She says they're not having an affair; but he makes sure she gets all the money she needs. *I'm* not paying for all those brushes anymore. This guy must have a fortune, but he's as crazy as her. Why does he send her all this money? Because he wants to free her. She says he's supporting her to do whatever she pleases, how do you like that? At first she was doing crazy things you wouldn't believe—walking around the house naked, going to Christian churches. Then she got exhausted from trying to do everything, so she concentrated on buying household goods from door-to-door salesmen. This guy, I can't understand what he wants from her. *She's* in love with *him*, I can tell that. She keeps raving about the way he dresses: always white suits with blue piping, is that really what they're wearing now? Do and be, he tells her. Do and be whatever you want."

"*Be* and *watch*," I corrected, my throat strained tight. But I couldn't edify him further at the moment, because my knees were buckling, the world went pale and lost its breath, everything vibrated and bulged, and my field of vision became a dance floor for spots of light. Then the world went dark, and I heard myself say, "Being and watching," like hearing a radio signal in the blackness of outer space, as I swooned to the Persian rug in a faint.

8.   A Youthful Indiscretion

The Flimes fired me for causing a disturbance in their office.

"Now things will get back to normal around here," Ardith growled, shoving me a severance paycheck. If I hadn't been there, would the birthmark have always stayed in place, the white shirts been ironed and sewn, the sisters kept their noses quietly in their dunning letters like normal business people? I don't know, I don't know.

"Mr. Litovsky," Ardella said—when I say "Ardith" and "Ardella," of course, I'm referring to their clothes and mannerisms; as to which body inhabited which garments, I doubt if they themselves could have said—"Mr. Litovsky, we'll assign our top writer to your project, and we'll try our very best to help rid your wife of that delusion about buying and watching—"

"*Being* and watching!" I shouted, and before they could make the slightest Flimeish reply I ran out of the office. I passed the empty reception desk, and the unmarked door of the good old writers' room, with the dried apricot stains around the doorknob, and the good old writer snoozing amid cigarette fumes. I went to the front door and flicked the three locks . . .

The coffin slid up the gangplank.

The criminal slid up through the gallows trapdoor.

The arrow flew out of its target.

I was out!

"It's true," I said to my fellow elevator passengers and lobby transients and to the security guard and to the revolving door and to the air that hit me with pretzel smoke and fresh oxygen and to the huge library with its stones full of sun—to the peace and order in the library and the sleaziness crawling around it. "Being and watching is true!"

I watched my shadow travel along the sides of the parked cars. I stopped to stare at people, and my shadow stopped to cool a car door. On the sidewalk at the foot of the library steps, a teenager in a black suit, narrow black tie, and military crewcut waved a pointer in front of a blackboard covered with the words "God—Creator," "Jesus—Redeemer," "Sin," "Damnation," and preached to an audience consisting of another youth dressed exactly the same. The pretzel man and the hot-dog man ignored each other from the shade of their pushcart umbrellas. A bowlegged little man wearing a blue sun visor handed out sightseeing-company flyers. A black man in a red dress, black net stockings, and high heels stole a pocketbook from a sidewalk display while the proprietor wasn't looking, and wiggled away to his escape. A woman, sitting on a bench with two shopping bags at her feet, held an aluminum V under her chin to catch the sun rays. On the line for the Fifth Avenue bus, six people took turns stepping into the gutter and squinting uptown on tiptoe.

"That's the way!" I said. "Keep watching!" And I thought, What'll I tell Laurie?

Without a job, I couldn't afford to find my own place; but after sharing her expenses, I couldn't have respected myself if I'd gone back to sponging off her.

I walked around the block, and then around many blocks; and wondering made me slow down, so that I didn't get home till after most unfired workers.

I stepped into her building, testing explanations. Laurie, I got fired from my false job but I still have my true one, and in fact I've had proof that it's real. . . . Laurie, this guy will send me money too, as soon as I have faith that he will. . . .

I entered the loft. She was sitting on her bed, looking out the window. I saw her right profile in bronze dusk-light. She was wearing white shorts and a red tee shirt. "Hi, pal," I said. She turned her full face to me, and she was crying.

93

"What's the matter?" I walked toward her, but when I tried to sit beside her on the bed, she put her arm out stiff like a turnstile to block me.

"Get yourself a beer," she said.

I shrugged, walked across the loft, got a beer can from the refrigerator counter, set it down on the counter after my first gulp as she'd known I would—

On the counter, right next to where I'd set the beer can, was a thickly stuffed white envelope with a San Diego postmark and an aroma of strawberries.

I touched the edges with my fingers, and moved the envelope aslant on the butcher-block surface. I flipped it over with a thumb-flick, not wanting to get too close to it. I saw the broken splotch of red sealing wax on the back.

"His latest diary entry?" I asked. I put my hand around the cold, wet beer can.

"He describes," she shouted across the loft, "he describes all about how he found a new hole to put his sperm in."

I got so angry that I started crushing the beer can. I forgot that there was still a lot of beer in it, and it started spilling. Then I wiped the beer suds off my wrist and shirt cuff, and guzzled more beer from the dented can while I walked back to Laurie. I saw that she was going to let me sit next to her now; she had put her hands in her lap. I stood next to her bed, and felt my lips tighten so that they wouldn't quiver in fury—they quivered in fury anyway—then I said to myself, What am I doing trying to get next to Larry's woman? and I crushed the beer can all the way, and with a terrific side-arm, as if I was whipping Larry, I threw the can out the window.

"That cheating son of a bitch!" I yelled.

The can hit cement, thank God, not hitting a pedestrian. It had been a thoughtless, immature gesture, but I felt good about it. I felt revengeful and protective, just like I'd always wanted a woman to make me feel on her behalf; and I sat down and hugged Laurie and said, "How can he do this to you?" I could smell her hair. I tried to

94

nudge her into tilting her head down onto my shoulder, but she didn't; and, the eternal fantasizer, I thought, She's free for me! She's free for me!

I put my hand on hers—and it made her sob out loud. I wanted to take my hand away; but then I thought, Maybe I can keep my hand here if it's a fraternal hand rather than a lover's. Maybe she won't reject me then.

I looked at my hand on hers, and I thought, How caddish do you want to get, Redstone? You're taking advantage of her unhappiness. If she felt my hand at all, she felt it unpleasantly; but I couldn't take it off hers, I couldn't, I really did want to hold her hand and comfort her. I knew she loved Larry and wanted to be back with him; suddenly I wanted that for her, too; I wanted her to be happy with him; I just wanted to keep her hand until she could go to the airport and fly to him. And the more I started sharing her grief, the more rotten I felt about inflicting my hand on her. But the more rotten I felt, the more I needed to be soothed and loved. So I kept my hand on hers.

"He's going out with a veterinary intern," she sniffed, and ground her hand under mine as if she half wanted to extract it. "She works at the San Diego Zoo. She takes the lemurs' temperatures. She cures the elephants' infections with antibiotic darts. She tests the old lion's eyesight. I just hope she tries to make the rattlesnake say 'Ah.'" Laurie pouted, as if waiting for that wonderful event to happen. "The letter's very explicit. He met her when he went to the zoo on a Saturday. When do *I* have a Saturday free to go to the zoo? Either I'm working or it's the only day I can buy food and clothes. The elephants wrap their trunks around her. They trumpet when she calls them by name. She helped deliver a baby proboscis monkey. She likes giraffes, but she doesn't like bison. Her name is Jane. She's a very promising intern at the best zoo in the world. All her life she's known she's wanted to be around animals. Now she's around Larry. They feed each other peanuts after they make love. Why did he have to tell me that? What do I care how honest he is? I didn't tell him about *you* in *my* diary." She looked into my eyes

95

enraged, as if I'd hurt her. She pulled her hand out from under mine, and began to sob. "I hope she lets the rhinos wrap their horns around her. Look at that diary entry."

I hesitated.

"*Look* at it," she said.

I stood up and got it from the counter, and we read it together, with sheets of paper resting on our inner knees. I read it silently, finding the passages Laurie had already described, and she read it with interjections of "Ugh! Feh! That creep! I hate him!"

"You don't hate him," I assured her. I went on reading the diary:

> Perhaps Freedom like Death is something we prefer to observe in Others, & when we see signs of it in Ourselves it scares us. But I'm trying not to be afraid of it in Laurie or myself. I hope she is exscersising Freedom too. My new friendship won't decrease our Feelings for each other, it'll just decrease the pressure of our artifiscial way of Life. We'll still get together someday & live together. In the meantime I'm learning a great deal about Myself and the day to day practises of corporate Capitalization. . . .

"That stupid bastard!" I said, because his fine phrases hadn't brought him nearer to Laurie. But she was still *his* woman, and that made me angry at him too. I wished I could force him to come back here and treat her well. I would join their hands together, and then I'd tearfully and contentedly wave goodbye to them as they walked off together. . . . No, maybe I should beat Larry up first for treating her so badly. . . .

"What are you staring at?" she asked.

In my romantic reverie, with the diary pages bobbing on my lap, I had been staring bug-eyed through her and letting all the changes of emotion show on my face. When you love someone, you unconsciously let her see all the primitive faces behind your civilized one, as if you're dreaming.

I debated with myself: Should I tell her why I was staring? I'll make a fool of myself. But even if I make a fool of myself, she won't mind, she's a friend and true friends can forget. Okay, I'll tell her why I stared through her without even knowing what I was staring at.

"I love you," I said, as quickly as I could, wishing only half of her could hear it.

She laughed, with that I've-just-tasted-lemon expression which suited a short, brown-eyed blond so well.

"Well, at least I stopped your crying," I said. Quickly I recomposed my face muscles into the mask of businesslike friendship. I lose at least half of my debates with myself.

And I hadn't even stopped her crying. She started sniffling, rebuking me for making her laugh. "Think I'd be this sad if *you* slept with another woman?" she said.

I took a guess: "Yes?"

She laughed and shook her head as if I was pathetic.

"I've been with you for months," she said, "and both of us have been talking about how we really want someone else. I've been telling you to go out without me more."

"You've been telling Larry to go out with other people, too."

"But he didn't have to *describe* it to me in clinical detail, complete with camel tranquilizers and panda sperm counts. If he slept with someone who wasn't important to him, someone he could leave out of his diary—"

She bit her lip. She must have seen that she'd hurt my feelings. My chin sank, as if it was suddenly too heavy to hold up. I looked at the scuff marks on my buckskin shoes.

"I'm sorry," she said. "I *should* have put you in the diary, that's the point. I tried to deceive Larry, and now I'm being punished. Of course he has a right to sleep with her, after what we did. And he's so good, he tells me about it."

I inched my legs against hers, and pulled her closer to me. A mistake. I knew I was going too fast; but I was thinking about little Constance and Prudence and Grace, and how I'd take them on being-and-watching training walks while Mommy worked at the bank. . . .

I could feel Laurie's muscles tighten, like strawberry yogurt hardening in the freezer.

"I'm not sleeping with you again, that's one thing," she said. "If I keep away from you, maybe Larry will drop the animal girl. She's my punishment for you. What I'll do is, I'll write about you in my diary, apologize for not doing it sooner, and Larry and I will forgive each other and that'll be that."

"That'll be that!" I said, with a cheerily sick and hollow feeling.

I wanted to touch the bronze light between the blond strands of her hair. I wanted to swim in the coal-tar-and-hyacinth smell of her shampoo. I said to myself, You're only sad because you're losing something, not because of what you're losing. The thought made me feel glummer and glummer, as if I was losing even more.

"Well!" She bounced up from the bed. Her mood was improving rapidly. She was ready to take on the world. She clapped her hands once, and walked around the bed to the end table where she kept her diarizing equipment. She got out her looseleaf notebook and fountain pen, and sat down with her back to me.

" 'August Whatever,' " she said, testing out loud, " 'it's time for me to confess a terrible sin. Rich and I have engaged in sexual intercourse a certain number of times recently . . .' "

"Why don't you call it sexual congress?" I said. "That has the impersonal touch you seek."

She didn't look at me. She stepped around the bed with the notebook clutched high at her chest, and her head up drum-majorette style, as she marched to one of the tatami mats on the floor. She began writing. Humming. " '. . . Sexual intercourse. It's all over, and was of course merely a youthful'—that's right—'a youthful indiscretion.' " Pleased with the phrase, she tucked her legs in so they drove me mad, those clean, tan, plump, bare legs, and she resumed writing, her tongue appearing in the corner of her lips. " 'I understand what Larry's been going through and I bear him no malice'—et cetera— 'Rich and I are on a sound footing now, with his salary paying for half of the expenses, and he reports that his work is going—' " She looked up at me with the pen tip between her teeth. "How do you report that your work is going?"

"Great, I got fired today."

She tore out the diary page, crumpled it into a ball, and threw it at me. She glared at me until she was sure I was telling the truth, and then she glared some more. Maybe to entertain her, I punched my thighs. When my thighs protested, I got up and started lightly pounding the window with the edge of my fist. Then I rested my forehead on it.

"It's been a great day," I said, and the strange thing was, I meant it. "Laurie, I want you to know that my mission in life is being and watching. I'm completely secure in that knowledge now and I'm gonna follow through with it wherever it takes me. It would be nice if my best friend understood that, but if not, okay."

I heard her pen, that deceitful invention, scratch its way along the pages. " 'Unfortunately, Rich finds himself jobless again, and this is the conclusive reason why further sexual intimacy between us is out of the question. Rich knows my feelings about men who are not middle-class professionals, and if I'd obeyed those feelings in the first place, everything would have been fine.' "

" 'A pinstripe suit is the greatest aphrodisiac,' " I suggested, looking back at her over my shoulder, then turning my whole body in her direction. Not that she looked at me.

" 'I've repeatedly pointed out to him that women who respected themselves just wouldn't go out with a man who couldn't pay at least half of the check. So our project of finding him a lover must be inextricably intertwined with the project of finding him a career. . . .' Oh, that idiot!" she said about Larry, always Larry. "Why couldn't he get better grades in school?"

● ● ●

The next couple of weeks, I was so miserable I watched TV. I watched game shows. I watched soap operas. I watched old movies. I watched cartoons. I watched puppet pedagogy for preschool kids. I watched daytime talk shows for women. I watched daytime news for women. I watched evening news for men. I watched situation comedies about truckers, sheriffs, waitresses, high-school students, blacks, butlers, and disk jockeys. I watched dramas about cops, stunt men, cops, lawyers, cops, paramedics, and cops. I watched British soap operas in fancy dress on the public TV station. I watched more news, more talk shows, and more movies. That was my watching.

And my being became a function of Laurie's letters and diaries. Into September, comments about me flew from coast to coast, deciding my worth. Larry was completely magnanimous, understanding, and forgiving about my desire for Laurie—"which was a purely Sexual desire," he wrote all-knowingly. He even admired our supposed honesty. And as if he were a disinterested judge, he agreed that, yes, it was probably a step forward in personal growth for Laurie and me not to sleep together anymore.

Apparently he was still seeing Jane—an ocelot ate too much popcorn, a toucan's eggs were dangerously thin-shelled—but he became discreet about his sex life and emotions. Laurie acted pleased about that.

The whole tone of the diary had become sickeningly grown-up and factual. And I remembered when that diary was a treasure of unguarded emotion and honest self-disclosure! It drove me up a wall to think that I was responsible for the change. I kept waiting for Laurie to repent and tell him the real truth: tell him how we'd learned all the lovely individualities of each other's body, and how we'd smile to ourselves in the dark when our hands recognized the bumps and asymmetries and boninesses and fleshinesses, the hairs, the pores, the pimples, the wrinkles, the dry spots, the loose skin, the This is Too Small, the This is Too Big, the This Sticks Out, the This is Out of Shape. . . . She wouldn't tell him we knew that about each other. I kept waiting for her to tell him how, when our thighs were bucking and bumping against each other and my eye patch was practically slipping off, we'd each silently get angry at the other for not loving more, and the anger would make our bodies more passionate.

Well, I said to myself, if she's not telling him all our secrets, maybe it means she still wants me. So I hung around. I was waiting for her to beckon. I was waiting for clues to appear in her diary. I was waiting for her to ask me to atone. But all that happened was that she mentioned me less in the diary, over time.

I was intensely interested in the new TV season, because the TV was in Laurie's loft. I could lie on her bed, watch the set, and sniff her sheets, while she was out for the evening at some corporate seminar on Women in War Profiteering. Rich, I told myself, you're a disgrace! You're totally captivated, straining forward over the edge of the mattress and toward the screen, as you watch a network promo! "What do a handicapped ex-basketball star from Indiana and a telepathic kung-fu expert nun from the inner city have in common? Watch for the season premiere . . ." I was so far gone, I started thinking, Gee, what *do* they have in common? Was that Tuesdays at eight, seven Central Time?

Then a commercial came on, and a Western landscape filled the screen: a long, red, rocky vista with a butte on the right. A man on a palomino horse trotted into view, strumming a guitar. He strummed soothing, nostalgic Western chords. He was wearing a red-white-and-blue plaid shirt, blue jeans, and a white Stetson hat with a silver buckle that glinted. There was a close-up of him: tall and rangy, crinkly-eyed, smiling through tan wrinkles. Then he was standing in the open, on an old pioneer trail, speaking to a cluster of eight or ten men and women who represented about twenty different groups, among them an American Indian nurse, a black hardhat, a white housewife, and so on. The man with the cowboy guitar tipped his hat back, revealing a thatch of hair that somehow looked boyishly silver, before answering a question from a Mexican-American college girl. His crinkles bunched and unbunched so interestingly when he spoke that his words seemed to come from the corners of his eyes rather than his mouth. His voice was as vast and airy and hushed and certain as the west wind on the prairie.

"Good question, miss, and my answer to you is, well, shucks." He paused and strummed his guitar, and the members of the crowd smiled at each other as if his chords had made them all want to set aside their differences and be friends. "I've heard some folks claim that the basic liberties we hold so dear will be hurt if I'm elected. They have the right to say that, under our system. But I say to them and to you: Well, now. Look at this beautiful land all around us. Our land, our natural resources, is one of the most priceless parts of

101

America that we have to preserve for our children. If you want to preserve a natural resource, you plumb gotta be careful how you use it—not squander it wastefully. Well, the way I see it, freedom's one of our greatest national treasures, too."

The members of the crowd nodded to each other with bright eyes, as if he'd just told them about a new brand of vitamin-fortified breakfast cereal.

"Well, then," he went on. "As a great national resource, it's our duty not to squander and use up our freedom, but to conserve it wisely, just like our air, our water, and our minerals under our ground."

He flashed a smile, like an applause sign, and everyone applauded, and one black woman and one white woman jumped up and down clapping as if they'd won new refrigerators on a game show. The picture zoomed and froze on the three-thousand-mile-wide smile of the man in the white Stetson; then we heard some relaxed country guitar picking, and the man's voice sang, "Freedom—don't use it and you won't lose it."

And a sign came on the screen: "Jason A. Fleece—Our President in Eighty-Four."

I screamed. I jumped up from the bed and screamed curses at the TV; and I turned off the TV, screaming more curses; and then, muttering curses because my throat was getting sore, I packed my suitcase; and I walked out to find some freedom to squander.

9. Shelters

"A room for a week," I said, and threw my fountain pen on the hotel desk.

The desk clerk thought I was crazy, of course, but it was the pen with my hundred emergency dollars in it.

"Goodbye!" I cried to my hundred-dollar bill when I saw it go into the cash drawer.

The desk clerk no longer thought I was crazy, because it wasn't up to him to think ill of anyone crazy enough to rent a room at the Elephant Hotel. It was called the Elephant Hotel not because it was especially big, and not because any large animals had ever stayed there, but because of the grotesque protuberances all over its Victorian face, and the frightening deformities in its skeletal structure. People had been known to collapse in dread upon seeing its rooms for the first time. Since this isn't a horror story, I won't describe in detail what my room actually looked like. Nor will I describe what kinds of spots and lumps I found after sleeping in the bed, nor what kinds of lotions and powders I had to apply to cure the spots and lumps, nor what specimens of the medical profession I consulted and what their manners were and what they charged, nor how many different subtle and learned diagnoses I received for one and the same rash, while it spread from my fingers to my wrists to my armpits to my chest to my . . .

Nor will I enter in too much detail upon descriptions of the meals I ate at lunch counters up and down this blessed isle over the next week: the fried eggs swimming in gray oil, the pork sausage juicy-red in the center, the coffee with rainbow swirls floating on top, the egg-salad sandwiches runny with warm mayonnaise, the chopped liver crusty-brown on the surface, the roast beef with its antique green patina, the salad which I unknowingly shared with the cutest family of baby cockroaches, the layer cake that my fork cleaved in two like a brick, the hamburger that was charcoal black on the outside and frozen inside. Nor need I delineate the emergency room where I took my food poisoning, and how long I waited, nor divulge the names and mannerisms of the interns and nurses who tended me, the deft witticisms they made, their wise and sure surmises as to my condition, their respectful and dignified discussion of my finances. Nor will I waste words acquainting you with my companions of that period: the drunk from whom I snatched an empty green bottle of Night Train Express before he cracked it over his partner's head; the fire-escape crawler whose head *I* cracked with a snap-kick when he stuck it into my window (I stood shaking by the window for the next three hours, a lamp in my hand, until I started dreaming with my eye open and sleepwalked back to bed); the desk clerk who, each night, made a new pyramid of beer cans beside the hotel register, claiming the pyramid emitted longevity rays; the old lady who wore iridescent-green toreador pants and showed me photos of her son's execution for rape and murder; the two-hundred-and-fifty-pounder who stood in his room in a Boy Scout uniform eight hours a day, shouting, "Right face! Left face! About face!"; Rex, the one-eyed white cat with protruding ribs, who slashed a vein in the top of my hand when I tried to pet him; James, the ten-year-old shoeshine boy who worked from eight in the morning till midnight; Bobbie, the lesbian sculptress who had chopped off her left hand because a hook was more seductive; June, the secretarial student who wore matching gold necklaces with Roger, her Great Dane; nor—especially nor—poor Mr. Rodriguez. He was the one who rigged a pulley to lower his ass onto a twelve-inch piece of broomstick which he had clamped to his toilet bowl. One evening, five minutes after he'd returned from his job as an ice cream man, I heard groans from his room. I knocked on his door, he told me everything was okay. Later the groans grew louder. He began to sob, he called out the names of saints and of the Virgin, I knocked again, he told me it was okay again, he groaned a big groan and was silent, I told the desk clerk, the desk clerk's hand shook from palsy as he tried to place the last beer can on top of the pyramid, the beer cans tumbled over the registry desk, the clerk was a mild and resigned man, he simply closed his eyes and shook his head in pain and said, "O mighty forces of the pyramid, Isis, Osiris . . ." but he said he'd go up and check on Mr. Rodriguez, but he must not have, and the next morning Mr. Rodriguez' ex-wife came with their little son to ask Mr. Rodriguez for money. That's when everyone found out about the broomstick and the pulley. She found him dead, impaled up to his intestines, a human popsicle. The pulley rope had snapped, and Mr. Rodriguez had learned that it can be dangerous to fall too deeply in love; and that when you finally learn the lesson, it may be too late.

Maybe this isn't freedom, I said to myself when I saw Mr. Rodriguez that morning. Maybe I could squander it equally well in someplace more . . . polite.

The thing was, I didn't know how much rent I could afford, and I couldn't prove to a landlord that I could afford any at all. I was living on the horse luck that had returned after I quit Yer Press; but the luck seemed to appear only when I got desperate. Whenever I tried to build a cushion, I lost; but I always won enough to replace the hundred in my fountain pen and to keep food money in my pocket. One day I hit a five-hundred-dollar Perfecta, and as soon as I stepped out of the OTB parlor someone came up behind me and stuck a knifepoint into the left side of my neck.

"You wait around to see who the big winners are?" I asked as he emptied my wallet.

"The big winner," he laughed, "is the dude that only gets this."

And he drew a nick under my chin, the size of a big shaving cut, and I laughed, too, because he went away. A minute later, walking with my head down in sorrow, cursing my luck and pressing a handkerchief to my neck, I spotted a silvery paper on the sidewalk.

105

I picked it up—it was one of those supermarket contest tickets. I scraped away the silver coating, and the white panel underneath said: "$100 Instant Winner!"

How are you going to explain that kind of earning power to a landlord?·

After being laughed out of six or seven rental agencies, I took to knocking on the doors of building superintendents. The East Village was my target, because it had the greatest variety of cheap ethnic restaurants in which to spill sauce on my shirts. It had Indian restaurants to spill curry sauce; Chinese restaurants to spill soy sauce; Spanish restaurants to spill garlic sauce; Russian restaurants to spill sour cream; kosher delis to spill mustard; natural-foods restaurants to spill tahini. And it had Ukrainian social clubs; Carpathian relief organizations; Polish churches; red-and-black storefronts of the Puerto Rican revolution; theaters showing double-feature musicals from the thirties; late-night hair salons to restyle you into a parent's nightmare; babies crawling out on fire escapes; billboards advertising beer in Spanish; Turkish baths in a tenement; spice stores, incense stores, coffee stores, stores with signs in unidentifiable alphabets with unidentifiable brass utensils in the window; gray-bearded men in floppy sandals, their steps chemically springy or chemically sluggish, trying to recover from the experiments of twenty years ago; used-clothing stores, used-book stores, used-appliance stores with sidewalk displays of old refrigerators; rock clubs where you could dance like a broken robot; hundreds of derelicts hanging out in front of the Fourth Street welfare office; Hell's Angels headquarters raising the tone of Third Street.

Tenth Street, though, was the sedate part of the neighborhood. Privately owned brownstones instead of tenements. The residents swept their own sidewalks; opera came through the windows on weekend afternoons, and a corner church held poetry readings. I knocked on a house door.

A woman with graying black hair answered. She wore a floor-length quilted yellow housecoat, yellow pompom slippers, and half-glasses. She carried a *New York Times* folded to the crossword puzzle, and there was a yellow pencil tucked behind her ear. She was a foot shorter than me, and when looking up at me she bent at the waist and squinted up, with a bewildered but optimistic expression, as if I was an eight-letter space she hoped to fill in.

"Yes?" she asked.

"Excuse me, do you have an apartment available?"

She straightened up and took the pencil out from behind her ear. "Yes, of course. Welcome to freedom!"

10. How I Became an Outlaw

"I'm Bea Goldfish," she said. "Please come in."

I stepped over the threshold—and stopped. "Lady, I've seen a lot in the last couple of months." She was nodding and smiling dimly through her half-glasses. "I doubt if anything in here is gonna shock me after what I've been through."

"Well, of *course,*" she said, and turned away and walked through the narrow entrance lobby. The gold wallpaper was faded, but the mahogany doors to the main apartment, and the mahogany bannister on the staircase, were polished. I passed a mirror, with a chipped gilt frame, hanging above a high-backed chair, and saw that my face had acquired a permanently, cheerfully stunned expression, which is easy for it to do because of my eye. I winked my left eye—it's funny to wink when it makes no difference to your vision. "Of *course,*" she said. "You're coming here to rest and to work and to marshal your resources."

"Damn right!" I said.

"The last thing we'd do is put you in an anxiety-producing situation."

"I love it here!" I said.

"Good!" She turned and blinked rapidly at me with the far-sighted smile I was beginning to love. "I'll try to find the forms for you to fill out."

Forms? What kind of forms? What would I put on them? Name: Rich Redstone. Occupation: being and watching. Reference: man in white suit with blue piping. Filling out applications always makes me nervous for that reason. But I had a creepy feeling she knew about me already.

"And my husband, Judge Goldfish, will want to meet you—Oh!" she said, touching my arm, and I almost jumped. "Does his being a judge make you anxious? Don't worry, he'll approve whoever I approve. We've been serving as a halfway house for parolees for almost twenty years, and I've developed a kind of sixth sense for those who'll make it and those who won't." She pushed up her glasses and squinted up at me. "I'm going to go out on a limb now, at our very first meeting, and predict that you will henceforth have an entirely clean record."

"I can guarantee it, ma'am." The word "ma'am" was part of the reformed-criminal persona I was improvising on the spot. If I had to pretend I was an ex-con in order to get an apartment, so be it. If Bea Goldfish discovered my ruse, I hoped she'd consider it a misdemeanor entitling me to more rehabilitation. I was both proud and hurt that she'd immediately mistaken me for the real outlaw she was apparently expecting. I was unshaven, and my corduroy jacket and tea-stained forest-green tie looked as if they'd been donated to me by a charity organization. I liked the way I called her "ma'am." I thought of it as a word used by the good people in the social classes from which bad people come. I was brought up, as I've said, in a social class in which there's neither good nor evil, just a lot of complaining.

She was looking at me with three fingertips pressed to her lips. "I hope you won't think me inquisitive, but precisely what was the nature of—the reason for . . . your . . . your incarceration, I mean?"

Bea, did you want to provide shelter for veteran inmates who needed training in how to live outside jail but had never, never done anything nasty? I had an urge to tell her I was a mass murderer. But I wanted her to accept me; so, just as a real mass murderer would have, I said, "Nothing big, nothing violent. Got stupid once when I was younger. Thought I could make money without working for it."

She patted my elbow. "It upsets you to talk about it. Don't ever let me ask about it again. Anxiety is the last thing you need, with the difficult job you have in front of you. You'll have to cook your own meals, budget your own money, schedule your own time. You must learn to think of shopping at a store as more exciting than robbing a store. Then there are bills to pay, you must pay for everything in this life, and from now on you'll have to pay for them *honestly*. If you saw our heating and air-conditioning bills, you'd wonder how anyone can pay for anything honestly anymore. Judge Goldfish is always saying he'd like to throw the whole Public Service Commission in jail—Oh! I won't mention that place to you again!—You'll have self-responsibility, which is in a way the most difficult responsibility of all. . . ."

One item not included in her litany was "You'll have to hear me talk." She made everyday living sound so hard, I wondered why everyone on earth didn't leap into a jail cell at the first chance. After she had assured me several times that she didn't want to make me anxious, I was trembling. But her house was so much quieter than the Elephant Hotel! You could barely hear the street traffic. The air was scented with lemon furniture polish and a soupçon of dust, the hallway lamps were lit low and yellow, and unpainful sunlight slanted through the transom on serenely gleaming wood. I wanted to stay here and, just like she said, marshal my resources.

"I'll show you the downstairs apartment," she said. "That's where you'll live. The last person who lived there is now a consultant to the Internal Revenue Service, you'll be pleased to know. The one before him has his own school of locksmithing." She tapped her newspaper against her hand and showed me the crossword puzzle. Half a dozen of the short words were filled in, and none of the long ones. "By the way, do you happen to know a six-letter word meaning white of the eye?"

" 'Sclera,' " I said immediately.

She looked at me in astonishment. "You've been occupying your time constructively! I approve, I approve! I've often said to Judge Goldfish, if only all prisoners were given the *New York Times* crossword puzzle to do, there would be fewer crimes in the cell. People would be helping each other find the right word instead of shaking each other down with homemade switchblades. Sclera, that's a real buff's word! Have you ever made your own puzzles? No? I'll let you see mine! But later, later! Now let me find that downstairs key." She patted the quilted pockets of her house-coat.

And so, in her enthusiasm over my vocabulary, she forgot to get me the forms to fill out. Actually I hate ophthalmology and I don't understand anything about how the eye works; but after my accident, my doctor gave me all kinds of pamphlets as a going-away present: pamphlets from the prosthetic company, pamphlets from the ointment company, pamphlets from the makers of over-the-counter eyewashes, pamphlets from the makers of surgical instruments. . . . Each pamphlet had a slightly different illustration of the human eye, with the parts labeled: the macula, the fovea, the vitreous humor—all those good crossword terms. I don't even remember which part goes where, I just remember those other-worldly names crowding around the eye, with black lines piercing it. I had flipped through the pamphlets only once, in a boyish rage; but there are diagrams you see once and never forget.

• • •

At about six that evening, I was sitting in the living room of my new home when Bea called me on the phone to invite me to dinner. My basement apartment was cool and dark, as if a convict had to be aged carefully in a cellar like a bottle of burgundy. The furniture was a cot, a folding Formica table and two bridge chairs, and a vinyl sofa that maybe one of her former residents borrowed from a dentist's waiting room. And there were iron bars on all the windows— "to keep out the burglars," Bea had said. But I didn't think about the cheapness of the furniture, or the cracks in the dark-green linoleum, or the way the iron bars striped the wall with shadows. This was the first apartment I'd ever rented without a roommate, and all I wanted to do was sit stretched on the floor, with my palms on the floor to feel the heart of the place, and look at the pink-and-yellow dusk through the top halves of the basement windows, and go "Ah! My place!"

"Don't think I'm gonna just let you sit there!" she said over the phone. "You're gonna eat dinner with real people tonight."

I got the feeling she meant herself. Well, I told myself, you

111

didn't have any more choice of dinner companions when you were in the Big House. . . .

"Hide the silver, I'm coming upstairs," I said, and ran up the steps to the main flooor. I knocked on the door.

At the same instant, someone else's hand put a key in the lock. The hand was smaller than mine, and had gray knuckle hairs and brown liver spots. My glance followed the line of his arm: it was a short man in his sixties, wearing an old-fashioned gray hat that looked damp around the forehead, and a gray suit that was sweaty not only in the underarms but on the breast and down the back and on the cuffs and in the hollows of the elbows. He had small, bright, blinky brown eyes, thick dewy eyebrows that twitched drops of sweat onto his face, and a shiny brown-and-white mustache. He sniffed with his wiggling nose as he looked at me, the way a very brave squirrel might sniff at a dog on a leash. He treaded from one foot to the other on the welcome mat. A black attaché case banged against his left leg, and he seemed helpless to stop it. He was having trouble turning the key, and he was whining, "Hihng, hihng, hihng?" to himself in a tiny voice as he shifted from foot to foot in frustration.

"Rough day at the court?" I asked.

"Hihng, hihng, hihng," he nodded.

"Separating the good from the evil. Passing judgment. It must be exciting, but depressing too."

"The types you see." He looked down and shook his head; a drop of sweat landed on his black shoe. "People with no respect for anything. I'm telling you, it's a disillusioning experience. No one wants to take responsibility for his acts. Everyone just wants to get away with it. And then, to hear from their own lips what a cesspool they've made the city. How you can't set foot in the street anymore without taking your life in your hands. To find a single remorseful person is a triumph."

I was awed. I said to myself, Isn't it amazing, the guises power takes on? Here's this modest, measly old guy, looks like you could give him heart failure with one shout, even a gray suit doesn't make him look dignified, defendants must snicker at him right up to the moment he sentences them to life. This guy no longer needs to keep up a formidable appearance; he is a truly powerful man, and maybe a keen scholar too. When he gets a bad table at a restaurant, he just thinks it's funny—or doesn't even notice. It's too trivial to upset him. He sniffles through life, with the sniffle of wisdom. I'd like to be that way when I get old. Maybe I *should* go to law school.

He jiggled the key furiously in the lock; it didn't move. "A protégé of my wife's made this key. He teaches locksmithing. An excellent safecracker, but the simple things tend to defeat him."

"That's the criminal class for you." I shook my head sympathetically. "Here, let me try." I tried to turn the key—it was really stuck, a masterpiece of nonworkmanship. I tried pulling on the doorknob; the old man tried pushing, at the same time.

The door thumped so much that finally Bea heard, and came and opened it. She kissed her husband, spun him around to face me, and introduced him. "Judge Learned Goldfish, of the Traffic Court!"

"Judge." I shook his hand. It was such a weak hand I wanted to cry. The Traffic Court!

"Mr. Redstone is a parolee who'll be staying downstairs until he acquires some life skills," Bea said.

"What is he, a murderer?"

"Don't ask him, he's very sensitive about it!"

"It's all right, murderers make excellent chauffeurs." He blinked and peered at me as if trying to remember my face. "Have you ever come before me for any serious violations?"

"I'm not a chauffeur," I said, and I was about to tell him that I wasn't a murderer either.

"Who's a murderer?" said a new voice, coming from the next room on my left. I turned so I could see.

A beautiful young woman entered. She was frowning, and pulling at her eyebrows with her fingers.

"Are you the murderer?" she asked me.

"Yes. I mean no, I mean I'm the person they were referring to but I'm not . . ."

I wasn't too sure what I was, because *she* was five feet ten and

113

lanky, with a high-boned face and big gray eyes, wavy black hair parted in the middle and bouncing against her shoulders, and long, narrow, low-slung breasts that rolled this way and that under a white silk robe. She wore the robe over blue jeans, and she wore white pompom slippers that might have been bought in the same store as Bea's yellow ones. Her eyebrows were black, but extremely thin, almost nonexistent—but that gave her an exotic beauty. She looked about twenty-eight, and I was thinking, Five years older than me! How spicy! Maybe she'll make herself my tutor in the ways of adulthood! The breasts are still full, but beginning to sag, maybe there's a purple vein or two behind her knee, a few soft wrinkles in the belly—please let me look into this further!

Bea introduced her as their daughter, Debs Goldfish.

"Rich Redstone," I said, stepping toward her to take over the introduction before Bea could do any more damage to my reputation. "Reformed white-collar criminal extraordinaire."

"White collar," she groaned. "Mother, you're really taking the rough chances these days, aren't you?"

"He may not be a hardened thug, but he seems like a very nice young man anyway," Bea said.

"I'd like to see his record of violations before I give an opinion on that," the judge said. "Some white-collar criminals are quite conservative in their driving, but others have no compunctions about contributing to gridlock."

Debs pulled at her eyebrows. She grabbed the skin around the eyebrows, frowned with pain and self-reproach, gave several hard tugs, inspected the hairs that came away on her hands, and flicked them onto the floor. "Well, next time you kill someone," she told me, "give me a call and I'll try to get you off. I'm an attorney in the public defender's office."

"I have never killed anybody," I said, smiling because I was glad I was remaining so calm.

"Next time you rape some guy in prison, then. I mean, I know what it feels like to be a victim of this oppressive system." She threw a glare at her parents. "Last week I won a case for this guy who took a screwdriver and shoved it into— Actually there were four other guys with him, but I got his trial separated. But you look

114

like the type who'd *be* raped." She laughed me up and down. "Tell me, what did it do for your self-esteem, especially vis-à-vis women?"

"It didn't do a fucking thing," I said, smiling now because I was glad I *wasn't* remaining calm. "I've never been raped in or out of jail, in fact I've never—" I was so piqued, I was about to admit I'd never been in jail at all, and lose the apartment. Luckily she was laughing in disbelief at what I'd already said, so I couldn't say any more.

"How'd you get away without it?" she asked. "Were you in solitary the whole time?"

Pride, and desire for her, spurred my imagination. "No, someone tried it once. I happened to have a lead pipe."

"Good!" She didn't sound like my idea of a lawyer, but, as I've said, my father kept me away from his business. "But why are you still alive?" she asked.

I shrugged. "I did lose an eye."

She gasped with satisfaction. That eye sealed my credibility and, as so often, intrigued the female. She was delighted that I'd been so dashingly mutilated. She questioned me thirstily: How had it been injured, how was I treated by the prison doctors, had I sued the state? She made me let her look into my left eye until she was convinced it was really blind; made me let her run her finger over the eyelid so she could feel the hardness underneath; and, most fun of all, she stood to my left and laughed at me for not being able to see her. She took it upon herself to test my peripheral vision, moving a step at a time from left to right and laughing, "Can you see me yet? Can you see me yet?"

Bea warned her that she was hurting my feelings and causing me distressful memories. "Oh, it's terrible! To lose an eye, half of the most precious sense! If I were you I'd hate it whenever anyone even mentioned it! Did they gouge it or stab it or what? Ugh, don't even tell me!" That was Bea's way of giving me solace. Meanwhile Debs laughed at her, threw me eye-rolling glances to disavow her mother, and said that the loss of an eye was completely trivial compared to things her clients did, in and out of prison, every day.

"Well, if it's trivial, I'll go set the table," Bea said, and she did.

In a few minutes, we were eating at an oval table with a white linen tablecloth with a rip right underneath my silverware. Bea had thoughtfully placed all my dishes on my right side instead of in front of me. "It's so you can see them with your one eye," she said. "I don't want to make you feel inadequate by putting half your things where you can't even see them."

"Thanks a bunch," I said, and started eating my soup, with my hand shaking so much that half of the spoonful fell back into the bowl. It was some sort of chicken broth with canned bamboo shoots and bean sprouts and drops of Tabasco sauce floating around in it. Then we had a meatloaf that oozed purple-gray suet, was full of crunchy bits of something or other, and was completely tasteless except when the crunchy bits, fusing themselves to my tongue, turned out to be hot pepper and ginger.

"It's a Szechuan chicken soup and Hunan steamed meatloaf." Bea smiled euphorically through fogged glasses. Bits of meat fell from the chopsticks she was trying to bring to her lips. "They had the recipes in a special Chinese menu in the *Times* today. I left out the soy sauce and the wine. You know the judge's low-sodium diet."

I nodded, as if completely familiar with the feeding habits of Goldfish.

"And the doctor said to watch the alcohol," she added, pointing a chopstick at him.

"I hardly ever drink," he told me. "Cutting back the alcohol means leaving out the cooking wine."

"It's so important to be creative with recipes," she said. "I love the *Times*." With half-closed eyes, she inhaled a breath of rapturous devotion. "Debs, did you hear how Rich helped me with the crossword puzzle today? And, you know"—she pointed the chopstick sideways at her daughter—"you'd think a lawyer would at least be able to help her mother with some of the Latin words once in a while."

Debs plucked an eyebrow hair into her soup and frowned. She tried to spoon it out, but it kept slipping away and she ended up banging the spoon against the side of the bowl, making splashes with the underside of the spoon, and making almost inaudible whimpering sounds.

"White-collar bastards," she said to me. "I see you've got my mother in the palm of your hand."

I was about to blush under her criticism, and deny all crossword-puzzle expertise—but then it occurred to me that she was *jealous,* and that if her mother played up to me, it might attract Debs to me more. It occurred to me that there might be worse ways of getting to a twenty-eight-year-old who still clung to her parents than of cultivating those parents. And if she mocked her parents while clinging to them, you could mock them while cultivating them. There might be no better way, in fact, than by winking at each other over their heads.

I embarked on the most guileful project of my life. "Crosswords are a wonderful thing, they got me time off for good behavior." I gulped. Honest Rich Redstone—there goes another self-image down the drain. Exhilarated, I turned to the judge. "You know, I could tell on my first day out what a menace gridlock has become."

He looked at me as if suddenly admiring my intelligence. "Gridlock!" he spat out. "It's ruining the city. It's holding honest citizens hostage at green lights. It's causing normal people to go crazy in the middle of the afternoon. It's separating fathers from their families and making them miss dinner. I'm telling you, don't let a driver come into my hearing room accused of blocking the intersection! Taking their license away is too little! If I could give them a nice stiff jail sentence—then they'd have time to think about the person whose lane they were blocking!"

He sat back in his chair, breathing hard and red. "I myself refuse to ride in Manhattan anymore, that's all," he said. "I will not set foot in a cab or bus that might be responsible for blocking an inter-section and shattering innocent lives. As for the subways, you know what they're like. And a bicycle, you take your life in your hands."

"Daddy won't go anywhere he can't walk to," Debs said.

We looked at each other across the table and smirked. It was perfect for getting her to like me, even though I was a little ashamed of myself.

"I'm just getting my exercise, that's all," the judge said. "I walk to

117

Traffic Court; and if there's some entertainment I can't walk to, it's not worth going to."

"Ever since he became a judge three years ago. . . ." Debs rolled her eyes, and discreetly twirled a finger behind her right ear.

Apparently the elder Goldfish were the kind of sweet old liberal couple you could say anything in front of. I leaned across the table toward Debs and said, "I think he's cute."

"Your father is known to be the most sensible man in the entire Motor Vehicle Department," Bea told her daughter. "He just wants to live in a more simple mode, is that so wrong? 'Simplify, simplify, simplify, simplify, simplify.' Who said that?"

"You did," I told her. She looked quite pleased.

11.   There Is No Such Thing as a Free Brunch

"People often ask me what makes a great judge," said Learned Goldfish, walking through the medieval wing of the Metropolitan Museum of Art. "What makes a great judge is great judgment." He tugged the bulb of his nose from side to side and sneezed, then wiped his fingers delicately inside his pants pocket. He drew out a handkerchief and waved it at the gold-illuminated paintings on the blue wall. "Look at this art. This is art." He gave sharp glances to Bea, Debs, and me, as if challenging us to dispute him. "Those guys knew how to uplift the soul, all right."

"Oh, my legs," Debs moaned. "Is there a sofa in the next room?" She walked up to the guard. "Where is the next room with a sofa?"

The museum was four miles from the Goldfish house, and most of us had walked it. Debs had come along, which must have meant she'd wanted to be with me. The judge had sweated, huffed, and swung his arms haggardly all the way there, but he was faster than either of us and from half a block ahead he would turn to point out traffic jams and yell, "See? Would you rather be in that?" As soon as we finished climbing the steps of the museum and walked into the cool lobby, all three of us plopped right down on the rim of the central fountain—and waited fifteen minutes for Bea, who was stuck in a cab on Third Avenue. The judge *was* wise! The Met was his northern limit, though; I suggested going to the Guggenheim someday, but he shook his head decisively and said, "Too modern."

In the medieval gallery, Bea ambled from painting to painting with a dreamy smile on her face, crossing left foot in front of right as if being led by an invisible dancing instructor. She was wearing the headphones of a recorded tour.

She blinked away tears of emotion, clicked her tape machine off, and said, "I love gold!"

Debs laughed disrespectfully.

"What?" Bea said. "You think I said that because of its monetary value? How little you must think of your mother! Gold is a perfect artistic material, that's all I'm saying."

The judge bent toward the little white tag on the wall next to an Adoration of the Lamb. He read aloud: " 'Acquired from the Nate and Ada Grinspan Collection.' I've *heard* of that collection!" He walked to the next painting, a Madonna and Child. " 'Purchased with matching funds from the Sneerman Foundation.' I'm telling you, become a foundation!" He stepped sideways, crouching, to the white tag next to a portrait of an ecstatic saint wearing a monk's robe. " 'On extended loan from the Archdiocese of New York.' That archdiocese, they really know which way is up!"

We walked past the guard in his gray uniform, to a later room in art history. Bea wormed up beside me and held my forearm to stage-whisper in my ear, "All these guards, they give me the creeps, how about you? Oh, I forget: you're used to it."

"You really know how to make someone feel comfortable," Debs told her.

"Well, you see? I'm already thinking of him as a normal person, so I forgot!" She smiled at me with tremendous maternal fondness. "Don't worry, I'll let you know if there's anything worth looking at on the left wall," she assured me with a squeeze.

Judge Goldfish had walked up to a triptych of the Crucifixion and was looking at it, hands on knees, lips shaking with awe. "Remarkable! Look at the face of that Roman soldier! The heaviness of the brow, the sunken cheeks with blue-black whiskers. He looks exactly like a man whose case I heard yesterday. I'm not kidding: exactly! Talk about realism! I fined him two hundred bucks, and he was lucky I only suspended his license for thirty days." He glared slit-eyed at the Roman soldier, who, with the meek and sheepish expression of an elementary-school student standing in front of the class and pointing out an obscure city on the wall map, was sticking a spear into Jesus' side. "It shows you how types recur through history. The guy ran over a dog in full view of its owner, causing considerable emotional damage."

The Goldfish were introducing me to the splendors of art.

It was because I'd been deprived of culture, you see, that I'd grown up amoral and with a leaning toward crime. But with my benefactors' help, whenever I got the lust to steal money or clobber someone from behind, I'd leaf through the pages of a Picasso reproduction book instead. That was why they escorted me to the museum, not trusting me to find my own way through the galleries. That was why Bea kept trying to stick the earphone of her tour pack into my ear, and why she thought it was wickedly uncultured of me to twist away and refuse. That was why she sidled up to me, took hold of my elbow with all the joy of a lobster pinching a lobsterman's ankle, and half-whispered, "After the Middle Ages comes something we call the *Renaissance.*" That was why Debs got me in a corner, flicked a couple of eyebrow hairs at the glass case enclosing a fourteenth-century book of hours, and, confident she could read my thoughts, said, "What a distorted system of values, right? Astronomically priced art: the symbol of feudal oppression continuing from the past to the present. Someone should steal it and pay for the legal costs of indigent defendants who've been railroaded by the so-called system of justice. Listen, you can tell me now: when you were doing it with your cellmates, did you take the male or the female role?"

"Female," I said in exasperation, and watched her face tense up with the effort of hiding pleasure. Her gray eyes had brightened. "I took the female role in jail," I said loudly. The guard looked at me. Walking past him into the next room, I flashed him a smile worthy of a starlet.

Debs bumped against my side, and her long black hair lapped against my ear. "Past events mean nothing to me," she murmured. "I'm not trying to embarrass you, I have a professional interest; I want to relate to my clients better. . . ."

121

From the room we'd just left, we heard Bea's voice. "Judge? Judge?" She was turning this way and that. "He always gets lost in places."

Debs grabbed at her eyebrows briskly and angrily, just seeing her mother.

"Stop doing that," I said, and pulled her hand away. A little black hair came away on my finger, and I rubbed it, feeling its oil. A piece of Debs' body!

"I love culture," I said, looking at it.

• • •

Saturday was museum day, but Sunday was even more important. It was the day of—

The Sunday *Times!*

They invited me for breakfast, or, as breakfast is called in Manhattan, "brunch." Debs looked especially lanky and swingy in her white silk bathrobe over cleaned and pressed blue jeans; Bea especially judgewifely in a shiny green dress, pearl earrings, and stockings without shoes; me, especially probationary in dirty jeans and a white shirt—a demoted dress shirt—with yellowing spots. The living-room sideboard was set with cheeses and fruit and fish. Bea pulled me over to it. "I bet they didn't have smoked salmon you-know-where." "You-know-where" and "that place" were her tactful ways of not mentioning my shameful past; I heard such phrases at least six times daily from her, and another six from Debs, who, taking special savor in repeating them into her mother's face, always used them "parodistically."

The judge had gone out for the paper, and in the meantime Bea trotted over to the stereo console and put the ritual thumbprints on a record, before Debs took it away from her and turned it on. It was some late-Romantic symphony—the heavy metal music of 1880, what people were forced to write when they wanted their eardrums battered but they didn't have rock 'n' roll yet. Two guitars, a bass, and drums would sound infinitely cleaner and more dignified—the good classical music was written early, when people still danced to it and the instruments and tunings were still crude. But try telling

122

that to a person of culture. I got up and walked to the corner of the room farthest from the stereo. It happened to be where Debs was. She happened to have two tomato juices in her hands, and I took one, and we stood side by side and shook our heads pityingly, as we watched Bea sitting transfixed by the music.

"In seventh grade they once tried to teach us to like classical music," I said. "There was this music teacher, Mr. Fiebelwitz, who conducted the school orchestra. One day in assembly the orchestra gave a concert; he had chosen some piece that kids would like—I don't know what, something very rhythmic and melodic—and everybody loved it! The orchestra consisted of our friends and we were sitting in the audience saying, 'Hey, they're good!' and thinking it must be fun to play classical music. So I started clapping to the beat. My friend Sterling followed me, then all of us friends started clapping to the beat together, then different groups of friends started competing at clapping until practically the whole auditorium was clapping to this classical beat. Then Mr. Fiebelwitz turned around at the podium, looked at us—waved at the orchestra to stop playing. 'If there is any more clapping, this concert will end immediately!' "

Debs gasped. I liked her for that. I accidentally-on-purpose clinked our glasses together.

"Fiebelwitz tried to stare down the whole auditorium. He was the kind of adult man who thinks it's important to stare down two hundred seventh graders. Well, we wanted to hear the end of the piece, so everyone stopped clapping. But before he'd start the music again, Fiebelwitz told all the teachers in the audience to stand in the aisles and make sure no one clapped. We listened to the end of the piece—it was still real good, I wish I knew what piece it was—and at the end, Mr. Fiebelwitz *told* us to clap." I took a sip of tomato juice. "You might think we refused to clap. No—we clapped for our friends in the orchestra. We also booed and whistled at Fiebelwitz. All the teachers went scurrying all over the place blowing whistles, while the orchestra played the processional to get us out. That afternoon, a memo from the principal was circulated to the teachers, asking for the names of the ringleaders in that morning's disgraceful interruption of the concert. My teacher put down Sterling's name—she'd forgotten me. So naturally Sterling squealed and told her I'd started it all. My parents were called in, and when we got home my father took away the record player in my room."

And that, I thought, was my experience in jail. "And that," I said, "was my experience with classical music."

At that moment, a key jiggled in the front door lock, and when it jiggled so much that the door started to shake, Bea got up and opened it for the judge. He walked in carrying such an immense folio of paper under his arm that you wondered how people could read even a fraction of it and still keep any time for themselves, or fit any other information into their minds, much less clean the ink off their fingers.

"Here's the *Times*," he announced, and dropped it onto the marble coffee table with a grunt. "Whew." He shook the cramp out of his arm, and wiped his forehead with his jacket sleeve.

"Entertainment section!" Debs shouted, lunging.

"How cruel!" Bea said. "You knew I wanted to read that article on Nijinsky's ingrown toenails."

"Oh, Mother, haven't you learned to share yet? Why don't you take the magazine and do the crossword?"

"*I* want the magazine," the judge said. "There's an article in it on the Supreme Court."

We all looked at him as if to ask what possible interest he would have in the Supreme Court.

"You're just trying to take the magazine away from Mommy so she'll take the entertainment section away from me," Debs whined.

"Wait, wait," Bea said. "I've got an idea. Give Rich first choice which section he wants to read. He may not have had access to the Sunday *Times* in that place. Which section, Rich?" She leaned forward on the sofa as if coaxing a child to take his first steps. "News, sports, travel, business . . . ?"

"I'll just finish my tomato juice," I said. "I don't feel like reading the paper this morning."

She was intensely bewildered. "Don't feel like . . . ?"

"You mean he doesn't want to read the paper?" the judge said. "What does he want to do on a Sunday?"

Everyone looked at the *Times*. Everyone looked at me.

The fact is, I associate the Sunday paper with reading the want ads and dreading Monday, when you'll have to dress up in pretend grown-up clothes, carry a one-page summary of your life in your hand, and walk smiling into places where they don't want to know you. The other thing I associate the Sunday paper with is my father. When I was little, he used to bring home both the *Times* and the *News* every Sunday—trying to be a universal man—and all day my mother would be begging him to drive her to the clothing sales, I'd be begging him to take me to the miniature-golf range or the ballpark, and he'd be piling sections of paper between him and us, and grunting, "In a minute, in a minute." He was reading about hemlines in Milan, he was seeing what was on TV that week, he was just skimming through an interview with a horror-movie director from Bulgaria, he was looking over a feature story on the varieties and prices of lettuce, he was tearing out coupons for buying paper towels in quantities you couldn't store in an apartment cupboard, he was studying an in-depth analysis of our military position in the Gulf of Barbarbarann, he was learning what the *Times* had learned about the reasons behind the President's choice for assistant White House lavatory attendant, he was chuckling through cheerfully frazzled anecdotes about the ordeals of walking a dog/being a career woman/giving money to panhandlers/playing the latest racquet game in Our Great City, he was appalled at how homely the socialite brides were, he was admiring photographs of how people had made their one-room walk-up apartments into showplaces, he was glancing at the European stock prices just in case he became a big investor someday, he was reading the radio listings for old times' sake, he was outraged by a letter about teachers' pension funds, he was fascinated by a diagram of a quarterback's knee. . . .

He was learning who was more successful than him, who was more famous and made more money and said clever things that got in the paper. Who was the big actor? Who was the big criminal? Who was the big has-been making the big comeback? Who was better than my father, and what was their secret?

"Take me miniature golfing!" I told him, through the front page, so called because it was in front of his face.

"Here, read the comics," he said, nudging the *News* at me with his left foot.

"Pick!" Bea said. "You're part of our family now. Don't be bashful. Pick!"

"Okay," I grumbled. "Give me the section with the bra ads."

There were sighs of approval all around.

Freedom is being able to pick which section of the Sunday *Times* you want to read first.

• • •

"Your father and I are going over to the Schwindlers' for pinochle," Bea said after brunch. "I don't suppose you'd like to come, just in case Rhett is there?"

"Are you kidding, Mother?" Debs said. "Rhett Schwindler, that running sore? That pustule? That chicken-pox scab on the face of humanity? That rank and vaporous fen of a human being? That stagnant scum floating on the surface of the earth?"

"I always thought he was a personable enough young man," the judge said through his one unplugged nostril.

"Rhett Schwindler," Debs told me in a confidential tone intended solely to be overheard by her parents, "is the mucus that creeps out of the corner of your eye when you have a sinus attack."

"Who said you have to like him?" the judge said. "Are we telling you who to like? It's a beautiful day, that's all. A youngish single girl has no activities planned?"

"I'm gonna stay here and fuck Rich," she said.

Her parents started to gasp, but then they got wise: she was only taunting them. "Learned, leave her be," her mother said knowingly. "It's not our business. Imagine how anxious and upset it would

126

make a grown daughter feel if her parents started pestering her to go out."

"Who's pestering?" the judge said. "It's commendably prudent for a young woman to stay indoors these days, with all the types running around. I'm just saying the Schwindlers are always pleased to see her."

"Well, she's in a phase where she pretends that kind of thing doesn't mean anything to her. Debs, can we at least tell Rhett and his parents you say hello?"

"Yeah." Debs pulled at alternate eyebrows with a pistonlike motion.

"If it violates your principles, we won't do it."

"Do it! Please, go to the Schwindlers' and say hello for me! Hurry!" Debs and I were sitting near each other on the floor, in front of the scattered newspaper sections, and as I watched, her eyebrows became noticeably thinner, until finally she grasped and grasped and came away with no hairs at all. She had no eyebrows left. She looked up at me in astonishment and fear. Searchingly she patted the place where her eyebrows used to be. She began to cry.

"Well, I'm sure the Schwindlers will ask about you," said Bea, who had already turned and headed for the door. "We'll have to tell them something."

"We'll figure out something," the judge said, shooing his wife out in front of him. "We'll say she's working on a brief. Just don't offend them, that's all."

"Do I ever offend?" she said, as they shut the apartment door behind them.

Debs began kicking the floor, kicking newspaper sections to all corners of the living room. Then she squeezed and pulled her eyebrow skin until it was bloodless white, and sobbed.

"I feel so guilty," she said. "I'm still living with my parents, and you see how I can't stand them. I'm not here because I want to be. I'm here because in a public-interest job I can't afford a decent apartment. And our house is close to the courts. But it's torture for me to have my mother buy my clothes. She has time to shop and I don't, is that my fault? She buys me such expensive stuff I feel guilty. Last winter I went to the islands with them and I hated every minute of it. My parents aren't happy till they're spoiling everything for me."

She was leaning next to me as if asking to lean against me. I let her, and put my arm around her. I looked down and could see her bra under the white silk robe, bouncing with emotion.

"Listen," I said. "I read in a book that as you get older you're supposed to forgive your parents. Everyone's parents warp them, but when you're an adult you can understand that they were warped in turn and they couldn't help it. So the sign of being mature is that you forgive them."

"Do you forgive yours?"

"Sure, the hell with them, what do I care? See? I forgive them. It's easy."

It was fun being mature.

"Okay, I'll forgive mine too." She smiled.

"Congratulations!" I looked into her eyes from very close. They were red-rimmed and wet, but still beautifully gray. She pushed her black hair off her face, then hesitated, and raised her hands reflexively to her eyebrows. I put her hands down, and the sash of her white silk robe loosened a bit every time she shifted her weight. The skirt of the robe fell open on my pants leg, and Debs' legs scissored nervously, kicking mine.

I kissed her on the mouth. It tasted like smoked salmon and tomato juice, it tasted great.

"Do you feel different now that you've forgiven your parents?" I said, and we laughed in each other's mouth. I kissed her neck hungrily, I kissed her jawline, I dabbed her earlobe with my tongue and painted the waxy down of her ear-nooks with saliva. We wriggled each other's pants and underpants off, and she was bony in the pelvis, slim in the upper leg, as if her legs were the gates of a city, and when I first glimpsed the city through the gate, my breath caught in my throat.

"Urban, Innocent, Clement," I whispered in her ear.

"What?"

"Thinking of names for our kids."

She laughed, and while the laugh was trailing off I swooped my tongue down her neck, in loops on her breasts, and straight down between them, past her belly button, and I gnawed on her thigh-bones, they were better than spareribs. We tucked our knees up, grabbed each other's ass for dear life, and gorged ourselves like starving travelers testing the sauce of a strange city, until out of politeness we turned around, wiped our mouths, and lay greased together face to face, with me on top and rising on my toes so I wouldn't weigh her down. We didn't move for ten minutes, till we both went "Ah!" Then I let myself sink heavily onto her for a minute, with my ear to her pulsing chest. . . .

Then we lay side by side and held hands, on the living-room floor, surrounded by newspaper.

"I think twenty-three for the man and twenty-eight for the woman is the perfect age," I said. "I feel like I'm in the big time now. I've been accepted by a mat-oor woman." I stroked the hair above her ears. "Look, there's a little gray!"

"Get out of there!" She slapped my hand away and sat up. "Now you're making me feel guilty."

"Why, for ruining the morals of a youth?"

She tried to pull her eyebrows. When she remembered that they'd been used up, she looked at me with a desolate expression. Then she began to bite her toenails. She bit a toenail off and chewed it, the second right toe. I remained remarkably calm. I sat there, naked and wet, and looked at the wall behind her, thinking, Thank you for a great lay, while she sat naked and wet and swallowed one toenail and lifted her foot to bite off another.

"Can you forgive me?" she asked.

"I just wish you'd go back to eyebrows."

"No," she said, chewing on the toe itself. "I mean for guilt feelings—they're just neurotic, but—" She lifted her right foot and tried to tuck the heel behind her head. Done naked, it was quite appealing. "My guilt is something we'll have to talk about at the next HAH meeting."

"HAH meeting?"

"HAH: Humans Against Herpes. It's an organization of people who have herpes; we get together and discuss how it makes us feel, especially our inhibitions about going to bed with people when we have this . . . disease. When you find out you have it, you're so mortified for a while. But I got over it."

"You got over the herpes!"

"No, I got over my inhibitions. I'm really glad we fucked, it proves I'm able to live with myself. I never want to hide it from anyone, I'm very honest. And you're so nice, I knew it'd be okay."

"I'm so nice," I moaned.

"Besides, after the sordid sexual experiences *you've* been through . . ."

"Help me!" I cried to the ceiling.

"What I have is Herpes Nine," she said. "It's the latest strain. It's completely incurable, but—"

I groaned in despair and rolled back and forth on the floor. I pressed my hands between my legs and rocked and moaned.

"Please don't make me feel guilty," she said.

"I'm sorry, I'm sorry," I said, meaning, I'm sorry I ever touched her.

She crawled across the floor to me and rested her head romantically on my thigh. "Herpes Nine is only contagious every third week. That's when I get lesions and fever. I feel too shitty to go to bed with anyone then, anyway. The rest of the time, the disease isn't communicable. Except possibly a few days before and after the active stage, you can't be exactly sure. I'm only in the second week now. But you can come to my HAH meeting anyway—knowledge is the best prevention. It'll be fun learning to relate to my disease together."

"Fun?" I moaned. "Will you promise me I won't catch it? I mean, you'll always tell me when . . . ?"

"Oh, I'll always tell you when! A good lawyer never promises, though. All I can say is that if we're careful, it's more likely than not that we'll avoid the high-risk days. It would be unethical to say more. That rodent, Rhett Schwindler—*he* promised *me*."

12.   The Secret Goldfish

For three weeks I haunted the library, wore out the "H" and "V" sections in every medical reference book they had, studied the photos of viruses, and memorized the most tragic phrases in the science sections of the magazines. ("And now Herpes Nine, which may be the real reason why the man in the Nautilus machine beside you is grunting, or why the woman in the slinky sweatsuit can't lengthen her stride at the running track. . . .") For three weeks, every time I went to the bathroom, I stood holding my poor duped sex organ, and pinched the hole wider to look for signs. My three weeks were ruined—

But I didn't have to join HAH.

I was clean. Debs was telling the truth.

I know: illness, trauma, and misfortune make better stories; but this is *me*. If Faulkner would have run over his grandmother for the sake of his art, that's his problem; I love my grandma, and I'm glad to say that I remained in perfect health, except for the debilitating effects of avoiding one's lover. I was so lovesick, I even started plucking at my eyebrows. When I was lonely, sitting on the dental sofa in the basement apartment with barred windows, I'd take out an eyebrow hair for company. I'd examine its length and thickness, and the fatness of its white follicle, and ask myself, "Does this mean good fortune or bad?" I'd pluck more hairs to find out—then more, and more. I felt deeply troubled at losing my eyebrow hairs, but it made me feel close to Debs. I mourned whenever I saw the hairs slough off onto my fingertips, and whenever I blew them off into the air. "Goodbye!" I told them, learning how beautiful it was to

131

hurt yourself in order to mourn for yourself. "Yes, Debs is wise. It's fun to pluck out your eyebrow hairs. And why shouldn't she be a parasite on her parents and make fun of them? It makes them all happy." I understood her, and I wanted her body—and then I got it, but only on the safe days. I was extremely cautious, and drove her crazy saying no.

It became fall. I walked a lot, usually in an ivory-white wool sweater with a big loop coming out of the right sleeve, where I'd caught it on a fence wire. I wore a tie on my walks, because you should dress up when you're on the job. I always wore the tie flopping outside my sweater, because what's the point of wearing a tie if no one can see it?

During the daytime I had to stay away from the apartment, because I'd told Bea that I was rehabilitating myself. I'd told her I was working as a "youth counselor" at a recreation center. "Youth counselor" was the kind of title that made Bea glow with a nostalgic admiration that was one facial muscle away from pity. And it wasn't a total lie—having a lot of free time, I signed up as a tutor in a literacy program at the Fourteenth Street Y. One day I was coming back from tutoring—it was four o'clock, late enough for me to be justifiably home—I turned the corner onto Tenth Street—

Someone was climbing into the front window.

I ran fifty yards to the house. I jumped onto the brownstone bannister and ran up that. I didn't even ask myself what if he had a gun—I was Debs Goldfish's protector, and, besides, I had all that prison experience behind me making me tough. The housebreaker's head was disappearing into the front window, but his toes were still on the bannister. I pulled his legs out from under him. He held on to the window frame, and dangled, kicking the stones and looking back at me.

"Drop!" I shouted.

He let go and dropped into the front yard, and I jumped after him. I forced him down so his head banged against the pavement, and I pressed my knee to his chest.

I noticed that my knee was pressing on the white seal of a crimson Harvard sweatshirt.

And the housebreaker wore brown tortoiseshell glasses that sat crookedly on his nose; he had a new haircut and such a good shave his pale skin looked like a baby's; the unbuttoned collar of a pink Oxford shirt hung outside the sweatshirt; his fists were pressed tight against his chest and his eyes were shut, as if that was a way of hiding from me.

"Please take my money and go away," he gasped. "You've done enough psychic damage already. Although I do have a severe castration complex, so if you want to kick me in the balls it might prove a useful catharsis."

"Oh, shit, he's middle-class," I said. "Just when I want to hit somebody and be a hero. Who are you, a boy friend?" The thought made me so jealous that I pressed my knee harder into his ribs—but only in the act of getting off him. I stood over him, and watched him slowly and timidly uncurl.

He lay there, panting, staring up at me in fear, and whisking dirt off the Harvard seal. He was wearing scuffed brown deck shoes and he looked in his early thirties. Suddenly I knew who he was. He was Rhett Schwindler. And that got me really steamed.

"Get up!" I yelled; and I pulled him off the ground just so I could slam him against the brownstone wall. "You son of a bitch, you infected her and now you come romantically window-climbing, waiting for her? Let me tell you, *I'm* her boyfriend now, and you're breaking into my house . . ."

"Your house?" he said. He looked at my dirty jeans, stained tie, unshaved face, uncombed hair. "What are you, my mother's latest pet?"

". . . and if I get your disease I'll climb into *your* window and cut your cock off— Wait," I said, after his question finally made its way from my ear to the proper Redstoneish brain cell. I looked at him. "I'm Bea Goldfish's latest pet, if that's what you mean."

My fingers were gathering his sweatshirt, his Oxford shirt, and any chest hairs he may have had into my fist. My mind hurried to catch up to my fingers, shouting, Better leave him alone!

"I'm Norm Goldfish," he said. "Elder brother of Debs the Great. Have you ever heard of me?"

"No." I let go of his sweatshirt. He stood straighter, and gave a deep, clearing sigh—and I started saying I didn't know how to apologize, what do you expect from a person with my record, I hope you won't tell Bea and ruin her opinion of me. . . .

"I won't tell Bea. I never see my parents anymore. I'm independent of them. I live on the top floor, independently." He tucked his hands under his armpits, and fluttered his elbows.

I was staring at him. "I've been living here for months; they've never even mentioned you."

"Tremendously glad to hear it. Nice to know there's something my parents keep their word at. Two years ago I decided to keep my existence a secret from the world." His elbows gave an abortive flap. "You see, I've been giving everyone so much trouble in this crisis of mine—it started when I was five, but a couple of years ago I gained a new grasp of it. I accepted the fact that the world would be a much better place if it didn't have to be burdened by people like me who demand constant attention and babying. So I went upstairs. My parents were very supportive. If I'm in the hallway and they happen to be opening the door, they'll close the door again so we don't meet. It's taught them politeness. And of course it's made me a much stronger person. For instance, I'm not in a state of collapse that you jumped me. I can see that it might have been just the right thing for me today. As Nietzsche said, 'That which does not kill me makes me stronger.' "

"Not even Debs told me about you!" I said.

"Debs is ashamed of me. I'm not a lawyer. I'm on welfare. I've been declared psychiatrically incapable of working."

"You mean they give welfare payments for—"

"Well, I didn't make the rules!" he said. "My doctor told me about it; what should I do, refuse? I didn't want to offend him, he's a very bright analyst. For instance: when I was climbing through the window it was because I forgot my key. Why did I forget my key? Because I long for the irresponsibility of childhood; I want to climb into the womb symbolized by my mother's window. I forget my key all the time, but I wouldn't understand *why* without my doctor." He turned to pick at a fleck of mica on the bannister. He couldn't chip it off. He sighed with satisfaction. "It depresses me to

134

analyze myself; I do it all the time. Self-analysis is an addiction; it stimulates the natural opiates in the brain, which produce a pleasant paralyzing depression. I learned that about myself very recently, and I've thought about it a lot." He squinted up at the racing, gray sky; he fluttered his elbows against his sides again, hiding his hands from the October breeze. "Why don't we go upstairs? I'll tell you some new insights I'm pretty proud of."

I wasn't interested in his insights; I was interested in *who he was*. I opened the front door, and followed him in to find out.

• • •

Three flights up, there was a landing I'd never been to. There was a door with a "Beware of the Dog" sign on it. "That's me," Norm laughed. "There is no dog."

The apartment was three rooms in line. I suppose the big room was the living room, another the bedroom and another the study, but they were all the same except for size. There was no bed—sleeping bags rolled up in two of the rooms. There was no desk—two trunks stacked in the middle room, with a desk lamp and a paperback dictionary on top. There were no kitchen fixtures—a hot plate and a two-foot-high refrigerator in a corner of the big room. There were no bookshelves—piles of books in every room, mostly paperback psychology books, flung and spread open with creased covers. The top-floor sunlight fell on two wall posters: one of a unicorn chained in a corral, and another of a damsel in a see-through shift riding a white horse through a meadow. The horse's gray mane and tail, the damsel's champagne-colored hair and shift were all blowing to the right as she leaned forward over the horse's neck. Norm kissed his fingertips and blew the kiss at her—then he blushed and shrugged at me, as if to say he was only trying to be silly.

But what you noticed most in Norm's apartment were the instruments. Walking through, I spotted acoustic guitars, electric guitars, a mandolin, a fiddle, a string bass, an electric bass, an autoharp, a zither, and on top of the toilet tank a row of harmonicas in blue plastic cases.

"You're a musician," I said.

135

He shook his head vehemently, as if offended. "No, I'm *nothing*. I used to be a musician. But when I joined a group and we started writing our own songs, I'd think, 'These aren't as good as the songs on the radio.' And when we played other people's songs, I'd think, 'Why am I playing songs other people play better?' That was a few years ago."

"A few?" I wondered exactly how many. Two? Ten? What had he been doing since? Regretting his rock group and doing nothing else? I thought of myself. No, that was dangerous—anyway, I had something to do, I was busy watching him.

He sat on the floor and picked up a blond acoustic guitar from an open case. The wood looked waxed, the tuning pegs shone silvery, and I'd never seen anyone hold a guitar so tenderly. He kept shifting it on his leg, lightly hefting it, as if afraid holding it firmly would hurt it. He ran a finger up and down its neck to wipe away one or two motes of dust; when the strings sang from the friction, he quickly stopped them. He tested chord fingerings, barely touching the strings, as if trying not to make a sound. A sad expression came over him, and he looked at the poster of the damsel far away.

"My parents gave me this guitar for my birthday last month." He looked into the sound hole. "They left it in front of my door. Long ago they stopped asking me when I'm gonna get a job."

"When are you gonna get a job?"

He ignored my question, and began tuning the guitar. He plucked the six strings one after another, so softly he had to bend his head to hear the notes. I edged forward to hear. Soon I thought he got all the strings tuned. But he shook his head as if berating himself, and retuned the bottom string; then he plucked them all again; then shook his head in disappointment; retuned the next-to-bottom string . . .

He forgot all about me and became completely involved in tuning the guitar for at least fifteen minutes. Even the first time it had sounded in tune to me; but each time he retuned it, it sounded better. I kept thinking, Now it's in perfect tune, now he'll be satisfied. But he kept turning the pegs and plucking the strings, and each time, it sounded better by so little that it couldn't have made a difference to anyone but the worst perfectionist. Finally he shook his head with a slow, bitter smile, and said, "Oh, give up." He looked deep into the sound hole for a long time, and ran his fingers over the strings with an eerie scraping sound until he shuddered and stopped the strings. Then he lowered the guitar into its case.

"I have superperfect pitch," he said. "Ordinary tuning forks sound out of tune to me. I can't listen to music anymore; I can't stand how out of tune it is. If rock groups hired guitar tuners, I'd have a job. That's just about the only job I could stand, I think. But it's not a job in this world. I try to keep my own instruments in tune, as you see, but it's a lost cause. They go out of tune in five minutes. Whenever I'm awake, I'm trying to tune them. It's futile."

The word "futile" made him laugh with quiet satisfaction. His laugh was a hesitant waver that refused to settle on any one pitch—perhaps because if it tried, it wouldn't meet his standards.

He stuck his hands under his sweatshirt, and one of them crept up and out through the collar, to pick at his neck.

"If I have so much trouble tuning a guitar," he said, "imagine what it's like trying to tune my *mind*. I'd like to do something with my life—it sounds like a sort of neat idea—but my unconscious doesn't want me to. I'll have to stay here tuning my unconscious until it lets me take some sort of action, I suppose. I'll have to keep learning more and more about myself."

"You seem to know pretty much about yourself already," I said naïvely.

He scoffed. "I don't know a thing about myself! I mean, I do know enough about myself to be aware that I'm not some sort of sensitive flower. I'm not hiding from the world because of fear of rejection. I'm hiding from the world because I fear being *ignored.* Because the world doesn't give me a medal for going out there; the trees don't bow down when I walk by. I'm just a disgusting, spoiled, infantile narcissist, that's all," he said, beginning to glow, and stepping over instruments and books with exhilarated high steps as he paced the room with hands tucked into armpits. "I'm not recoiling from some terrible pain. I've never been seriously hurt, unfortunately. The tragedy of my life was simply that Debs the Great was born. I was thrown down from my pedestal as pampered child; I began to sulk; and for the last twenty-eight years I've been failing at everything I could, to get back at my parents, and to try to recapture the status of a coddled infant. But, you see"—he stopped pacing, and faced me, and put each hand through the cuff of the opposite sleeve—"see, I don't even begin to know enough about myself yet. Everything I've just said, you could find in one of these books." He swept his foot over a pile of paperbacks, with a kick that missed. "Every time I realize something about myself, it's something that's already described in print—in Freud, in Horney, in any of those people who happened to be born before I was. I'm a textbook case; do you realize what a blow that is to my ego? I have to find my own neurosis; I have to discover that deep original core of me that isn't in the psychology books. I won't even believe I'm a person till I do that; I won't be able to do anything. But when I find it, I can do anything: drive a cab, give music lessons, anything!"

13. The Bar Scene

Norm needed emergency treatment: he had to get a job, punch a clock, ride a rush-hour train, gobble a sandwich at a desk, or die. He had to collect a paycheck and find out exactly how much he was worth, or he would be worth zero.

The trouble was, he felt a nostalgic longing for worthlessness. "It's a nostalgia for the womb," he explained. "Or nostalgia for before existence. Hey, maybe that's the deep core!" He straightened up on his barstool, and his nondrinking hand crept up through the neck of his sweatshirt and tapped his lower lip.

"Great, you're cured!" I said. "Now you can start playing music again."

"No." He shook his head and grimaced as if my enthusiasm made it impossible. "That's still not the real core of me. I still don't feel in tune." He took another sip of beer, the great tuning lubricant; and in frustration I ordered a second plate of knockwurst and cabbage.

We were in O'Bleary's, a bar on lower Second Avenue, where the street outside was still cobbled. The storefront sign was green; a leprechaun hat sat tilted on top of the "O"; there was masking tape on a broken corner of the window. There were white cards with the prices of cheap drinks above the bar mirror. Along the opposite wall was a cafeteria counter serving manly-type boiled meats, sandwiches, cabbage, and potatoes.

It wasn't that *I* liked O'Bleary's. The idea, if anything, was to leave O'Bleary's; but it was the only place where Norm felt at ease. For the past couple of weeks I'd been coming here to help this thirty-two-year-old, as if he was a college freshman and I was his upperclass adviser. My method was very basic and unsubtle, and therefore exactly what he needed. I just kept telling him to get his ass in gear and get a job. I was an expert on that subject, and if I told someone to get a straight job, he must have really needed one.

"I have every intention of playing the guitar again," he quavered, "but I need a repertoire first."

He took a sheet of yellow paper out of his pocket, unfolded it, and smoothed it out on the bartop. It was a veteran piece of paper, torn and creased into eight floppy sections, furry and bleached from handling, and it soaked up a ring of water from where a glass had been. The whole page was smudged with song titles in pencil, and ninety percent were crossed out. They were good old songs from the sixties and seventies, ones my older brother Joe sang while he was checking the length of his hair in front of the bathroom mirror; ones whose lyrics I half heard from the radio in his bedroom; ones whose titles gave titles to my earliest memories—songs that now sounded innocent, by those fab singers of the past: "I Wanna Please Me," "Time is on My Cloud," "Just Like a Changin' " . . . .

Norm said, "The trouble is, as soon as I decide to play a song, I learn something more about myself, so the song seems like it's from my immature phase."

I would have put my head in my hands, but I sipped beer instead. "You don't have to worry about the songs being too immature for you."

"Oh, no? Know what it's like spending a whole week learning a song, then realizing it's not right for your repertoire? I don't want to waste my time like that, do I?"

"You pathetic shmuck," I groaned. Unfortunately, that was just the kind of thing he liked to hear. He smiled and contentedly fingered his list. He was the kind of person who picked his friends by acting helpless and seeing who stopped to help. That made it dangerous to be his friend if you really wanted to help him; but what could I do except try?

"You can't understand my problems," he told me. "Your life hasn't been anything like mine. You've done things, taken chances,

140

been punished, gotten stronger through the punishment. You've had it easy. You don't know how hard it is, not getting the chance to suffer."

I looked around, trying to catch the eye of someone who might side with me. Not likely, at O'Bleary's. In New York there's a bar for every taste, every kind of person; and O'Bleary's was the bar for people like Norm. The bartender didn't even want to serve drinks—he was a round-shouldered redhead who looked like he would duck under the counter in case of a fight; and when you tried to call out for a beer, he always made sure to be talking to someone at the other end of the bar, so that you'd have to wait in suspense to learn if he was feeling hopeful enough to serve you. And the customers . . .

Sitting near us was a fortyish man so fat he occupied two stools at once. He had walked through the door sideways, in a pair of black pants that looked like a punch bowl with legs. He must have thought I was rude, because I had to turn my head to the left in order to study him—an occupational hazard of being one-eyed; for instance, it's hard for me to watch a woman discreetly if she's going from right to left. He waved at the bartender and said, "Science fiction has become respectable." That's all. Apparently it was a code phrase: the bartender ignored him for the proper length of time, then said, "Oh, *all* right," then sulked his way over to put a pitcher of beer down in front of the fat man. The fat man took the whole wet pitcher in his hands and looked at it the way you shouldn't look at an inanimate object, and gulped half of it at once, white foam and yellow liquid, straight from the spout. He closed his eyes, licked his lips, and wiped his hands on his legs. Then, with his most urgent thirst satisfied, he poured a glassful, while sweat ran in trails from his hair. He lifted the glass and said in an alto voice, "Science fiction has become respectable. Science fiction has become respec—" He tilted the glass against his lips and guzzled.

"That's Skip Space, the science fiction writer," Norm whispered. "For the past twenty years he's only been able to say that one sentence. But he knows how to change the intonation in very subtle ways, so that it can mean 'A pitcher of beer,' or 'I'd like these cleaned and pressed for Thursday,' or 'Where's my advance?' Of course he spends his whole life in the same few situations, so he only needs the same few words. . . . Hi, Skip, how are you?"

Skip turned his head—he couldn't turn his body, or he'd slip off one of his barstools. "Science fiction—"

"Glad to hear it," I said, and asked Norm, "does that mean 'Fine, how are you?' "

"You have a good ear." And he actually was impressed, poor Norm—his awe of everyone else's slightest accomplishment made him seem like a nice guy. I nodded away his compliment.

"But how can he write?" I asked.

"Simple: he has a word processor. It's an advanced Japanese model with all his previous works stored in its memory. It also has a custom-made scrambler button. When he has to write a new book, he presses a button and it prints out a recombination of some of his old scenes."

Skip pounded his fist on the bartop, exactly the way characters do in pulp novels. "Science fiction has become re*spec*table!"

"He wants to emphasize," Norm interpreted in a frightened murmur near my ear, "that he still plays an important creative role by deciding exactly which permutations, out of thousands, will become part of the new book."

I turned and smiled encouragingly. "Way to go, Skip." I sank my head on the bar and closed my eyes. Oh, my job, my job! I needed a being-and-watching coffee break. In the darkness with my left cheek on the cool wood, I smiled and thought about what a nice job I had, but how I deserved to be better paid for it. I thought I was improving at the work, because even during this break I was sensing the temperature of the bartop, the vibrations from glasses being placed down, the warm breeze from the bartender moving past me to stare out the window, the babble of the TV of course, the squeaks of Norm's barstool on my right, the slowing of my own pulse, the reddenings and flecks of light in my visual center. . . .

"Goldfish!" shouted a voice at the front door, and my head sprang up.

A short man with a gray beard and long, hanked hair clumped in wearing brown hiking boots, one of them unlaced. He greeted Norm like a friend.

"This is Jonathan Done," Norm told me, and we shook hands.

Done sat on our left and took out a paperback book and began to write in it. I saw him cross out the first printed line and write on top of it in blue ballpoint pen.

"Got it!" he cried. "Goldfish, look at this."

He slid the book past me, and Norm picked it up. It was *Moby Dick*. I read over Norm's shoulder: "I who address you have decided to cloak myself in the name Ishmael."

"Bartender!" I called, because it was preferable to choking. "Another beer!"

"I'm trying to get it right," said Done. "There are too many books published in this world. An ordinary writer merely tries to add to the pile of mediocrity. I try to improve what's already there. A writer's first asset is patience: if I didn't get it right this time, I'll try again. If I mark up the whole book, I'll buy another copy. But I won't use pencil: that would imply I plan to erase. You must have self-confidence! Goldfish, the book." He opened his hand on the bar, and Norm slid the book back to him.

"I would be the last person on earth to criticize a person's choice of friends," I said to Norm.

"He's a great man," Norm said. "He was my high-school English teacher, but one day he decided to *do* instead of teach. He has a pure commitment. He's a writer who knows he'll never make a penny, because he rewrites other people's books. His first triumph was *For Whom the Bell Tolls*. His version is so much better than the one you can buy. It has the real Hemingway simplicity, while the published book is full of adjectives and long sentences. He knows the masses will never read his, but that doesn't weaken him. He makes me ashamed to be doing so little. I've got to decide on my repertoire right away!" Norm picked up his furry sheet of paper, looked at it, bit his lip with sudden thought—and put the paper back down. "Well, one thing Mr. Done's taught me is patience. I have to be willing to wait as long as it takes, and not rush into things."

"Bartender!" I called.

143

"I'm coming, I'm *com*ing," the bartender said, pausing to think about precisely which glass to give me.

"Okay, got it concise," Done announced. He slid the book back to us. The old handwriting had been crossed out, and there was a new first sentence: "Ishmael, speaking."

I grabbed the book out of Norm's hand and threw it against Done's chest.

"*Too* concise?" he asked.

A young Puerto Rican guy ran into the bar with five fingers raised. "Channel Five!" he called to the bartender. The bartender sniffed, served me my beer, served another pitcher to Skip out of pure spite, and finally strolled to the TV mounted on a high shelf, and switched from the basketball game to Channel 5. A commercial was in progress:

"But I *use* an antiflatulent," an old lady told her druggist.

"Not all gas remedies work alike, Mrs. Zepp. Try new Avoid, in the little brown box. . . ."

Jonathan Done stood up from his barstool in a state of inspiration. Holding *Moby Dick* open like a Bible, he cleared his throat, and read aloud in a ringing voice: " 'Let the name be Ishmael, then!' "

He had achieved exactly the same impact as Melville: everyone ignored him.

"Come on come on come on come on come on." The newcomer snapped his fingers at the TV set. He was five feet seven, wore a black leather jacket over a blue tee shirt, and had a pencil mustache. "Let's see that news, man, let's see that news. I'm a double winner, today's the biggest day ever in news history."

We all crowded close to the TV set. Skip Space lifted his pitcher in both hands and, while still guzzling, waddled in our direction, hip-checking his barstools out of his path. The bartender, smirking with disdain, moved to our end of the bar, and wiped a wet spot as if that was his main intention. They all seemed to know what was going on; and I wanted to find out, not only from curiosity, but because I like to gamble, and I thought maybe I could get in on something.

144

"What's happening?" I asked the Puerto Rican.

"Victor Colon," he said, answering my question and introducing himself at the same time.

"What's the story tonight?" Norm asked him.

"Tenants marching to City Hall for their rights. These land-lords, man, they really greedy."

The camera showed a crowd of people marching with signs, on the sidewalk outside City Hall. A newsman came on screen, and did the usual brilliant job of TV reporting: told how many people were at the rally, what slogans they shouted, which precincts the cops controlling the crowd were from, and what vacuities a mayoral aide had uttered from the City Hall steps, but gave no clue to the arguments for or against rent increases. He interviewed a marcher who claimed a policeman had shoved her; then the camera panned the crowd, and the reporter summed up: "And so, what is profit for some is, perhaps, when you really stop and think about it, loss for others. Wes McClean, News Five, City Hall."

The guys in the bar clapped. Victor held his hand on his belly and took a deep bow, and the bartender even poured him a free beer; but before he sipped it, Victor flashed all ten fingers and then an extra one. "Channel Eleven! There's two tonight, I told you." Then he punched me on the shoulder, with a small fist like a small steel hammer. "Hey, new member, how you like that story?"

"Fine," I said uncertainly. "What are you betting on, something the reporter says?"

He laughed. "You're not very observant, my friend." Not very observant! Talk about wounding remarks! My ego started shriveling; I felt vacuumed up inside. He had said the word "observant" with the gingerly lilt of someone trying to speak well. At least I observed *that*, I thought. "That landlord story?" he said. "Where Wes McClean asks the lady how the cop beat on her? You didn't notice nothing? Wait a second, here it comes."

Channel 11 had been doing the weather; now a story came on that made Victor raise his fist and shout, "All right!" A blind man's Seeing Eye dog had gone blind itself and had received a Seeing Eye monkey to help it. A blond female reporter was standing outside a blind people's association, interviewing the dog's master. She asked him a poignant question and made a sympathetic, pouting face; she asked him a lighthearted question about monkeys and gave a bright-eyed smile. The camera made sure to show us the whole range of facial expressions that the blind man couldn't see. But I was thinking, What don't *I* see? What are they betting on?

"And so, tonight, Somerset the Seeing Eye monkey has not just one blind master to guide, but two." The reporter grinned as if her stock portfolio depended on it, while the monkey's tail wrapped itself in a gray-furred loop around her journalistically concise right breast. She smiled sheepishly at the blind man, who wasn't looking. "Twinky McFloss, News Eleven, New York." The camera gave a last look at the monkey scampering from her shoulder to the blind man's—

And I saw it.

Standing against the wall behind them, next to two kids with braids who were giggling and popping bubble gum, was Victor Colon. He stood solemnly at attention, with one hand on his belt buckle, staring at the lens like a plantation owner in an old photograph.

The barroom erupted in applause. The bartender, shaking his head in defeat, poured another beer for Victor, and then Skip Space, with a subtle intonation, ordered a pitcher for everyone in the house. Norm patted Victor on the back and said, "Wow, you really know what you want out of life. If only my parents had spanked me like yours . . ." Jonathan Done raised his glass and said, "O Mana-hatta, enchanted isle. . . ."

"Good night, Punch," said the news anchorwoman.

"Good night, Judy," said the news anchorman.

And I must admit I was impressed, just like when I'd seen Brass-berg's picture in the magazine. "And you were in the first story too?"

"Two in one night!" Victor Colon said. "That's some record to beat. They'll all try to beat it, but they won't." He was talking manically and laughing with joy; he kept patting me on the back, as he wanted to be patted on the back himself. I wondered about him;

146

but that didn't keep me from smiling and nodding at him in congratulations. "It's my hobby, getting on the news," he said. "I don't make news; I get on the show without having to kill anybody for it. Look: you see somebody being interviewed, he's on the street or in a public place, and there's people in the background, right? They pass by, they wave, they laugh, even if there's a dead body on the ground. Well, you look closer, you see that almost every day one of the people standing with those passerbys is me, I."

He was so high on himself, and wanted so much to tell about it, that when I interrupted with a question, he had to clamp his lower lip tight over his mustache to stop himself; and he stared hard at me as if to ask why the hell I was interrupting.

"What do you do?" I asked. "Run all over town trying to track down reporters?"

He shook his head indignantly, the way you do when someone paraphrases your life in a way that's essentially correct but far too unglamorous. "It's hard, what I do, man, try it and see. I mean, it's easy for me now 'cause I know how; but it would be hard for an ordinary person. I wake up in the morning—I'm the superintendent in an apartment building—see, I can do all the repairs in the morning, if I don't I just leave them till the next morning. In the afternoon I'm nowhere near that building, they don't own my life. I'm finding out where the reporters are. I'm near the courts, the Stock Exchange, City Hall, I'm listening to the radio to hear what stories are in progress. There's news cameras all around Manhattan, man, if you know where to find them. This is a news city, you see, and I'm on the news. Millions of people see me on their sets every night; they don't know they do, but they do. They see me somewhere in their minds without knowing it, and they keep seeing me, and maybe one day somebody sees it and *sees* it, and pretty soon I'm famous—because how can I not be? I'm on the news all the time, what you mean not famous? Then there'll be news stories about me, myself. About all the initiative I use in finding the news stories; what do you know, I'm more interesting than the interviews in the foreground! Pretty soon every night there's people turning on their sets asking, 'Victor Colon been on yet? How long can he keep up

147

his streak of being in the background of consecutive news stories?'
There's public demand for a station to hire me for the background
of *all* its news stories. Finally, a dream come true: my own show,
The Victor Colon Show. Me and my crew we go anywhere we want
that looks interesting for the people. It's like news, but not really,
more like real stuff you'd want to hear that's interesting. I find some
block where they got good handball, some block with nice flowers
in the windows or something—I tell the people. It's like, 'This is
New York, you dumbasses, this is the city you see around you
every day but you don't notice it like I do.' And every show will
end with a sign-off, I got it memorized already: 'I'm Victor Colon
and you're you, but even if you're not a big celebrity like me, you're
beautiful.' "

The bartender banged another beer down in front of Victor, and
managed to make the act look reluctant. "Oh, here, you're so stupid
you deserve it." Then he looked at the window. "I can't stand it,"
he whimpered. "People hang around outside my tavern, gawking,
like they want free atmosphere but they don't want to pay for a
drink."

I turned my head to the left and saw a man outside, starting to
walk away from O'Bleary's window. I didn't see his face; I saw the
back of a head of curly black hair, and the back of a white sports
jacket with blue piping around the lapel. He was wearing a blue-
and-white scarf to keep out the fall wind. . . .

I ran out of the bar. The man got into a double-parked cab and
slammed the door. I was overjoyed to see him; I ran up to the cab,
shouting, "Hey, come back!" I pulled on the door handle; it was
locked. I looked through the window and shouted, "Don't you
want to talk to me?" I shaped my lips very emphatically so he could
read them even if he couldn't hear me through the glass. But he
wasn't even looking at me. He was looking straight ahead, at the red
numerals on the meter, with the bland, worry-denying smile of any
taxi passenger. The cab started up. "What were you, spying?" I
said. And did the one thing that's bound to make a driver stop his
car. I kicked the fender, hard. It was unearthly: the cabbie kept
driving.

"Come back here, what are you doing?" I shouted after him. And every moment, I expected that the cab would stop, it would back up, it would screech stopping in front of the bar again, the guy in the suit would bound out laughing and shake my hand and tell me it was only a joke to test my equanimity, and he'd tell me that even though my equanimity wasn't too great I was still doing a fine job. . . . I kept expecting that, as I watched the cab reach the corner, drive through the red light, and diminish down the street.

"You goddamn spy!" I shouted. "How about a raise, you cheapskate? If this is what you think of me, why don't you hire Norm?"

And I lost track of the cab's taillights, amid the other pairs of taillights driving down Second Avenue. I kept looking down the street until I didn't even know what I was looking at.

I felt the way a kid feels when he's first learning about the world and he asks the grown-ups to explain something to him and they won't explain it; they just laugh at his cuteness or they walk away to do something grown-up, and he thinks they don't love him because they won't explain. It was a November night and it was drizzling, it was the kind of night when the cloud cover reflects the orange of the sodium lamps, and every sign on every store window seems to have a letter missing. Are they always watching me? I wondered. Are they ever gonna tell me what to do?

I hardly knew the guy in the suit at all; but I felt desolate because he hadn't rushed up and praised me and told me how wonderfully I was doing.

At first, standing in the gutter, I'd been heated by anger and dismay at watching the cab drive off. The next moment all the chill of November pierced my chest; I had to clutch myself and hunch over, and I went into the bar shivering out loud. I was exhausted from seeing my benefactor drive away. I was irritated that in order to get home I'd have to walk through a cold drizzle. Why didn't they give me the rewards they'd hinted at? Would I always have to hang around lowlifes, or weren't rich and successful people worth observing, too? How about an uptown bar with polished oak walls, a warm crackling fireplace, and a piano-bass duo in the corner? Now, that would be worth observing.

I got my wool sweater from the coat rack and pulled it on. I put on my corduroy jacket, and last I took my green tie with tea-stained coats of arms out of the jacket pocket, and I knotted it outside the sweater. It was a little wrinkled.

"We're going home," I said to Norm, and pulled him by the arm. As soon as I did, I thought to myself, How lucky I am! I'm pulling him, he's not pulling me. I'm the one with the fantastic, wonderful job that I like doing and that I still want to learn more about. The guy in the suit didn't talk to me, but he's interested in me, he's watching, and from the little he just did, I know I'm not going wrong. Norm doesn't have anything. He might be fine at being and watching, but he wasn't recruited. That's the way it is with jobs: there might be many well-qualified people, but if only one or two are hired, the rest have to forget about it and keep walking the pavement.

"Next thing I'll run for mayor," Victor Colon said, pacing, and punching his hand. "Everybody'll know me from TV, they'll say, 'That Victor Colon, let's vote for him, he puts something back into the community.' I'll start a volunteer squad to stand in front of the news cameras seriously; we'll chase away the kids who clown around."

Skip Space gurgled something—we knew what it was—while he drank from two pitchers of beer at once, and beer spilled onto his collar from two spouts.

"Let's go." I tugged on Norm's arm.

He pulled back and gazed at the yellow paper on the bartop. I was starting to churn up with anger inside, angry at him for being like me and making me pity him. "My repertoire," he said.

" 'Hi, I'm Ishmael,' " Jonathan Done read.

"No you're not," I said, and I grabbed *Moby Dick* out of his hands. I threw it onto the floor and kicked it spinning, the length of the bar. Then I ran up to Skip Space and pulled one of his two pitchers from his hand. Then I ran over to Norm's yellow paper, and tore it into bits. I pushed Norm ahead of me out of the bar, before the bartender got up the energy to chase me out.

14.   Thanks

The trouble with the Goldfish kids was that they were on my own level. I mean, when I want friends on my own level, I have plenty of people my own age to choose from. When I hang around with people older than me, it's because I hope they can teach me something. But Debs still believed in the romance of crime, as if she was an undergraduate. After making love, she sometimes asked me why I hadn't stolen her father's credit cards yet. Her fantasy was that I'd become a kind of American Express Robin Hood, charging food processors and tape decks and giving them to the poor from the safety of a rented car. She felt terribly guilty to be living in an expensive, well-kept house on the fringe of slums; but she didn't take it kindly when I suggested going outside and dumping some garbage on the stoop. And when she got angry at her parents, she would start "rationally" discussing the possibility of moving out— she was twenty-eight, and still using that as a threat. I tried to bring out the mature side of her by asking her for help with her brother; but that always tensed her up. She said that she wanted everyone to be free and therefore she couldn't do anything about Norm until he rejoined his family of his own free will. It occurred to me that her career and his lack of one were the only things that made the world think of her as the healthier of the two.

Well, *I* helped Norm.

I got him to play music again, and my technique was very simple: I forced him. He'd never been forced to do anything in his life, and it was a revelation to him. We were sitting on the splintery floor in his big sunny front room with the unicorn and damsel posters on the wall. He was trying to tune a guitar—it sounded perfectly in tune to me, of course, but he kept shaking his head. At the same time he was telling me how he'd vowed to find a goal in life by the time he was thirty-four.

"What if you don't find it by then?" I asked, afraid he might kill himself.

"Well, I'm flexible about deadlines. I wasn't raised in a culture of firmness—"

"Enough!" I shouted, and sprang up toward him. It seemed to me that even a resolve to kill himself would have been more definite and constructive than this. He wouldn't have actually killed himself, of course, but it might at least have scared him into doing something better. So I figured it was up to me to scare him. At first I was going to grab his guitar, but I realized that would let him claim I'd put it out of tune. Instead, I merely stood in front of him, and jabbed a finger in his face with all the authority of my felony record. "Okay, the guitar's in tune," I said. "Now play something for me."

He tried to wave me away with a sneer, as if it wasn't for me to say whether it was in tune or not. But I insisted, I *ordered* him to play; and he laughed nervously to cover up his fear of me. I kept insisting; he kept shaking his head with nervous laughter; I said if he didn't start playing immediately I was gonna put my foot through the guitar—I was a hardened criminal, and he remembered our first encounter at the window. He knew I'd do it. For a second, I think he was tempted to let me, just so he could wheedle a replacement guitar out of his parents. But thank goodness he was more mature than that. "Okay, okay," he laughed, and plucked a couple of chords as if he didn't mean them, as if only trying to placate a dangerous lunatic. I didn't care what he thought of me; I only wanted him to play. I don't play any musical instrument myself. Once, in high school, three of my friends bought cheap electric guitars and asked me to buy one and join them in a group; I refused, because I thought that was cooler. Every so often, I think about that and really regret it.

I made Norm practice every afternoon when I came back from

my fictitious youth counseling. For a while he treated it as a joke—which was much better than if he hadn't let me in at all. After a week he was used to my bossing him around, and no longer needed nervous laughter to justify complying. He looked a little exasperated, but he dutifully played every day, with me watching—and after a month he was making himself practice, instead of being made to. I trusted him to play every afternoon without my going upstairs. He started a new repertoire sheet with up-to-date songs on it. And he collected ads from rock groups looking for guitarists—I waited eagerly for him to actually call them, but you can't expect everything at once.

My big plan of the season was to bring him downstairs to play for his parents and make them admit their son was alive. But he wouldn't do it. When I even suggested it, he threatened to put his own foot through the guitar. The idea of playing music, he said, was to make him independent of his parents; if he played for their approval, it would mean he was dependent. "If they don't like my playing, I'll be discouraged, and if they do, I'll rebel against them by quitting again." Like all Norm's psychological observations, this was so sharp he could have slashed himself with it. Maybe I should have insisted he play, but, after all, he was an adult, and I was trying to build his dignity, not demolish it.

The Goldfish invited me for Thanksgiving dinner. Four places were set at the table: for Bea, the judge, Debs, and me. I was shocked: even at Thanksgiving, Norm and his family couldn't face each other. Where would he eat his turkey dinner—in a coffee shop? I stood around the living room uncomfortably in my corduroy pants and white shirt, and studied the lithographs of Paris on the pale tan walls.

"Take some crudités," Bea called out, and with the yellow asbestos mitt on her right hand she pointed to a platter on the coffee table. I saw carrot and celery sticks, red radishes, the obligatory raw broccoli . . . "That's a special Barbarbaranni dip I made from a *Times* recipe," she said. "It's based on mint and goat's-milk curds."

I passed up the crudités, as a silent protest against Norm's absence. Bea didn't notice whether I had tasted her politically daring dip or not—she'd trotted off to the kitchen, where she had an appointment to argue with the judge about whether the turkey was done or not. The sounds of "The juices are still pink!" and "You're crazy, the drumstick is falling off!" resonated—as my old pal Lois would have said—through the long halls of the brownstone. Suddenly I heard a much more disturbing and yet more captivating sound—a crunching behind my left ear.

The sound of Debs chewing on a toenail.

She tried to circle in front of me, but I turned to the right, to keep her on my blind side for as long as I heard the chewing. I didn't want to approach Bea's turkey dinner pre-nauseated.

"What's on the menu for after dinner?" I said, stepping away to look at another lithograph—of a bridge, or maybe a cathedral, it didn't even register. "Coming down to my apartment?"

She hurried her chews for my sake, and politely swallowed before replying. "I'm feeling rather morose today, I'm afraid."

I turned and looked at her. Was she beautiful! With her narrow bony face, her gray eyes, her long wavy black hair in which I knew where some gray strands were hidden. . . . She was wearing a dark-blue sweater with a cowl neck, and blue jeans over bare feet. I wanted to kiss her, but of course I had to be prudent. "Well, if you're having one of your outbreaks . . ."

"Go to hell," she said, "I don't have one of your fucking 'outbreaks' today. I just feel so—I don't know how to put it. How would you describe it if someone felt guilty, but in a way that transcended ordinary guilt? I mean, if they felt as if they were really doing something *wrong?*"

"I would call that guilt," I said.

She sneered at me with pitying disappointment, then took a quick two-fingered pull at her right eyebrow, where a light hair or two was struggling to grow back.

"I can understand your feeling guilty," I said. "Here we are, having this supposedly joyous holiday dinner, and your own brother is sitting upstairs like a total outcast."

She stared at me. "Have you been bothering Norm?"

"I've been helping him, if that's what you mean. He does live here. In fact, I got him to play guitar again."

She laughed. "He doesn't want to play guitar."

"He is."

"What did you do, threaten him with your cell-block methods? You know, I'm really beginning to think that you'll never adapt to the civilized community." She sat down on the floor frowning, snatched up her foot, and took a nip of calloused skin from around the second toe. "Maybe I should talk to your parole officer," she said, chewing.

Fellow fetishists, I had a fierce craving to kiss that long, narrow toe on the raw spot; a toe so cute I wished it could have spoken. I wanted to grab her and ravish her beneath the crudité table before her parents could decide on the proper carving strategy. But the fact was, I was peeved at her for the way she treated her brother, and for desiring greater intimacy with her toenails than with me.

I sat down next to her. I grabbed her slim bony foot, rotated it in the ankle socket, felt the cool hairless metatarsel. "If you feel guilty and you don't know why, the best thing to do is to sin."

"It's falling, it's falling!" That wasn't Debs, it was her mother, trotting in circles around the judge, who was tilting the platter he carried in, as if giving the turkey a fair chance to escape.

"Leave me alone, I know what I'm doing," he said, as cranberry jelly slices, parsley sprigs, and whole walnuts slid to the front of the platter. Luckily, as soon as the turkey got one leg over the side, Bea scurried around her husband to catch the bird and push the trimmings back. With a moan of relief, the judge dropped the whole platter onto the dinner table, and though a garnish sprang onto the tablecloth here and there, really they had nowhere to go but back onto the platter in the hands of justice. Out of respect for his office, I will not describe how the judge tried to carve the turkey—the test cuts that were made, the screechings of dull blade against bone, the shredding of skin and dry white meat, the high-pitched fumings of frustration which came from his judicial nostrils.

Finally I walked over and said, "I have some experience filing through iron bars."

155

He gladly handed me the knife. It was serrated, of all things. I sawed, and smiled dauntlessly while Bea told me all about the better carving knife she had seen in the *Times* but hadn't been able to buy because she'd thrown out that day's paper without remembering to save the ad.

The turkey came off in chunks rather than slices; stringy and dry near the skin, red near the bone, covered with a translucent brown liquid in which lumps of half-cooked flour and chopped giblets floated together as tolerantly as dogs and suntan-lotion bottles on a lake.

"You didn't get turkey like this you-know-where," Bea said, as I subtly pushed my plate to the left so I wouldn't see it, and strained my jaw muscles trying to work enough saliva into the food to swallow it.

Finally I gave up on saliva, used a couple of glasses of California burgundy as lubrication instead ("We're being very American today," Bea had said, to explain why the wine wasn't French), and found myself saying tipsily, "I love Thanksgiving. Isn't the human race wise, to mark certain days on which you're supposed to think about things larger than yourself! I'm thankful that we have a day when we can put aside our everyday selves and talk about history, hope, and tradition. Because what is the everyday self anyway? It's a robot we send out into the world while our real self cowers behind it. I walk around the streets and I see well-dressed people who are as confined as prisoners and as underdeveloped as African nations." Debs smirked as if I was a young fool—this was the kind of situation in which she loved to show off her maturity. I went on, for her sake. "They don't respect others, but they're afraid to do anything others won't approve of. They're bitter because they're not cared about, and they're terrified of having to care about anyone. Each one will be glad enough to stay lonely if it keeps the others lonely, too."

"And they all read the *Post* nowadays," Bea said. "Whenever I take the bus, someone next to me has that horrible *Post* open to some lurid sex crime story, and of course you can't avoid reading at least the headline—"

She stopped, and looked at the ceiling.

Guitar notes were coming down, like American leaflets falling on a Barbarbaranni village. Bea stood at the door of her hut, watching the sky with alert peasant suspicion. I listened. I began to smile. I smiled broadly at Debs—she furrowed her nearly hairless brows.

"Ma-ry had a lit-tle lamb," sang the guitar.

I was overjoyed; for the first time in years, Norm was playing electric; all my lessons with him had been acoustic, because he'd still been afraid to make noise. Now it came down loud and sweet, though hesitant, as if he had to ask each note for permission before plucking it.

"Did Dr. Ripstein prescribe guitar playing for him?" Bea asked the judge.

"I prescribed it," I said.

"You? You're his psychiatrist?"

"Does he need a psychiatrist to prescribe the air he breathes, too?"

They looked at me as if I'd said the most obtuse, childishly contrary, unworldly, irresponsible thing imaginable. I loved the way they were looking at me! I wished I could scoff in their faces, but I really am somewhat naturally polite.

The nursery rhyme sang down from the ceiling and through the windows, louder and quicker, with a little bend to the notes; no longer as if he had to ask permission, but as if he had to debate with himself about each riff.

"Lit-tle lamb," he corrected himself. "Little lamb, little lamb."

"Doesn't he have more judgment than to play so loud when we're eating dinner?" said Learned Goldfish.

"We can't blame him," Bea said. "Holidays make some people anxious." A dreamy look came over her face. "Remember the holidays when the kids were children?"

"When you were all anxious together?" I said, in spite of myself. She looked at me, hurt, and I was a little ashamed.

But the guitar came louder, Norm's hesitation had become bluesy repetition. The word "lamb" was a hard-strummed chord. The walls vibrated.

Bea stood up. "I'm calling Dr. Ripstein."

Norm turned up the volume switch. I couldn't see him, but I could sense what he was doing and how much joy he was feeling. My protégé! My brother! He had broken through his barrier; with no more tentativeness, he improvised blues lines as sweet and tart as cranberry sauce.

"Hello, Dr. Ripstein?" Bea said.

The guitar faltered. Norm groped for notes. There was a beautiful fragment, then a gap, then another fragment a bit less beautiful and more apologetic. He couldn't hear his mother, but somehow . . .

"I know it's a holiday," she said into the phone. "Can you give me the number where he can be reached, please? I'm the mother of one of his most diligent patients."

A couple of briefer guitar bursts; and then Norm stopped. The walls stopped humming.

We heard, faintly, an electric guitar being tuned.

"Never mind, it's not an emergency," Bea said, and hung up.

We all watched her return to the table, as if she, not Norm, had become the important figure, the one whose moods and gestures would set the tone. She sat down sighing. "Oh, I wish he would resolve his problems one of these days. If only he would gain the slightest particle of self-insight. Tuning up is no better for him than playing."

"No *better* for him?" I repeated. I looked to Debs for support, but she sulked and picked at turkey skin as if it was her own skin. "Let me inform you, madam, that his guitar playing is the only good—"

The doorbell rang.

"Get it," the judge sniffled. "Who's getting it? Who's closest to the door?" Gripping the arms of his chair he turned this way and that and fumed helplessly. The bell rang again. "Who's closest to the door?" He threw severe glances at each of us in turn.

"I'll get it," I said. I went and opened the apartment door, and then the front door of the house.

On the welcome mat stood a short, round man with the left side of his hair dyed magenta and the right side dyed white. He wore a white suit with black vertical stripes, and dime-store wraparound sunglasses with black frames and cheap green lenses. He was smiling as if I was his best friend—as if everyone was his best friend, and wherever he went he would get his hand pumped in admiration and good fellowship.

"Goldfish residence?" he asked.

I pointed inside. He nodded and smiled with immense but easygoing gratitude, and, pushing past me, said, "Best Thanksgiving wishes to you and yours." He had a remarkable voice: a light, friendly baritone, with no strain in it at all but with a fullness that made you think it could project for miles. Not only was there an uncanny sincerity in it, but just hearing it made me feel sincerely touched and peaceful. I followed him in, smiling tranquilly, and feeling alpha waves spread through my brain.

He stood at the Thanksgiving table, drew a thick white envelope from his inside pocket, and took out some official-looking papers. "Hello, everybody; how are you on this fantastic holiday evening? I know you weren't expecting me today, but I thought we could share the glow of Thanksgiving together, as one. Hey, I'm Buddy Plastic, I'm sure you've heard my voice over WOLD, Where Rock Is Still Technically Alive." He looked at Debs for recognition of the famous slogan that was on subway posters in all the demographically correct stations.

"Buddy Plastic," I said. "I've heard that name before."

He gave a modest little chuckle that could have split an anvil. "I was the top-rated deejay on FM radio till I 'ran afoul of the law,' as they say."

I snapped my fingers. "That's right! Your station ran a contest with a lot of publicity; the prize was a date with you. The winner was a sixteen-year-old girl. You took her to your apartment, served dinner, then killed her slowly with her own utensils and ate her raw liver while a news cameraman kept taping."

"Wow, computer memory!" Plastic pushed his glasses down to the tip of his nose, and looked at me with absolute friendliness. "That was a classic moment in rock history, from way back last year. But the judge was really enlightened; he commuted my sentence to a series of benefit appearances against child abuse. (How

159

are you tonight, dear?)" he asked Debs. "And my station hired me right back, but they do ask me to kind of live in a group setting for a while. Which is a really neat idea—not that I expect to hang around here too much anyway. But, you know, I think that what the world really needs—I'll just say this one serious thing and let me know whether you do or don't agree—I think that the one thing the world really needs is more understanding and trust. We're all human, we all have our frailties, hey, let's agree to understand them. Here are my parole papers—"

"Oh, I'm terribly sorry," Bea said. "You seem like an excellent tenant, but we already have a released offender living here." She nodded toward me. "Mr. Redstone."

Plastic frowned, and flipped through his papers. "Those pseudos, those retros, those oids—they told me you had a vacancy."

"They must have made a mistake. Mr. Redstone came here this summer with all the proper credentials—" Bea stopped with her mouth open, and looked at me. "You did show me your papers, Rich, didn't you?"

"Uh, no," I said. And after months of lying and living a double life, I confessed and admitted that I wasn't a criminal at all, but a fraud.

Bea shrieked. "You—you uncultured person!"

I hung my head. I felt terrible. Poor Bea—she'd trusted in me for months, thought of me as her greatest triumph, and now I had to tell her that I'd been deceiving her—that I was really an honest citizen. She was pouting at me furiously, but mostly she felt betrayed. There were tears in her eyes.

"Hey, Turkey Day should be happy," Plastic said. "Like we're thankful for our blessings, but nothing too heavy."

He elbowed me away from my chair, and stood behind it expectantly. Bea sniffled, wiped her eyes, and beamed at him. "Mr. Plastic, won't you sit down?"

"Wait a second," the judge said. "Have you ever had your driver's license suspended for more than thirty days?"

I started walking backward, on tiptoe, toward the door. "Well, 'bye, folks. Sorry . . ." I looked at Debs, and couldn't finish. I stood blinking and gulping, while she patted her mother's hand to calm her.

"You rodent," she called me. "You marmot, you cavy, you capybara! How could you betray the trust of innocent senior citizens? Don't worry, Mother, he's leaving. He won't lie to us anymore."

"So much for the girl who wanted to steal her parents' credit cards," I said.

"Liar!" she screeched. "Nothing you say deserves a particle of credence."

"I love you," I said, and watched her hand rise to her face. But then an amazing thing happened. Before it could touch her eyebrow, she stopped her hand in midair. She looked at it, thumb pressing hard against two fingers, and she frowned with deep bewilderment as if she suddenly couldn't remember why she was doing such a self-destructive thing. Her hand dropped to her side.

"I feel tremendous compassion for you," she told me, and she averted her eyes. She looked at Buddy Plastic. "I bet your virginity lasted about ten minutes on Riker's Island."

I turned around and headed for the door, to pack my suitcase.

15. How I Found My True Love

Thanksgiving night, and I was lugging my suitcase down Second Avenue, wearing my corduroy jacket over my sweater and tie. It was breezy, the old clouds kept being replaced by new clouds, the air smelled good from lack of traffic, and I passed two hatless cops sitting in a parked cruiser, eating turkey dinners from aluminum-foil plates. A Puerto Rican father and son with pushed-up shirtsleeves checked under the hood of their car, while a little daughter with a pink hair ribbon hopped in a circle around her chattering mother and grandma. "Happy Thanksgiving!" I wished them, and tried to hurry away before they got suspicious. Once, I passed through a current of air that for no apparent reason smelled of turkey, and a couple of blocks later it was pumpkin pie. I didn't know where I'd sleep that night. My arm was tired from the suitcase, the suitcase kept banging into my leg. I turned west on St. Mark's Place. There were metal gates in front of the stores. The rebellious young record salesmen and haircutters and punchers of belt-holes had gone home for Thanksgiving, and I said to myself: Everybody has a place to be during the holiday, and see, Redstone?, so do you, your place is right here in the world. All of a sudden I started taking huge breaths of empty-street air, and looking at the row of closed stores alternating with open restaurants, and I felt lucky, as if the whole world had been given to me. As I walked I kept imagining that Debs had come with me, or that she was running after me. She would have to become a whole other person, in order to get up the courage to leave her parents, but she'd still be Debs. Soon I'd hear her fast footsteps, and her voice calling my name, and I'd turn around just as she threw herself into my arms, and we'd find a hotel to sleep in together, some hotel that had been built especially for us. . . .

Somebody tapped me on the left shoulder. I almost jumped—the touch came from a spot where a person with a left eye could have seen blurred motion in the corner, but I couldn't. I turned, and saw a man with oily hair and olive skin, wearing an unzipped gray parka and a yellow polyester shirt, carrying a clipboard and a ballpoint pen.

" 'Scuse me, sir, do you have a moment to participate in a survey?"

I looked around. A survey on St. Mark's Place at seven-thirty on Thanksgiving night? There was the answer: the store behind him had a sign, "Reader and Advisor," in the window. Two coatless little girls chased each other in and out of the store; the smaller one started to run up to the clipboard man, but her sister pulled her back in a language I'd never heard before. I watched them go into the store, in matching black dresses, and thought, I'll bet the little one gets all the big one's hand-me-downs, and she'll be wearing the identical black dress for years.

"I'm doing a survey on discrimination," the man told me. He checked his watch; I saw that it was a Cartier with a gold case. "Are you aware of the terrible discrimination that exists against gypsies?"

"Oh, give me a break," I said. "Find someone else, I've been through too much today." But I didn't leave. In fact, I used this as an opportunity to put my suitcase down and flex my aching arm. The two girls were staring at me through the window, from different heights, and I would have bet anything that they wished they were part of the regular world like all the other girls they saw on the streets. Maybe they wished that a handsome man like me would take them away and raise them to be normal Americans, with school and good clothes and friends.

"Sir," the man said, checking his watch again, "I know you've heard a lot of innwendoes about our time-honored methods of character reading. Wouldn't you be pleased to learn that all those inn-

163

wendoes are absolutely false lies? And wouldn't you like to learn something about yourself in the process? Would you care to answer a few survey questions to help us educate the public about gypsies, and my wife will be honored to give you a palm reading absolutely free, normally five dollars? Would you step inside for just two minutes to answer these simple questions, they're vital to the security of us, your law-abiding, proud gypsy neighbors?"

The smaller girl leaned out through the storefront door, lifting one leg behind her. "It's on, Papa!"

He checked his watch again. "All right, all right! *The Muppet Show* is going on, sir. We always watch it together, you see what kind of a family we are. Please, I invite you into our home."

"*The Muppet Show!*" I said, wondering who was the special guest star tonight. Then the bigger girl appeared in the doorway, and leaned out in exactly the same one-legged way her sister had, and I started to smile; I thought about sisters growing up so close that they learned all kinds of unconscious gestures from each other—I knew how she'd blush if anyone pointed it out. I tried to imagine how good it must be to grow up with a lot of affection between sisters or brothers. She was eating a floppy slice of turkey white meat, and I thought, Turkey! They have Thanksgiving, too! I'd had no idea what gypsies ate or what holidays they kept. Maybe they *are* trying to be like normal Americans, I thought. They actually are discriminated against. Do you have proof that every gypsy is a cheat? Are you being nice to those two girls by automatically considering them accomplices to theft?

The girl had gone back inside, and I wanted to go inside, too, just to show them that someone from the outside world could treat them civilly. And I wouldn't let them victimize me, either, I thought; I was alert to the possibility, so I wouldn't let it happen; I'd simply honor them with my American decency.

"Okay," I said, "but no funny business." I picked up my suitcase and walked in, planning to ask the girls, "Do you go to school? Make sure you go to school."

The man trotted behind me. "No funny business. No funny business, of course, sir. Please sit at our family sofa. It's our own sofa we sit at, a traditional ethnic sofa." He gestured toward an old ripped sofa, with a bright-red flower pattern and a fringed bottom placed against the store window. Next to it was a little round table with a red oilcloth. There was fake wood paneling peeling off the walls, and a purple bedsheet, scissored down the middle, partitioned the room. From behind the bedsheet came the voices of *The Muppet Show*. Miss Piggy was trying to get Kermit the Frog to give her a part in the day's production. I leaned forward and peered through the gap in the curtain, in order to see whether the girls were enjoying the show.

I saw their eyes, between the halves of the purple sheet. They were watching me. I was the show. They were watching me eagerly, because they wanted to know whether Daddy would be able to buy them new dresses soon. I was their income—except that if I was smart, I'd be their poverty.

I wanted to be smart. I wanted to leave, and not let them rob me. But I wanted to give them all the money I had so they'd have their new dresses. But then I thought of how they would laugh at me, and even if I willingly gave them all my money, they'd think I was a sucker. I stood up.

The curtain parted, and out stepped a tall, thin woman in a clingy dark-green dress with small flowers on it, and a bright-green kerchief in her hair.

"Sit down," she said. And she looked straight at me as if she knew me. Under the kerchief, her black hair was sprayed into enamel waves. She wore backless black slippers with the vinyl flaking off, and when she pushed past her husband to get to me I heard the soles flop. The purple curtain stirred behind her. I started to sit on the sofa.

"No. Here," she said, and pointed to the round table.

I rushed over and sat down. Her voice made you want to rush to where it said to. We sat opposite each other, in wooden chairs with rickety legs. I put my hands on the red oilcloth. They left sweat on it.

The man said, "The gentleman is interested in our survey—"

"Quiet!" she told him. "Go watch *Muppet Show*."

He muttered something in their language, opened and closed his fist at his side. Then he smiled at me and said, "My wife is a great seer. She will enlighten you. Have a pleasant time, sir."

And, like any American family man, he stalked off to watch TV. From behind the curtain came his shouts; then the TV channel switched and a game show came on. The girls shouted back in high voices—then there was a slap, but no cry. The game show stayed on. Dim-witted contestants in Hollywood were about to win thousands of dollars, and Rich Redstone was sitting in a gypsy's parlor on St. Mark's Place trying to hold on to his last few. I couldn't walk out yet, either, because I had to observe the surroundings. I decided that I would be wary: like a turtle deciding that he will fly.

"Well," I said, to show her whom she was dealing with, "anyone walking by can see that I'm the one sucker in a thousand—"

"Quiet!" she said, and it was such an original way of treating a customer that I shut up.

She looked at my face.

That was all she did for a long time.

I couldn't even smile, because it gets very uncomfortable smiling at someone who is calmly staring you out of your mind.

I could feel the passersby, in turn, staring at me from behind, and I could see the woman's three relatives taking turns staring at me through the parting in the bedsheet. Well, why not? I thought. I'd always felt as if I deserved to be stared at for a fool.

But after a while, I no longer felt like a fool when she stared at me. I felt as if I was undergoing some kind of expert examination. She knew what she was doing. She was seeing me. Her eyes moved, tracing the outlines of my skull, my mouth, my nose. It was as if she traced every line on my face with her eyes—I say "as if," only because I'm a little abashed to admit that that's what she really, actually did. Then she leaned close, and stopped still. She was staring into my left eye, my glass eye, from two inches away. She'd found my secret, and was staring deep into it. I didn't consider her impolite. She stared for a long time, as if she was looking past the glass into my mind, and I wish I could see what she saw.

She lay one hand on top of the other on the red oilcloth. Her fingers were bumpy and red-nailed. "Your name?" she asked.

"Rich Redstone. What do you do now, read my palm?"

"No. For you I do it for real." She stretched one hand toward my face, lifted my chin, and looked at it from underneath. She turned my face left and right; looked at lines, shadows, tracks of experience or inexperience. Then she took her hand away, and my face dropped. She gave a small, close-mouthed laugh that might have been her laugh for the decade. She pushed her chair back, squeaking.

"Now I tell you a story," she said. "You pay me as much as you think it's worth."

I stood up. I laughed nervously. "Gotta go—"

"This is story about Rich Redstone," she said. "Story of his perfect mate, the woman who was born matched with him, the woman to make him happy, to be made happy by him, and without each other neither of them will ever be happy."

I sat down. She looked at me questioningly—she stared me into fishing out my wallet. What am I doing? I asked myself. Smiling with the longing to trust somebody—to trust the most untrustworthy—I handed her five dollars. "This is a large percentage of my worldly assets."

She shrugged, and put the bill into her skirt pocket. "Rich Redstone. He has loved so many girls, he forgets which ones he liked and which he didn't. They were all nice, smart college girls, but none of them was for him. A long time ago he knew that one long love was the best; but he forgot, and he started to think a lot of short loves were just as good. He forgot to be afraid of growing old alone."

"Hey, where's the story?" I said.

"One evening Rich Redstone is walking in the Village with his suitcase. . . . I'm starting the story," she said, and held out her palm. I told myself to leave—I half rose—I dug into my wallet, and put five more dollars into her hand.

"He's walking, it's the night of a big American holiday—I even

167

let my kids get turkey from the place on the corner, I read the owner's palm once a month and she gives us a dinner. Rich Redstone is wondering where to go. It's dark. He's so sad he wants to punish himself, so he keeps walking with his heavy suitcase, thinking, When will I find the person who's made for me?"

"That's exactly what I think all the time," I said. I would have been embarrassed to tell almost anyone else, but I knew I could tell her. I felt as if I would gladly walk all over the earth with my suitcase glued to my hand, and my arm hanging numb, if only I'd find the person who was made for me. The gypsy woman looked at me and understood. I didn't care if she was a mercenary, I knew she understood.

"Rich Redstone walks to Washington Square Park," she said; and I thought, I do? I will! "He's thinking, Should I sleep in the park? Should I check into a sleazy hotel? Should I call my parents and tell them I give up, I want to go to that law school on the corner?" She opened her palm and smiled, and I smiled and gave her another two dollars for knowing about law school. My money was draining away and it made me feel giddy, the way you feel giddy when you're bleeding and you feel your blood draining away.

"Before he decides," she said, "he just wants to sit on a bench for a while. Sit on a bench, look up at the bare branches, and remember who he is. He's crossing the street, but not really looking where he's going, because he's looking at the benches where he wants to sit down. He hears wheels come at him from the left side where he can't see. A young lady's voice goes, 'Yow, no brakes!'—Give me all the money in your wallet and I'll tell you the rest of the story."

I didn't hesitate a second.

She wet her index finger and counted my money. She smirked, shrugged because there were only seventeen dollars—I smirked, too, because I had refilled my fountain pen with a hundred from my biggest Goldfish-era racetrack win. It was in my jacket pocket, but there was no reason to tell her that. She put the seventeen dollars into her skirt pocket.

" 'Yow, no brakes!' Rich Redstone can't see her till he turns left.

By that time she's crashing into him, a young lady on roller skates, with her arms stretched out forward like a sleepwalker, and when she closes her eyes she's laughing. Her hands they grab Rich Redstone's coat; one of her skates trips over his foot. He grabs her to stop her from falling, but he topples over his own suitcase and lands on the sidewalk.

"She has a braid of blond hair pinned in a circle around her head, and a bobby pin shines in the lamplight. She wears a green down vest over a red sweater, and tight blue jeans with big cuffs, and white skates. She is laughing to say she's sorry. She picks him up. He helps her pick him up.

" 'Why do you want to stand in the way of someone who's just learning how to skate?' "

"She has a Southern accent. Rich Redstone realizes that she has the most beautiful voice, she is the most beautiful woman, he has ever met. He also knows that this is true because it is not a fact. There are taller women, women with thinner noses, women with larger busts, women with longer legs. He would like to make them her dressing maids.

" '*You* were the one who assaulted *me*,' he says.

" 'I gave you fair warning. You acted like you didn't see me.'

" 'I'm blind in my left eye,' he tells her.

" 'Well, then, you are obviously the type of person who enjoys getting into trouble.'

"It's not the funniest joke, but they laugh, and while they laugh, they watch each other get better-looking.

" 'Would you like to go somewhere and discuss exactly who was at fault?' he asks.

"So they go to one of the coffee places where the students hang out. But not at the sidewalk terrace; they go deep inside, for couples who don't want to see others. They sit under a painting of a volcano in Italy, and half their talk is to ask each other what they're smiling at. Their cappuccino cups are very close at the center of a little round white table. They hardly drink. The young woman's name is Novella Swan. He hasn't even realized he loves her yet. Then they tell each other about themselves."

I leaned forward over the red-oilclothed table. She paused just long enough to scare me—what'll she make me do before she tells me the rest? I had to hear about Novella Swan. Novella, my Novella, I think I knew your name already but I'm first remembering it now. . . . I hungered for the gypsy's voice like a baby hungers for its mother's breast. I sweated onto the oilcloth.

The woman said, "She is a social worker; she studies for the master's degree. While she studies she has a part-time job. She works at a residence for children whose houses burn down. Sometimes their parents have been killed in flames or smoke. Sometimes their parents are in the hospital burn ward. The parents have thrown the babies out of windows to save their lives. Or the children have run out of the house without waiting for the parents. Or the parents ran out without waiting for the children, but the children they got out anyway. Sometimes there are three, four, five brothers or sisters with no more parents. Sometimes only one child left from all the brothers and sisters. They are accident fires or arson fires. Sometimes the children set the fires, for fun or because their parents turned off the TV too early. Sometimes their friends set the fires. Or their landlords. Sometimes their enemies set the fires but the children are afraid to say who. This is in the Bronx, Brooklyn, Queens, Manhattan, and Staten Island. All the children are very very frightened. Some they are hysterical crying. Some walking with dead eyes. They lost their dogs. They got nowhere to live. They're afraid of everything. Afraid of the staff, afraid of the other children, afraid of sirens, afraid of orange and red, afraid of being inside, afraid of being outside. The white ones fear blacks, the black ones fear whites. Most of all, afraid of fire. There's a girl who howls like a dog whenever she sees a cigarette. There's a boy who will not eat any cooked food. When the TV shows a fire, the whole room cries. At night they wake up screaming that they're burning.

"Novella Swan comes to see these children every morning. She talks to them, smiles at them. At first they're afraid of her. In a week she is their best friend. She plays with them in groups so they'll start talking to people again. She plays with them one at a time so they can sometimes tell about their fires. She takes them on trips outside to show that not everything burned down. She gives them drawing paper and crayons, orange and red too. They draw their houses. They draw her.

"In the residence there's a special kitchen, children's size. It is the most important therapy. These kids have lost normal life. No more house or Mama or Papa—gypsy kid would know what to do, but not American kid. They're terrified of the stove. Stove is death, fire, nightmare. Novella teaches them how to cook breakfast. It takes a very long time to teach. They're afraid to even enter the kitchen. Maybe in a week they can go in, but only take milk from the refrigerator. A while later she lets them crack the eggs into the bowl before she cooks. She asks them to put bread in the toaster, put water in the cereal pot. The older children help the younger ones. Everyone gasps when she turns the flame on. But look: the flame is cooking our food! The flame can be good! There's a boy who had five skin-graft operations on his face and arms. In the beginning he hid under the kitchen table when the cooking started. But now he can fry his own eggs. He used to hide his hands behind his back because of the scars. Now he leads the newer children by the hand. The children with the worst losses make the most progress, because they stay with Novella longest.

"Novella asks Rich Redstone what he does. He can't answer for a while. He's overwhelmed with love.

"Finally he tells her he's a writer. For lack of anything else to tell her, he has to lie. What can he tell her? Not even she would understand his real job. But he has to tell her a job to make her love him. So he says he's an unpublished writer traveling to find experience. She shines with admiration. She knows he has great talent and wonderful messages. He's ashamed of himself. He tries to act very gallant and tender, and tells her about his unpublished stories, which do not exist. He makes them up just to tell her. 'I try for a very natural style.' She likes that. It's wise to love people for their work.

"When they finish their coffee, he pays with the hundred-dollar bill from his fountain pen, which is all the gypsy woman left him."

"How'd you know . . . ?" I said.

171

"Quiet, they're finishing their coffee. Now, the romantic thing is to linger in a café, but the more romantic thing is to leave it. But when the chilly air hits them outside, they get scared. Where are they to go? Rich has only his parents' house. Novella was raised strictly, not to bring men into her bedroom. She lives in New York, but her Southern upbringing comes back. Rich feels bad for lying to her, too. He worries it would be best for her if he left. Neither tells the other, but they both fear that this will be their only meeting. They will separate. They'll promise to call each other, but they'll have second thoughts and doubt their own memories, and put it off, and lose their phone numbers. Then, years later, they'll remember each other as a funny person they ran into in Washington Square Park, and they'll think about it for a minute, both at the same time.

"But five seconds after leaving the café they're happy again—the fear was only a waking dream. They hold hands. Rich walks beside Novella while she learns to skate around the park. Then she skates him to her building in the West Village, and invites him into her third-floor apartment. This is more important than her strict upbringing. Hey!" the gypsy shouted behind her. "You girls, shut up and let your father watch!"

And behind the purple curtain, the voices subsided. I hadn't even noticed them while she'd been speaking. She turned in her chair, narrowed her eyes to hear what was going on behind the curtain. "Novella takes off her skates—" she said. She stopped, to be sure her daughters were silent; then she turned to me. "Sitting on the stairs inside her building, she takes her skates off and wiggles one foot with a white sock on; she looks up at him, and they giggle. Like they have it in writing that they will never be separated.

"Her apartment is small and very nice. Begonias hanging in macrame baskets. Linen tapestries with African designs; and crayon drawings by the kids at work. The kitchen—tiny, no wonder she likes to cook at work. There's one main room, like a dormitory room, with a narrow bed.

"Does he want some more coffee? she asks. No. Well, does he want a brandy? No. Well, then, what does he want?

"They laugh, and they kiss. They stand in the middle of the room kissing. It's better than heaven. It's better than nirvana. Heaven is not a void, it's two tongues. They kiss, not hard and greedy, but with countless, countless flicks. They would like to sit on the bed, but they refuse to break the kiss in order to move. Sometimes they close their eyes; but sometimes they look all over each other's face, like exploring a new country, and their smiles press together.

" 'Your eyes are blue with green rays,' he tells her, but he has to shut up to taste her lips again right away.

"Without her skates, Novella is almost a head shorter than Rich. Bending his neck, he feels like a swan. While they kiss, they rub each other's flanks with their hands, to feel who each other is. Fast, up and down, laughing.

" 'What do you want to do?' he laughs.

"She kisses him again.

"If I took as long telling you about the kisses as you take kissing her, I would have to charge you more money. If kissing was the only thing humans could possibly do, Rich and Novella would be happy. This is it, he says to himself. This is it, she says to herself. Let's kiss some more, they think—like the earth saying, Let's spin some more. Their palms burn from rubbing the hips of each other's jeans. Their mouths are tired. Their bodies are damp.

" 'What do you want to do?' he asks.

"She says, 'I'm burning!'

"They look in each other's eyes, and it makes them hug each other as tight as they can. They are seared together. They're burning, their skin is as hot as flame. They both feel it at once: they have to take their clothes off. Is it hot in the apartment? No, it's November and the landlord isn't giving steam yet—goddamn landlords. But Rich and Novella are sweating, their clothes are sticky. They have to tear their clothes off to make sure their skins aren't on fire. And when they see each other's body for the first time, they gasp, and feel like crying for joy. They hug, and feel the cool sweat that is keeping them from burning up. They touch each other, so each can cool the other's skin.

173

" 'I'm burning!' he says. Then they both say it at the same time. They have to keep looking at themselves to believe they haven't burst into flames.

" 'Let's take a shower,' she says, and, burning, they run to the bathroom. She puts cool water on, and they jump into the shower together, and it cools their skin so much, they wonder why steam doesn't hiss from them like from hot stones. They hug, and if you saw them from outside the pink shower curtain, they would look like one double-thick body. Standing under the spray, they touch each other slowly with one hand, down the wet chest and the wet hip, just to make sure they're still there. They kiss again, closer than the last kiss, which was the closest possible kiss. They can't tell the difference between their saliva and the shower water on their lips. All they want to do is kiss, like children who don't know about anything more. Their kissing is better than anyone else's anything. But they're adults, they have to do more, and when they do, he leans his head on her shoulder and they both cry from happiness. The cool water sprays on them and doesn't make them feel cold. When they are joined, Novella says, 'A gypsy woman told me if I rode a bicycle on Fifth Avenue tonight, I'd meet my true love. To show I don't take orders, I put on roller skates.' "

My gypsy woman tilted back in her wooden chair, rested her hands on the red oilcloth, and closed her lips. I wanted to ask questions, but really the only thing I wanted was to be in Novella's shower. My lips were dry, I needed Novella's shower. I stood up— it was hard to, my legs were shaking—I stood up not for any reason but because I couldn't stay in my seat. I tried to make my voice not shake.

"That will happen to *me?*" I asked.

"She is your perfect mate. You and she were born to make each other happy."

"And I'll meet her if I walk right out of here to Washington Square! How do you know these things? But you must know it— you knew about my fountain pen, and law school. . . ."

She shrugged, as if my groping for explanations was dull. "I know one more thing I'll tell you now, the biggest thing of all. It will cost you a hundred dollars."

I touched my breast pocket. "That hundred dollars? Then I won't have a cent. How will I pay for the cappuccino?"

"Don't you know yet not to worry about money? Besides, why you pay? I thought you were a feminist."

"Yeah, that's right, let her pay," I said happily, and sat down. I took the pen from my inside pocket, unscrewed the cap, tapped out the tip of the hundred-dollar bill, teased it out the rest of the way with my fingernail, smoothed it flat, and pushed it across the oil-cloth to her. I smiled at the bill as I gave it up, the way you'd smile at a winning lottery ticket when presenting it to the judges.

She put it into her pocket, moved her chair closer to the table, and waved me closer with one finger. I tried to grasp the edge of the table, but my hands were so sweaty they slipped off. I needed Novella's shower. . . .

"You'll never meet her," the woman said.

I shouted out, "It was a fake! A story. She doesn't exist, I knew it. I gave you all my money for a lie."

"You think that?" she sneered. "I give you all your money back if you think that. Here—" She pretended to start digging into her dress pocket, but she didn't get very far. She decided to content herself with an indignant scowl. "I don't cheat you, I tell you the truth. I don't make up things from thin air. Novella Swan is a real person. She is for you. She is your perfect mate. I find her in you when I examine you. Everyone has such a mate. Very few people as lucky as you, to be told who it is."

"But I'll never meet her?" I was hoarse, I was half standing. "How could you give me that whole story if it wasn't going to happen? I thought you told the future."

She shook her head. She looked above me, because, I think, she didn't want me to see sympathy on her face. "What I told you was based on truth. But it was a story—I told you that, right at the beginning. And a story is something that won't happen. Has there ever been a story that happened the same way later in real life? No, that's against the law of the world. Once someone tells it, it's like it happened. It won't happen twice. That would bore the world."

"It wouldn't bore *me.*"

She shrugged. I wondered if anyone had ever been killed because of a shrug. "I'm sorry you didn't like my story," she said. "You want me to tell you what will really happen? Well, we gypsies know many things, but fortune telling is illegal in New York City. I can read your palm, read your character, tell you about yourself, give you advice about your problems, but I can't predict your future or I go to jail. What if you're an undercover cop? I run an honest business, I am mother and housewife. So if what I tell you about Novella is only a story, blame the City Council."

"Give me my money back," I said.

She tilted her chin up and to the side, and called out something in gypsy language. Through the curtain came her husband. He looked as friendly as ever, but in place of the clipboard he held a baseball bat.

I cursed them, and hauled my suitcase out of there.

I walked to Washington Square Park.

My right arm was sagging like it was carrying iron. On the corner across the street from the park, I set the suitcase down and flexed my hand. Then I scanned the street like a high-powered telescope. The university buildings were lit from above their doorways, and a uniformed guard was sitting in the vestibule of the main building. The benches in the park were almost deserted. The trees were lit pink by sodium lamps. Down the block, the arch was lit white. A man in a yellow nylon sweatsuit jogged by across the street. Who would be out roller-skating on Thanksgiving night? Someone who celebrated the holidays she declared for herself, not the ones other people had declared for her; and the day we met would be the greatest national holiday of our two-person country. Roller-skating had seemed like a silly fad before I heard the gypsy's story. Now I wanted only a girl who skated, and only one who skated on Thanksgiving night, with a blond braid wrapped around her head.

But the sidewalk was empty, except for the jogger in yellow, and a slow old couple walking a Siamese cat on a leash.

I picked up the suitcase and walked across the street—with my head down, so I'd bump into somebody. I walked up the wheelchair ramp rather than the curb—I was too unhappy to lift my feet. Then I heard skate wheels.

176

I turned to my left. A young woman was skating toward me, with the high, clopping steps of a learner, her arms breast-stroking to keep her balance. She had rolled onto the sidewalk from inside the park, and she was curving wildly toward the gutter, going too fast for her skill. There was a look of amused fright on her face. She had blond hair—not up in a braid, but long and loose, flying into her face as if, in her inexperience, she'd forgotten to tie it.

I stepped in front of her.

"Look out, you fool!" she shouted, and her amusement vanished. She flailed with her legs and arms to get around me, but I had dropped my suitcase deliberately in her path. Her right toe dipped, and the front bumper of the skate hit the pavement. She stumbled, hit the corner of the suitcase, started falling to the ground . . .

I caught her forearm. It was light and bony: a woman's forearm in a thick blue sweater, a typical arm, a unique arm. I steadied her, with the joy of taking the arm of the one I loved.

"Novella!" I said.

A gold necklace jounced outside her sweater, and its gold letters spelled the name Charlotte.

She had forgotten the down vest too.

She wrenched her arm away from me; gave me one glance to see if I was crazy, then shoved away without looking at me again. Leaning too far forward, her legs slipping out behind her, she skated past me. She grabbed the railing to propel herself around the corner, and in the lunging of her legs and arms there was something more than awkwardness. There was hate and fear of me—need to escape from me. From *me*.

I was appalled at what I'd done; but I was so desperate, the only thing I could think of to call out was, "Did you visit a gypsy woman?"

She didn't turn around. She was skating away from me so fast, I was afraid she would hurt herself. "Did she tell you to ride a bicycle?" I asked. I was asking the air she left behind.

I started walking on the path. "Novella. Charlotte. No, Novella, Novella," I said.

I touched the railing in the exact spot where she had touched it. "I'll wait till she circles the park. . . ." I could still see her skating away, grabbing the rail at intervals the same way I was; and why didn't she look back and see me doing it?

Halfway down the long block, where the railing opens for the arch, she skated into the arms of a tall, thin, long-haired man who was wearing white skates and blue sweater to match hers. They hugged, and he bent his neck to kiss her under the white light of the arch, and they looked back in my direction. I stopped, and turned sideways against the railing to hide in the shadows. But they skated off, hand in hand, and forgot about me. A steel drum was playing calypso music in the park.

I turned around, walked back to the corner, and would have picked up my suitcase, except that it was no longer there.

16. Assertiveness

"Better to travel without needless luggage," I said out loud; and I walked into the park, calling, "Novella Swan! Novella Swan!" I was thinking, My suitcase is gone—good. My suitcase is gone—good. It seemed to me that since I had lost something valuable, I'd have to gain something valuable in return, namely Novella. That was my state of mind.

A few yards along the diagonal path, there was a round cement clearing. A blond young woman was sitting on one of the stone benches, smoking a cigarette whose smoke looked white against the night.

"Are you Novella Swan?" I asked, and by way of saying no, she looked away and blew smoke at me from the corner of her mouth.

I spotted another young woman sitting on a wooden bench in the brick-paved clearing to the left. She was listening to two old Italian guys playing mandolin and guitar. She was a brunette, but it was worth the chance. I ran across the grass, and jumped the foot-high railing to the paved area.

"Are you Novella Swan?"

She wore a bulky white sweater with a shawl collar and brown leather buttons. She was huddled into herself, and her hands in her pockets wiggled to the music; but when she looked up at me and said, "No," she smiled. Suddenly she looked down again, as if she thought that to smile too much at me would be dangerous.

"Do you know anyone named Novella Swan?" I begged.

"No, sorry."

She was good-looking and friendly-looking, and maybe I should have told her my story. Maybe she would sympathize. I wanted to say something to her—but I had forgotten what you were supposed to say to someone who wasn't Novella. I had to keep searching. I wanted to leave her with a pleasant thought, though.

"I lost my suitcase," I said jauntily, and dashed away, past the drinking fountain and down the main path. A couple was necking on one of the benches.

"Paging Novella Swan," I called to them.

The lucky kids, they didn't even look up.

I came to the roller rink. In Washington Square Park, the most skillful skaters use a netless volleyball court, with the spectators serving as rink walls. But on Thanksgiving night there were no spectators—who would come here on Thanksgiving night?—and only five skaters inside the court lines. Four of them were male; the fifth was a Chinese woman in a skin-tight black vinyl jumpsuit and black skates, with the jumpsuit's big gold zipper open to her navel, and no breasts. She glided in figure eights, up and down the court, with her hands behind her. She didn't look at anyone, and she was smiling a little, as if listening to music through earphones; but she wasn't wearing earphones. She glided without speeding up or slowing down, without making any sudden moves; she didn't do anything fancy; you couldn't tell whether she *could* do anything fancy, if she wanted to. But she was so smooth, she never had to jerk out of the way of the four men who were frantically spinning, leaping, dashing, twirling each other by the hand, and doing splits and cartwheels from one end of the court to the other.

She sure outskated Novella. But maybe Novella would come here and take lessons from her. . . .

"Novella Swan?" I called out. "Anyone know a skater named Novella Swan?"

A blond-haired man in a black leather jacket raced up to me, arms swinging behind him like gorilla arms, wheels making slashing sounds on the pavement. He was dashing from all the way up the court, he was going too fast, he was going to crash into me. . . .

He stopped an inch from my shins; sparks kicked up from the pavement, and his red wheels flashed in the mercury light as he skated away.

That was all the attention I got. The Chinese woman kept gliding, the four men kept spinning and kicking, and I walked away. I kept looking back, so I wouldn't miss any blond who might join them.

I came to the big paved circle in the middle of the park. The fountain in the center was dry; I sat on its rim, and I tapped my feet to hurry the world along to bring my love faster. "Novella Swan?" I shouted, turning this way and that. The name echoed, and no one answered. The park was dark and mostly empty, but at one end the Washington Arch was lit up, and a few people were standing and bobbing under it, singing and listening to singers, sheltered from the wind that threw their voices to me. Maybe Novella's there, I thought. But I was tired and starting to despair. I told myself I'd get up and look as soon as my legs felt rested. The inner sleeve of a record ran across my feet and blew away down the dark, mica-twinkling pavement. The air didn't smell like turkey anymore; it smelled like cheap wine. I heard rapid footsteps coming toward me on my left.

I turned to look.

A tall woman was walking up to me. She was six feet tall, like me, and had long, slim, long-striding legs; she wore a red down vest, a flannel shirt, an orange aluminum-frame backpack, baggy blue jeans, and hiking boots. She had a big mane of hair heaped up messily above her head and tumbling below her shoulders and sticking out in loops you could put your finger through. She walked toward me in the light from the arch, and I could see that her hair was dark red, and that she was about seventeen.

I stood up and took a step forward, and was about to ask . . .

"Angelo!" she cried.

I turned around to see who she was talking to.

There was no one behind me.

She ran up and hugged me. "Angelo!" she said, and pressed her

181

cheek against mine and rubbed the hair on the back of my head. When she broke the hug to look at me, she was beaming and almost crying.

"Sorry," I stammered. "I'm—I'm not Angelo." She was a great-looking big young redhead with a square chin and maximum bright eyes. "I *am* sorry. I'm so sorry. My name's Rich."

She took both my hands, stretching our arms out and swinging them like kids playing ring-around-the-rosie; and, smiling into my face, she swore I was Angelo.

"Angelo, I know you don't know me yet, but it's me, Assertiveness."

"Assertiveness? That's your name?"

She tilted her head and ran her hand through her hair-loops. "My Mom and Dad named me Rainbow. I was born in 1967. Then in '76 they changed it for me, to Assertiveness. They figured, like, people used to name their kids after qualities they admired? Like Prudence—or even Patience? So they called me Assertiveness. Actually I don't like the name all that much, but if I changed it again I'd offend them."

For a second, her eyes unfocused; she looked at the ground behind me as if thinking; but then she snapped upright, and tightened her grip on my hands. She pressed me against her chest; I could feel the straps of her backpack shifting; then she stepped back and looked at me, as if her greatest imaginable joy would be to hold my hands and look at me for all time.

"I almost caught up to you in Austin," she said.

I said despondently, "I've never been in Austin."

"I waitressed there for a couple weeks. Then I went up to Boulder, then Iowa City, would you believe it? Someone told me they saw you sniffing around the creative-writing office. I said, That's my Angelo. You wore a seersucker jacket all summer, right? In Iowa. What a comedian. Then, let's see, I hit Madison—worked in a record store. Evanston—mother's helper for a professor's kid. Ann Arbor—stamped tuition checks in the Student Accounts Office. Columbus—blech, forget that. Princeton—they threw me out of town for wearing the wrong brand of boots. But before I left,

I heard a rumor you were here in the Village. I recognized you from across the fountain, by the tie outside your sweater—only *you* wear it like that, Angelo."

I squeezed my tie in my fist, and wondered whether I ever *had* been in Austin. "When was the last time you saw me?" I asked.

"Well, never physically; but my dream showed me exactly who you are. I saw you in a dream. I don't mean a sex dream, where you see some misty lover and get hot. It was just you standing there, like a police lineup. I saw every detail of you in one flash, heard your voice and everything. What you said in the dream was, 'This is a sample of Angelo's voice. This is a sample of Angelo's voice.' Over and over, like a tape. Say it."

"This is a sample of Angelo's voice," I said.

"Yep, that's you. And next to you—" she motioned up and down in the air on my left—"next to you there was like this instantaneous computer printout with everything about you on it. I wrote it all down in a memo book that's in my backpack." She reached back and tapped it. "For instance, your shoe size is ten."

I swallowed, and tried to hide it.

Never underestimate the power of total bullshit. My shoe size was ten. I said to myself, It's an easy coincidence; she's so nice and sweet, I can't lead her on. She's so eager to take a risk, so unafraid of sounding foolish. God, I can't disillusion her! But I can't send her away; she'd approach some other man and he'd turn out to be a creep who'd hurt her. And my shoe size *is* ten. . . .

I pressed her hands. They were calloused and gritty from travel, and the look in her eyes was innocence trying to pass as experience. She's only a teenager, I said to myself. On the other hand, she's more independent than Debs Goldfish.

"I told my friends about you," she said.

Gee, I thought, I hope I made a good impression.

"They didn't understand. The only ones who understood were my parents. I said to them, 'Mom and Dad, I'm going to search for the true love I saw in a dream. Can you write my school a note saying I'm pregnant or something and I can't be back till finals?' And they said, 'Sure, far out.' My mom and dad used to be hippies, don't you think that's neat? We live in Big Sur, you'll like it. They used to be these poor hippie cobblers trading sandals for organic peanut butter, but now they're wise and they make customized cowboy boots for rock stars and entertainment lawyers. The rock stars tend to be clones, but some of the lawyers are like really neat people. They have it all planned out, and that's what you have to do in life. Oh, Angelo, I can hardly wait to show you to my parents! They have this really futuristic workshop on a hill; they employ about twenty of the local burnouts—they're incredibly philanthropic for some reason, but I don't tease them about it anymore. And like my mom was this early feminist, and when they go out to a restaurant or something, it's so quaint—you should see them taking out their identical buckskin purses and making sure to split the check exactly in half. I told my mom, If you want power, why not make him pay the whole thing? But she couldn't see my point; she's mired in the past."

"That reminds me," I said. "Let's sit down here." I tugged her gently down to the rim of the fountain. Our knees touched, and we held hands. "I can't even buy you a cup of coffee right now. Someone took all my money—"

"Oh, but you'll get it all back and you'll become very prosperous and you'll be able to buy me whatever I want in just a couple of years!" she said, shining her young eyes on me with such complete, joyous trust that I did want to give her whatever she wished for. And that made me sad, because I couldn't, and, besides, you never can. "Besides," she said, "if we go up to my place now, we won't have to spend any money at all."

I shook my head, downcast and wanting to protect her. "My name isn't Angelo, it's Rich Redstone."

"You'll change your name for me."

• • •

Angelo, I said to myself. Call me Angelo. But our kids' names will be Viking names, Leif and Astrid and Erik, and they'll be tall and raw-boned and red-haired, could I be starting to—the feeling is familiar—could I be starting to love her?

184

We were in Assertiveness' furnished room on Thompson Street, on the second floor, above a coffeehouse, next door to a souvlaki stand, and across the street from a Mexican-and-Hindu restaurant and a souvenir shop with "I Love New York" undershorts in the window. Past the rusty fire escape, we also had a view of a chess club, two drunks walking in circles around a fire hydrant, and a man squatting behind his dog and holding a plastic bag under it. Assertiveness' room had dark-yellow walls, and was heated by a metal radiator and a corner steam pipe. The pipe kept banging, as if it was tired of giving heat and wanted to give sound for a change—like an artist tired of one medium and wanting to try another. The bed was an old fourposter, or more accurately it was four old posts: the thing in between was supposed to be a mattress, but if you sat on the cover you'd fall six inches before you hit anything solid underneath. But it was perfect for romance, because we gravitated together in the middle of the bed-valley, and to avoid a row of springs under the mattress I had to spread one leg over her.

"Angelo, when we get to California let's raise horses," she said. "God, it's freezing in here!" She pulled the army blanket up to her chin and moved in tighter to me, shuddering.

We were naked, our feet were cold, and we rubbed the soles against each other's shins, but we didn't seem to warm up. Lying on our sides, we wrapped ourselves around each other and rocked. "Brr!" we said together, and laughed; our teeth chattered, and we laughed at that too. I rubbed her thighs, and she rubbed mine, but it only rubbed the cold deeper into our bones. We kissed, and it felt like ice cream. "Whew!" I said, because I was so cold and she was so beautiful. We were the same length: when we kissed, and her red hair fell all over my face, our icy toes interlocked six feet away. And when my weight was on top of hers, it didn't seem unfair; but when she got on top, I felt oppressed like a woman; and when I rolled out from under, I felt like I'd accomplished something. But every time we touched each other expecting to get warm, we got cold. "Why don't *you* give a little heat?" I laughed. I felt her kneecap, her thighbone—they were like marble sculpture.

"Let's raise horses on the hill next to my parents' workshop," she moaned, teeth chattering. "The pasture slopes down to this cliff, and you can see the Pacific foaming up on black rocks. . . . Oh, you're freezing!" she said, and I thought she might cry. "You'll get pneumonia, you'll die! Aren't there city laws? Angelo, make them give heat!"

I wrapped her in my arms, but her back got colder and I could almost feel my fingers turning blue. I rubbed her feet with mine, but our toes got as stiff as rocks, and the blood drained from them. I ran my hand over her hair, but the red locks turned to red stalactites, and a coating of frost formed on my fingertips. I lunged my hands between her legs, and she pressed her legs together, but it was like a crevice in a glacier. I kissed her, and our tongues stuck together like tongues sticking to the inside of a freezer, and we pulled them apart with a sound like paper tearing, and I tasted little spots of blood rising from my tongue.

"What's happening?" we both said, and we both started crying. And when we touched each other's tears, they turned to icicles in our hands.

"Why are you doing this to me?" she said.

"You're doing it to me!"

We pulled the blanket tighter around us, and when that didn't work, we got the sleeping bag from the backpack, unrolled it in the bed, and climbed in, with the blanket over that. We clung to each other, and the nylon shell of the sleeping bag seemed to stiffen into armor plate.

Then we looked in each other's eyes in the darkness, and saw ice crystals growing in the irises; and we wanted so much to love each other that we got furious at the cold and at each other. We rubbed each other as if to do harm; we shook each other, but we got colder, the saliva congealed in our mouths, and the pain sang through our teeth. Then our hearts slowed down, our blood slowed, our limbs got sleepy, we could hardly rub anymore. If we kept hugging, we would freeze into a statue of an embrace.

"I want to raise horses with Angelo," she sobbed; the tears froze white over her eyeballs, and I held back my own new tears, and kept blinking so my one good eye wouldn't freeze over.

186

"Horses," I agreed, but my vocal cords were freezing shut, and the sound cracked frozen in midair before it reached her. . . .

I screamed, and kicked through the opening of the sleeping bag, and rolled out. She climbed out after me. We crawled across the bed, and dropped to the floor. We scrambled for the chair where our clothes were. We picked up our garments, and cursed from pain when our cold arms brushed. I buttoned my jacket over my sweater; she snapped on her vest; we laced up our shoes, and ran out of the building.

When we reached the street, it felt like summer by comparison. People around us were knotting their scarves against the breeze, and hunching with their hands in their pockets, but we straightened our backs and unbuttoned our outerwear. Our limbs softened and moved freely; we felt the blood flow again; and the tears on our cheeks melted, and were joined by new tears. We shivered one more time, at memory and in fright, and we wondered whether we could touch each other again. We stood on Bleecker Street, in the light of theater marquees and bar signs, and cried.

She stretched her hand toward me, but pulled it back. "Goodbye, Rich," she said.

17. How I Spent My Day

Poor Assertiveness, I thought, I hope she finds Angelo. But now to keep looking: for the right person, the right place, the right house, the right street, the right path, the right word, the right look, the right touch, the right sky, the right earth, the right leaf, the right roots, the right hour, the right season, the right weather, the right light, the right hair, the right mouth, the right clothes, the right nakedness, the right food, the right hunger, the right flame, the right sea, the right desire, the right satisfaction, the right sound, the right soundlessness, the right number, the right infinity—for Novella.

Under the Washington Arch, the four black singers were still bobbing, their voices shredded by the wind but amplified by the stone overhead. They smiled at each other over the heads of their listeners, and lifted their chins to sing, "Oo!" A boy on a skateboard glided around the crowd, and veered among people who were entering or leaving. A bright light shone from the top of the arch, but the singers were in shadow.

"No-vella," they were singing. "No-vella."

I ran up to join the crowd.

This is it! I thought. Novella is one of the singers' sister; he wrote a song about her. In ordinary life I wouldn't meet her—my ideal love!—because she happens to be black and in a different social circle from me; but by chance I've heard her name and it's opened the world. If he doesn't want me to see his sister, I'll see her anyway. . . . I pushed between people, to the front of the crowd.

"Oh-well-a," they were singing, "Oh-well-a," and I walked away, scuffing the cobbles, and shoved my hands so hard into my jacket pockets I felt the shoulder seam start to separate. Outside the arch, I looked back at the circle of bobbing people. Though I knew otherwise, the shredded words still sounded like "Novella." I was the only one who heard it, and though that made me lonely, it also made me possessively warm and glad. The wind blew my green tie over my shoulder; I pulled it forward again, and smoothed it down outside my sweater. "Tie," I said, while I walked toward the dry circle of the fountain. "Good old tie."

I put my foot on the fountain rim. I scanned the area: a dog loped through the fountain, a drunk peed against the spout. . . . Then I heard grunts and movements echoing inside the rim, right at my feet. I peered over. I saw a blanket, and four shoes sticking out from under it. The blanket went up and down, a mountain range rose and fell under it.

"Novella?" I asked.

The blanket slid off the bodies: two men stood up, pulling up their pants. One man was black, one was white, both were whiskered.

"Lebanese hash?" the black one asked me. "Ludes, tooies, meth, perc, Jersey City blotter acid?"

"*Jersey City* blotter acid?" I shuddered. "No, thanks."

"Then fuck off."

I saluted, and walked away. Looking back, I saw them kneel and pull the blanket over themselves. Just a couple of businessmen unwinding after a day's work.

I heard a whoop, then glass breaking, and I looked back at the arch. Somebody had liked the singers so much that he'd thrown a beer bottle against the base of the monument. The light from the top of the arch shone down on brown shards sprinkled over the cobbles. The circle of listeners had become dented when they'd pressed forward to avoid the glass. The guy who'd thrown the bottle was standing bent at the waist, and staggering as he tried to pick up pieces of glass. I sighed, and looked up to breathe the cleaner molecules of air and see how stark the arch looked at night. At the top of the arch I saw an inscription, in letters brightly lit and deeply shadowed:

"Let us raise a standard to which the wise and the honest can repair.—George Washington."

I turned away, shutting my eyes tight and covering them with my hand. My glass eye hurt. I'd seen too much, and the socket stung and itched as if a baseball was stuck into it. I wanted to take my eye out for the night, but I didn't have my patch. I wanted to tear my eye out and violently rub the itch out of the socket, and splash water into it from the drinking fountain; but I was afraid of scaring people with my empty socket. I needed to rest and I wanted to hide. So I sat down, with my back against the side of the arch, and stretched my legs out straight, and closed my eyes.

In the dark, the black men's voices flapped at me like a flag; I could tell the shifts in the wind by how loud I heard them. They sang soul songs that I didn't know, but all of them were good, and the fact that I didn't know them made them sadder when they were sad, and lovelier when they were about love. I listened to the songs with my eyes closed: the singing, the rhythmic hand-claps, the applause of the audience, the pause to collect donations, the movement of feet and bicycle wheels around me, the next song. . . .

"Okay, at least I know two things," I said in the dark. "I know who my true love is. And I know that I'm free to do what heaven wants me to. Those are things everybody knows, but to others it's told only in their sleep."

I opened my eyes and looked around, worried that someone had heard me babbling to myself—hoping that if someone had, it was Novella. But no one was watching me. In front of me was the playground, where preschool kids played in the daytime, and now teenagers with glowing cigarettes sat at the top of the jungle gym. Behind me was the cool stone of the arch; on my right was the main ring of the park; on my left was Fifth Avenue, with its streaming headlights.

"Novella Swan," I called out. Saying the name made me smile with happiness; I felt as if the city was domed, protected. "Novella?" I asked a young woman who walked by in an ankle-length purple down coat. "Do you know Novella Swan?" I asked the cop who drove the cruiser that crawled by. He didn't tell me to move; but in my state of mind, I felt as if he was secretly telling me to take the subway to my parents' house in Queens. No, I said mentally; if I leave, she might skate by for ten seconds, and I'll lose my whole life.

The singers had stopped singing. The sky was red-gray, there were four stars above the park, and the next time I looked there were five. The last skaters skated out of the park, the teenagers climbed down from the jungle gym, the romantic couples stopped strolling through, I heard a conga drum from down the block, but it stopped. Only a handful of young drinkers were left in the park, and they sounded as angry and oppressed as gobs of paint must be when a painter's brush mashes them against the canvas. I looked at the stream of headlights on Fifth Avenue, and I couldn't help smiling, it looked so great. There was an inspired harmony between the motion and stopping of cars and the motion and stopping of pedestrians. The bunching of traffic looked restful and intelligently planned. The vehicles looked like a series of witty variations on a splendidly designed basic shape, many of them with dents added as casual, last-minute master strokes to improve on sterile perfection. Two drivers trading licenses after a collision were unaware that they rhymed with two youths trading shoves on their way to a rock club. A cabbie stopping to straighten his broken radio antenna matched a wino flailing a broken umbrella stem. And I hoped I would find the person I rhymed with. . . .

I heard shouting from under the arch; more broken glass skidded into the stone; a man in a Burberry trenchcoat staggered out, guzzling from a bottle of Bordeaux.

"*You* don't love me," he shouted, turning this way and that. There was nobody with him. "You don't care about me, but I care about myself." He staggered out to the center of the footpath, shouting about how well he could take care of himself, shouting to his companion to get away from him. I sat in the eye of the wine-storm, with a big quiet smile, and all troubles seemed natural and graceful and fitting. Many other dissipated people and dangerous events must have passed in front of me, but I didn't know, because I fell asleep at the foot of the arch.

• • •

I woke up. The air was dark blue, a cold wind pushed a dream away and slapped me alert. Bare trees, concrete paths, shady lawns: they were all a blue-gray sky color, and the park looked spacious, the bare branches held the air like wineglasses. I looked up at the bleaching above the college rooftops, and said, "Up at dawn! Best thing for you!"

I groaned.

My neck hurt so much I had to straighten it with my hands. All my joints were sweating; they were chilly, stiff, and damp. My tongue was thick, and it was good my nose was stuffed, so I couldn't smell myself.

My glass eye hurt even more than it had the night before. The socket felt like a parched throat, and I had a fierce craving to splash the crud off it. I wished I had a mirror, but I was glad I didn't. My knees cracked when I got up, and I had to prance in place for a minute before I felt confident about walking anywhere. I started toward the water fountain, put my hands in my pants pockets . . .

My left fingers went through the pocket and ended up outside my pants. I looked down—hm, so that was why I felt a chill on my leg. My left pocket had been slashed away during the night. My wallet was gone.

I laughed. The thief hadn't gotten anything, and he hadn't killed me. I was ahead of the game.

I bent to the water fountain—God knows what kinds of mouths had put what kinds of germs on that spout—and splashed my face, then took a good drink. I looked around. I was the first one up. At scattered points, bums slept under blankets, dreaming of freedom and of their perfect loves.

"I've got work to do," I said, and walked off to start begging.

There weren't many people to beg *from*, at that hour. Not the

192

sunrise joggers; not the dope dealers rising up from the subways and taking their places at the compass points of the park. Finally the wave of students came for eight-o'clock classes; but people going to eight-o'clock classes aren't in the mood to give you money, and I'd never panhandled before, I had no technique. It wasn't till the nine-o'clock wave that I got my first quarter.

A quarter! I looked at that coin like it was a hundred-dollar bill. Time to go to the bank! I walked over to a savings bank I knew a block away.

The reason was that at this bank they had telephone books for public use. I flipped right to the S's.

I found no Novella Swans.

But there were a couple of N. Swans and N. Swanns. I used my quarter to call one of them—and it wasn't Novella, it was some guy I bothered during breakfast. I was sorry to bother him, but I couldn't help it, I had an important mission.

I stood on the street corner till someone gave me a dime. I dashed back into the bank to memorize another phone number; I made another call—again it wasn't her . . .

I called them all, and none of them was her. Then I called the burn units of all the hospitals, and spoke with head nurses and social workers. I got referrals to social agencies that dealt with burn victims. (I told them I had a relative who was a burn victim, and wanted to talk to his social worker, Novella Swan.) I called everywhere I could think of. All morning I stood in a phone booth on the corner of Waverly Place, becoming a local curiosity. The pizza makers, staring at me through their window while they tossed dough, must have thought I was illegal. At first I was so excited to get each coin that I immediately hurried to the bank, memorized the next phone number, and raced back to the phone booth in a panic because someone else might be using it. Later, I saved up enough change to buy a Bic pen and a memo pad, and I wrote down a few numbers at once. Besides, shopping gave me time out from hearing "There's no such person here."

About noon, my knees and hands started to shake, and I realized I was sick with hunger. There was an ache pipeline from my stomach to my head. I could almost feel my brain cells burning up for fuel, and I wondered which ones would go first: the common sense cells? The cells for sartorial taste? I knew I didn't have too many to spare, so I went into a supermarket and gave up all the rest of my money for a quart of milk and a half-pound loaf of wholewheat bread. Natural foods to the end! I ate on a park bench, threw the end pieces onto the sand for the pigeons—I was far gone, because I hate pigeons, and on a normal day I would never give them anything— and I strolled through the park. I felt full and steady, pleasantly sluggish, proud of noticing the movement of the sun along Washington Square South, and I said to myself, Okay, back to the phone booth.

But I didn't know who more to call. I had called all the places I could think of that might have led me to her job or school. All that remained were a couple of Swan—not even N. Swan—phone numbers where no one had answered.

I called those several times, until evening; she wasn't at any of those places either. My detective work had failed. And it wasn't bad detective work either. If she'd had a job like the one the gypsy had described, my calls ought to have uncovered her.

I sat on a bench and watched the sky turn dusky. The wind worked on the clouds, a pink-bellied gray one coasted over the Main Building, a guy in a purple-and-white NYU sweatshirt threw a white Frisbee to his Irish setter, and I said to myself, There is no Novella Swan.

But the gypsy said there was, I argued. She said Novella was real but that I'd never meet her. She hasn't been disproven yet; in fact, she can never be disproven.

Wait a second. The gypsy said that her story was fiction. My job is to find the facts underneath, but I can't really count on any of the specific facts the gypsy told me. She told me I'd meet Novella roller-skating last night; and I didn't. Maybe a dozen other parts of the description were dispensable, too. Maybe Novella looks different. I was ready to believe she was black. Maybe she's Puerto Rican or Midwestern or Jewish. Maybe Novella was a fictional name. Maybe she was skating at a different park. Maybe the park was in

194

another city. Maybe she has a different job—but it would have to be a good job, a noble job. The outer description was just story detail. What I have to find is the real woman who has the spirit of the one in the story. She'll be the real Novella. When I find someone with the spirit of the girl who crashed into me on roller skates, and took me to her apartment and kissed me as if it was the only thing we wanted to do, and held me so tight as we rubbed each other's flanks, and gasped when we saw each other's body, and leaped into the shower with me to cool off the burning of our skins, and even this hottest sexuality was only a lukewarm translation of our spirits' love—when I find that person, I'll know she's Novella. Maybe she'll be a first-grade teacher named Kris, and she'll be Novella. Maybe she'll be an art therapist named Ann, and she'll be Novella. Maybe I'll have to discard every outer detail of the story before I find the reality; but when I do that, I'll also discard the part that said I'd never meet her.

I sat in the twilight. A night bird sang in a tree, above a dope transaction, and all the clouds, skaters, Frisbees, dogs, and sweatshirts were turning gray. Oh, that gypsy! I thought. She tells you a story, you can't tell if it's absolutely true or totally false, but it takes hold of you. And you'll have to spend a lifetime checking it out.

And I was getting hungry again, my belly was empty and queasy, my eye felt like a hot stone, there was crud in the corner of it, and I had no money. What woman would take me in that condition?

I felt wonderful for knowing what I was after, and terrible for being so far from it. Around me the nighttime life was starting; someone behind me started playing saxophone like he was proud of how much he'd learned in his very first lesson. I walked away and thought about how to get some food, maybe a slice of pizza, or was McDonald's a better protein buy? But I thought I looked too bad to go into a store.

I walked over to the water fountain and splashed water on my face, but it burned my glass eye like lemon juice. I was getting very worried about keeping the eye in, uncleaned, for so long. I decided to take it out and rinse it. People might see me and be horrified, but I was past the stage of fastidiousness.

I took a long drink of water first, for courage, then cupped my left hand against my cheek and popped my eye into it. Then I held it under the spout and rinsed it—ah, that feels good, I thought. My eye glistened up at me from the palm of my hand. The socket felt cool and airy. I decided not to put the eye back in place—it would still have germs on it—it needed a rest. I would wrap my green tie with tea-stained coats of arms around my head, as an eye patch.

With the eye in my left hand, I tried to undo my tie knot with my right. Now, I thought, Novella will step up behind me, waiting for a drink, and say, "Ugh, what are you doing?" and five minutes later we'll be holding hands. I stopped, and sighed. Fumblefingered with reverie, I yanked the tie off with one hand; but I'd need two hands to tie it around my head. I put my eye for safekeeping in my left pants pocket—

But I forgot about the slit. My eye fell the length of my pants leg, onto the cement step of the drinking fountain, and cracked!

18. The Elephant Hotel

My eye, my eye, my beautiful ornament, the horrible foreign thing that had been part of me for years! It was ruined, what was I going to do, I was left empty and grotesque, what was I going to do about my eye?—I was finally free of it!

I thought the above, while I was falling to the ground.

I fell kneeling at the cement step of the drinking fountain. The mica in the cement shone. I grabbed and clutched my glass eye, and it shone, too. I held it in the palm of my hand; I saw my reflection in it, with half a face normal and half a face monstrous and a crack through the pupil splitting me diagonally. It was like your first glimpse of yourself when you stumble into the bathroom and hit your forehead on the mirror after waking with a bad hangover. I was slack-mouthed, pouchy, wincing in pain. I was also kneeling on the footpath, moaning with loving distress at my eye. I must have seemed drunk. I could see a street lamp reflected in the convex glass of the eye; also I saw the little red capillaries that they paint on for realism, beneath the white glaze. Before I blacked out, I imagined all the kind people in the optical factory taking measurements and testing pigments to make a perfect match for a stranger's eye. How nice it must be, making something to fit one special person, in this age of mass production! I remembered how friendly my ophthalmologist had been when I'd had my accident, how he'd made me feel better by acting as if it was an everyday event. I remembered how hysterical my mother had been—she's still terrified if I even get a speck of dust in my live eye. I remembered how angry I'd been at my father for trying to act as unworried as the doctor. And that shmuck Sterling, how calm and capable he'd turned out to be when taking me to the hospital, and how nice he'd been when visiting me the next day.

And now I'd disappointed them all. It was *their* eye, their precious gift to me, and I'd been negligent with it, and I'd have to go beg them for a new one and confess, not only that it was their eye, but that I'd been a young fool. Which is a very embarrassing thing to confess, because it's inevitable, and everyone else has seen it all along. I was enraged and embarrassed at being a young fool, and I clutched my eye tighter; but I knew I'd ruined it and couldn't wear it anymore. I got so mad at myself for ruining my eye, I wanted to smash it totally. I howled, and threw it down onto the pavement. I closed my good eye, to avoid glass splinters. . . .

• • •

When I opened my eye, I was sitting on an examination table, in daylight.

Someone's hand held open my left eyelid, and the other hand put something round into the socket. It felt like cool glass. It was a new eye, filling out my face and blocking the air that wanted to get at my cheekbones. It fit perfectly, with the right snugness and the right lubrication. I moved my eyes from left to right, and rolled them, and I could feel that they were rolling in unison. A hand put a mirror in front of me, and I looked at myself . . .

I looked different. I looked *better* than I had for days. I was clean-shaven; I had a haircut; my face looked washed and pink, without even any city oils or grime. I batted my eyes at myself, and smiled with all my teeth. My new left eye looked better than the old one had: the old one had been a tiny bit browner than my fleshly eye, but the new one was a perfect copy. I looked closer—yes, it was a *perfect* copy; every capillary in my right eye was duplicated in my left. A slight darkening of the white, near the inside corner, was also duplicated. With each blink the new eye felt more natural, less hard, less foreign; it was definitely better than the old one. Usually the best you can hope for from a glass eye is that you'll forget it's there; you won't feel it bulging or wobbling or itching—and you can always feel it uncomfortably if you stop and think about it. But this one felt actively *good*, as if it was sweetening my face.

"How is it?" said the person standing over me.

"Amazing," I said. I looked up.

It was my employer. The guy in white and blue.

I was so stunned and delighted and terrified and bewildered all I could do was look at him—an activity he must have approved of. But I have no memory of any bodily sensations in those seconds. And all I could think of to say was, "Where am I?"

"What do you remember?" he asked.

"My old eye cracked. I blacked out. I was in Washington Square Park. You were there, weren't you! You were watching me and you rescued me!"

I stepped down onto a rubber footstool, and then a tile floor. I was so overjoyed to be safe, I didn't mind a little amnesia—it added intrigue, and I'd always wanted to have a little intrigue in my life. I knew who I was, that was the important thing; and I knew who was protecting me, I sort of knew.

He was wearing a white hospital gown and white slacks, with a blue stripe down each side. I looked at my arms, and saw that I was wearing an identical suit. The examination room was white, except for blue wall molding. It was a narrow little room with a blue steam pipe in the corner, and the floor sloped toward a window set in a curved wall. Our faces and hands were the only things visible that weren't blue and white. The light from the window brightened one side of my employer's face. His cheek glowed porelessly smooth and tan; his black and springy curls were lined with daylight. He didn't smile—he kept his arms folded, as inquisitive and detached as a doctor—but I was smiling for two. The more I smiled, the better my new eye felt, as if it was getting used to my face muscles; and everything around me looked slightly magnified, like when you put on a pair of reading glasses. I noticed the gleam on my employer's forehead, the oblique shadow alongside his nose; I followed the left-to-right vibrations of his dark eyes as he observed me; and I kept being distracted by the weave of the threads in his tunic, and the shiny spots on his white shoes.

199

It all made me smile, but I didn't feel as if I knew enough to smile about it. It was as if I'd found my face to be smiling ecstatically, independent of me, and I'd agreed to go along with it.

"I knew you'd rescue me," I said. I hadn't known any such thing at the time, but now I felt as if I secretly had. "I can hardly wait to see what else will happen to me.—There's a little white thread stuck to the tip of your left shoe!—You must have looked bizarre," I laughed, for it was beginning not to seem bizarre to me, it was starting to seem normal, "descending on Washington Square Park in that suit, to pick up a derelict with his eye in pieces. I wish I could remember it—why don't I remember it?"

"Because your eye was broken."

And slowly, after a few seconds, I began to nod at this completely normal and comprehensible piece of information. "So I was unconscious? I passed out?"

"No. You were stepping into the street trying to adjust your tie over your head. You don't remember because you'd destroyed your organ of being and watching. You were functioning, but as an automaton, without thinking or absorbing." He sounded the way my ophthalmologist had when he'd tried to make me feel that the loss of an eye was no cause for extraordinary comment. "A cab was turning toward you from the left; it stopped short, and hit the material of your pants leg. I happened to be the passenger in the cab. I brought you here."

"You take a lot of cabs?" I asked.

He shrugged. "It's convenient."

I nodded—then, looking around, I laughed, I felt like a baby looking through a prism. "You've really perfected glass eyes." I rubbed my left eye. It felt too *good*. I wondered how the implanting of a ball of glass could make my whole head—no, my whole body, my whole person—feel cleaner and quicker and healthier, like antibiotics. It was like having a crystal ball stuck in my eye socket. "There's a strand of cobweb forming in that corner by the window. The blue stripe on your jacket looks as if it's been washed exactly four times. So you happened to be in the same cab that stopped in front of me? Of course. That's the way it happened, therefore it's possible." I nodded with enthusiastic understanding. "And you brought me to your secret medical lab. Where are we, in some kind of invisible hospital of another dimension?"

I went over and opened the window, and looked down and up.

I saw wave-shaped walls and funhouse-mirror windows; wrought-iron fire escapes with S-shaped ribs; huge round window boxes and tiny square balconies; gargoyles, awnings, columns, and cone-topped turrets. The bricks were uneven, the protrusions seemed to hang without support, the structure looked like a Victorian wedding cake that was collapsing from decoration. . . .

The exterior of the hotel had been repainted in white and blue.

I stepped back into the room in fright. But I had to go look out again.

In front of the entrance, a sky-blue taxi with a white roof unloaded a passenger. He was wearing a white trenchcoat, and a white hat with a small blue feather in the band. He stuck his hand into the window opening to pay the driver, who was wearing a navy-blue baseball cap with a white Yankee insignia. The cab was then hailed by a young woman, wearing a white down parka with blue arm-stripe, and carrying a white vinyl portfolio. The cab entered the stream of traffic, in which every vehicle was white and blue. I looked down to the street corner, and saw the traffic start up when the light changed from blue to white.

A woman in a white fur coat, walking a poodle, stopped at a white fire hydrant with a blue top. The poodle was black. But it was wearing a white knit sweater with a blue snowman design.

A vendor pushed his frankfurter cart down the street. He wore a white hooded sweatshirt with blue drawstrings, and blue sneakers with white stripes. His umbrella was divided into blue and white pie sections. A thief walked down the line of parked cars, testing doors, hunched inconspicuously in a blue-and-white plaid windbreaker. A prostitute stopped and scratched her thigh through white fishnet stockings. She wore a tiny blue skirt and a bulky white mohair sweater, and she licked her white lipstick. A cripple leaned on clicking metal crutches, his legs dragging, in blue-and-white checkerboard pants. . . .

Everything. Everyone. On the building across the street, white bricks alternated with blue ones. On the building next to it, all the bricks were pale blue and there was white trim on the windows and cornices. The wind that slapped my face was blue and white, and it made my good eye—my right eye, the human one—water.

"I'm not afraid," I said, terrified. I couldn't look back at him, I was too scared. "It's a mystery, but it's your mystery and I trust you." Because the only alternative was to be scared to death. "I can handle it. I mean, look at the walls. Are they scary? Why should they be scary? In fact, they might as well be telling me—I can almost imagine they're telling me—like they're saying, 'Don't be afraid. We're here for your benefit.' "

I heard his footsteps come up behind me, and I ducked in from the window to face him. My adam's apple started to spasm and I knew I was going to cry.

"What's the matter?" he asked.

"Well, nothing, nothing," I wept. "I guess it's still the same world, but now I know more about it. Do the other people know it's this way? I hope they do, so we can talk about it. I mean, is it really like that, or is it just the way I'm seeing?"

"What way are you seeing?" He stepped closer. He pressed his fingers to my forehead, lifted my left eyelid with his thumb, and frowned. I tried to keep my throat from gulping and my eyelid from twitching.

"If they all look like that, they ought to recognize each other, they ought to say hello to each other," I wept.

"Move your eyes from side to side," he said.

"What about my green tie?" I suddenly remembered. I stepped back, and knocked his hand away from my face. My tears made the blue-and-white walls look blurred. "My green tie with tea-stained coats of arms. I like it the way it is; can't I have it back? Can't I keep one thing the way it was? One little thing, it wouldn't hurt the rest of the world, would it? This glass eye feels cool and minty. Soothing waves are spreading through my skull, they're scaring me, make

202

them stop! Just let me see everything blue and white but with my tie staying green. Maybe that way I could get used to the new look." I stepped back farther; I backed into the examination table.

"I'll fix everything," my employer said. "Sit up on the table, please."

I did, and I watched him go to the white dresser with blue knobs. On it was a white case with blue latches. He opened the latches, and inside, on pale-blue velvet, lay eleven glass eyes, and a hollow for a twelfth. They were arranged in three rows of four; the empty place was on the left in the middle row. My employer put on a new pair of white surgical gloves, and picked up the eye that was displayed to the right of the empty hollow. He came toward me.

"I think this will fit you better," he said, in his light foreign accent. "If you'd please take out that one." He gestured at my left eye.

I popped it out into my hand, and it was lifted from my hand, and then a new thing entered my socket. I blinked it into place. My eyelid met a hard and foreign surface that it would have to learn to ignore. When I moved my eyes from side to side, the glass one was a tiny bit slower than the real one. It was at room temperature, warming up to body temperature, and it sent out no sensations of its own.

"How is the fit?" he asked, pulling down my lower lid and inspecting. "Is there anything at all disturbing?"

I shoved him out of the way, ran across the room, and put my hands all over the wall like a blind person.

The grimy, flaking, yellow wall, with dried brown tomato-sauce stains.

I turned around—I spun in circles, looking at things. The chest of drawers was brown, and two of its brown knobs were missing. The steam pipe in the corner was painted metallic, with silvery flakes lying at its base like pine needles under a Christmas tree. The linoleum on the floor was gray, with rings of rust where old cot-wheels must have been. There was a lump running along the middle of the linoleum, and it was stained a darker gray, as if someone had spilled something on it a long time ago. Against the opposite

203

wall, where the examination table had been, there was a bed—a ratty thing with stuffing coming out of a hole in the side of the mattress, and a gray wool blanket with a rip sewn up with purple thread, it was beautiful. Under the bed was—

"My suitcase!"

I pulled it out to the middle of the floor. I knelt in front of it and felt the cloth sides; they had a green-and-red tartan pattern, and it was *clean*. That suitcase had been gray with age from the time I was a boy, but it was clean now. There was a brand-new name tag of black vinyl hanging from the handle; I picked it up and read the I.D. card behind the clear plastic window. It said:

"Rich Redstone

"Being and Watching."

I unzipped the suitcase. I pulled back the plaid cover, and inside I saw:

"My tie!"

It was my forest-green tie with little silver coats of arms, and it was lying on top of a pile of clothes. It had been cleaned, pressed, and folded, and it was sheathed in dry cleaner's polythene. I lifted it up, looked at it front and back, poked my thumb through the polythene and stroked that wonderful dacron-and-cotton blend and pressed it to my cheek and kissed it. "My tie," I crooned to it, and I looked it over for tea stains.

There were none. I was momentarily stunned, but I took up hope. "They've taken your stains away, but I'll put them back on, don't worry, tie." I kissed it up and down, like a woman's arm, tearing the polythene off so I could reach the whole length. I twirled the polythene around for pure joy and flung it against the beautifully vomit-yellow wall, and I squeezed the tie in my hand, and, when I opened it again and patted it flat on the bed, I wept with happiness to see the creases that hadn't been smoothed out. I put it around my neck, outside the hospital gown, and tied it; my fingers were shaking.

"I'll eat spaghetti and meatballs tonight and get sauce stains on it!" I bent down in front of the suitcase and started lifting out the other clothes. "My ivory sweater! I'll eat spareribs and get barbecue sauce on you!" I held it up, rubbed it all over my face like a towel, nuzzled it, kissed it, got its fibers on my tongue, and dropped it on the floor next to me. "My corduroy jacket! I'll lean against some wet paint as soon as I can!" It was neatly folded lengthwise with the arms tucked in. I kissed it, and dropped it in a heap on top of the sweater. I was going to take all my clothes out and inspect them one by one, but I was so overjoyed to see my sweater and jacket that I just kept lifting them up, covering them with slobbery laughing kisses, and dropping them on the dusty linoleum. I kept pausing to lift the end of my tie up and look at it through tears of happiness.

"Thank you," I said to my employer. "Thank you, now I'll keep being and watching all over the place." He was lifting his eye case off the chest of drawers, and was heading for the door. The case was still blue and white, and of course his suit was, too. They now looked loud and incongruous, but only in the same way that royal robes would look loud and incongruous. "Wait a second," I called as he opened the door. "There are twelve eyes—what are the other ones like?"

He stopped, turned around, and looked at me. "Enjoy yourself. It's a pleasure to work with you," he said, and walked out, and closed the door behind him.

Should I have run after him? I've often asked myself that; but I think that, in my confusion and dazed joy, I did right in letting him go. What was I going to do, chase after him and ask all kinds of questions: "Who are you? What world are you from? Who do you work for? Will I ever be like you?" He had rescued me, showed me a vision and then saved me from it, given me belongings cleaned and pressed; I couldn't ask him for much more. Besides, he'd complimented my work! That's the kind of thing that makes you sit back and smile, not chase people. As soon as he walked out, I was filled with a peaceful, knowledgeable feeling, even in my confusion—because look at how much I'd seen already. I knew I wasn't ready for more yet; and I had to trust the evasive one to know when I was ready.

"I trust you," I called out. From all appearances, I was talking to

205

an empty room; but you never can tell. It felt good to return his compliment.

I picked up my clothes from the floor and smiled at them. "Good old tie, good old sweater." Then I almost had a heart attack.

"Money!" I didn't have any. I'm always forgetting the little things.

I had to run after him and ask him what to do. I rushed my arms into my jacket sleeves. You won't catch up to him, I thought. When he wants to be gone, he's gone. You can't call him if he doesn't want to come; but if he wants to come, he's there instantly and you can't keep him away. Nevertheless I started for the door; but then I felt something hard in my inner jacket pocket.

I reached in, and took out my fountain pen.

As soon as I finished gazing at it and kissing it, I unscrewed it; and the hundred-dollar bill inside was so new it had never been folded, just rolled once into a tight cylinder. It was so neatly packed, it was hard to tap out of the pen, but finally I did it, and it dropped into my palm like an egg or an eye, and I kept opening and closing the bill between my two hands, to hear the beautiful baritone snap of new money, and to see the picture of Ben Franklin disappear and appear, the way money itself does all our lives. I was so happy to see this clean, virgin bill that I immediately wanted to take it downstairs and change it for older, more well-used and usable small bills. I intended to buy a racing form without further delay, and, after lunch at the Elephant Coffee Shop, to try my powerfully supported luck at the nearest OTB parlor. I put my hand on the doorknob—

At that same moment, someone knocked on the door.

"Who is it?"

"Voider Brush Man," said a high voice.

19. How Things Stand; or, Don't Mention the Moon

I opened the door.

"Larry!" I said.

We rushed toward each other with a big, brotherly hug; I pulled him into the room and pushed him down to a seat on the bed. He smiled up at me in his anxious-to-be-nice way, and tapped his feet like a little boy who had to go to the bathroom. His clasped hands bounced in his lap. There was a pink milky mustache on his upper lip. He was wearing a Burberry trenchcoat over a gray, window-pane-check Brooks Brothers suit, and on the floor beside his black oxfords was the green vinyl sample case of a Voider Brush salesman.

"What are you *doing?*" I asked.

"I'm back in New York." He smiled, and accelerated his toes.

"I guessed that. What happened, why are you doing this? You've got strawberry ice cream on your lip." I reached out to wipe it off, but he raised his hand to his lip and did it himself. Larry the Self-Reliant. I said, "You're back in New York; so you and Laurie are back together!"

"No, Laurie hates me." He turned his palms up and smiled as if to say, I'll recover. "I called her when I came back, but she never wants to have anything to do with me again except to read my diary. She appreciates my diary as a document of human folly."

"No it isn't!" I said, thinking, Well, I guess it is.

Both of us sighed and shook our heads. Larry rubbed the linoleum from left to right with the sole of one shoe. "I came here to be with my girl friend Jane. She was working at the San Diego Zoo, but a great slot opened up for her at the Bronx Zoo. Anyway, she

207

left, and about two weeks later I'm sitting in San Diego, looking at the marina and saying to myself, 'What am I doing here when everyone I care about is in the place I left?' So I gave two weeks' notice and followed her. They were very upset I only gave two weeks, but I was getting sick of banking anyway."

I tsked, and we both laughed. "So you're living with Jane?"

"No, Jane knows all about animal instincts. Pair-bonding and all that. She knew that when I came back to New York I was really trying to get back to Laurie. I didn't realize that at first, but she told me and I had to agree; she's very bright. She didn't want to be anyone's second choice, and anyway she's living in the Bronx to be near work. How can you live in the Bronx? So here I was, rejected by the person I'd followed, so I went over to see Laurie. Laurie slapped me in the face." He touched his cheek, as if he could still feel it. "From her diary, I never knew she was so jealous about Jane. And of course she blamed me for making her sleep with you." (I blushed.) "When I told her I'd quit my job, though—that was it. She threw me out and told me I was a coward. She said I'd obviously found my rightful place in San Diego but was afraid of it. She doesn't want to speak to me again until I can call her long distance. She was right: as long as she hates me, I'm better off in San Diego, the weather's nicer. But I was already here, and my parents gave me my old room back; so I started sending out resumés—"

"To the Voider Brush Company?"

"That was after no one responded to my resumé. It seems I've blown my opportunity in high finance. No ones wants someone who walked out on a good job for love. I won't tell you what I went through before I found this job—"

"Good, we can skip *that* sort of narrative."

"—but I did end up here."

" 'Enclosed you will please find a list of our best customers.' "

"Hey, right! You know that guy?"

"I interned for Voider, I think I told you once. By the way, how's Zipporah?"

"Who?"

"You never heard of her? I'm shocked, she— Forget it, let's just say you missed a good customer. Gee, Larry, I'm no example, but don't you want to improve yourself?"

He smirked. "Rich, do you see this outfit I'm wearing? I'm the only Voider salesman who dresses like a respectable businessman. I'm also the only Voider salesman with an M.B.A., though naturally I didn't reveal that fact at the interview. I'm not gonna erode the pavement much longer. I have a diabolical career strategy. I'm gonna outclass everyone at Voider. In a couple of months I'll have the branch manager's job; then the regional manager's, and before long I'll be vice-president for sales. I'll be president of the company before I'm thirty, and then my plan begins. I'm gonna revitalize our capitalization and switch to up-to-date Japanese samurai management methods." From his sitting position, he gave a little bow. "I'm checking out companies that we can buy up in related fields. After I take over, we won't be the Voider Brush Company anymore—we'll be Voidco, a home-appliance and personal-products conglomerate. *Then* Laurie will want me back."

"I'd say let's go get some ice cream, but you've already had some," I said.

We looked at each other. I looked away, and smiled as if the knobs on my chest of drawers were slightly and pathetically amusing.

"I gotta get going on my route," Larry said. He stood up, and tugged the folds out of his trenchcoat. "Hey, would you like to see some really nice brushes? In addition to what's here"—he patted the side of his sample case—"I'd love to show you our catalogue, it's got—"

"No, thanks, Larry," I said.

He shrugged without discontentment. "Well, seventy-five percent of our customers are women. I do, however, carry the Bushwhacker line of extra wide natural-horsehair brushes and cowhide shaving strops—"

"No thanks."

He turned away, and now his head was a little bent. I felt bad for him, and as he walked away I said, "Wait. Give me a toothbrush."

209

He practically leaped over to me. It almost made me choke up: in an instant he was opening his sample case on top of the chest of drawers, he was digging out brush after brush, blowing the dust off the plastic cases, thrusting them at me—pink toothbrushes with yellow stars, black toothbrushes with purple polka dots, toothbrushes that changed color with your mood, children's toothbrushes that grew to fit the growing mouth, executive toothbrushes whose handles showed the time in four time zones . . .

"Got any plain toothbrushes?" I asked.

"Wait, wait, I'm looking."

He dug into the case like a dog going at dirt, and threw brush after brush behind him onto the floor. Finally he dumped all the contents out and squatted down to pore over them.

"Here!" he said, lifting up a nice light-blue toothbrush with white bristles. "I knew we had one."

He gave me an order form to sign, and pumped my hand with extreme gratitude while explaining that I would have to wait three weeks for my actual toothbrush, the one in the case being merely a display sample.

"It's always a boost to get that first sale of the morning," he said, giving my hand the last five or six shakes. "By the way, do you happen to have any suede clothing? Our laboratories have developed a new technology in suede brushes—"

"No, thanks, Larry. Really," and I patted him on the shoulder and knelt to help him put his brushes back in the case. A minute later I was sending him through the door. "But let's go to a movie or something next week," I said. "I'm always free."

"Okay, that'll force me to sell a lot of brushes."

He moved on down the hall. With the door ajar, I leaned my right eye out to watch him knock on the doors of lunatics (hallucination-cleaning brushes?), welfare recipients (sneaker-polish kits?), and poets (vocabulary dusters?). Very soon he was finished with our floor, and took the stairway. I took the elevator down to the Elephant Coffee Shop, ate scrambled eggs and bacon and the special week-old coffee, and, while thumping my belly to make it stop complaining, I looked for a telephone. I saw one in the lobby, but someone had put a torch to it as a joke, and the plastic receiver was melted and misshapen into the Elephant Phone. Rather than go back up to my room, I left the hotel and strolled down Eighth Avenue, but after trying three phones I'd found fifteen cents and no dial tones. I stopped in at OTB and bet two dollars on the letter *B*, to win, in each race, and then I said to myself, What the hell, it's only a few blocks away, and since when do I have to call for permission before I visit?

So I pressed the downstairs buzzer at Laurie's loft.

"Hi, kid, how was your Thanksgiving?" I said when she opened the upstairs door.

She grunted in surprise. Then she looked me up and down and smiled in disappointment, because I was the same as ever.

I walked past her into the open area of the loft, and looked at the pictures on the walls, and remembered the things we'd done here, the sweet guilt we'd felt. My shoes squeaked on the polished wood floor. Five vertical windows, as grimy as ever, but with gray November outside. No sunlight coming in, but the papered globe lamps warm overhead.

"I'm not lending you any money," she said.

"That's okay, I have some sure winners at Aqueduct. Listen, why did you throw your lover out?"

"Rich, you remember how complicated things were getting." She stepped away from me and turned her back. "I still think we shouldn't have fucked in the first place. We lost our innocent friendship, our ability to just talk to each other or go places separately—"

"I mean why did you throw *Larry* out?"

She stopped walking away. "I refuse to discuss Lawrence." The tail of her beige blouse shook; she was wearing it out, over jeans, and she was barefoot. Her blond hair was still cut short, and she wore pink lipstick that I suddenly wanted to taste. "Lawrence and I have grown to a new stage in our relationship. We hate each other."

"He doesn't hate you."

"Then he hasn't grown enough yet." She faced me, looking a little ashamed. "I should have left him as soon as his grades started falling. I should never have stood for that from him. It was a signal to me—if he'd still been attached to me, he could have done well in school. When we couldn't get jobs near each other, maybe that was what he really wanted. As for the animal girl, I wish him the best with whatever animal, vegetable, or mineral girl he finds. First he pretends he wants me, then he pretends he wants her, then he pretends he wants me back—"

"He does," I said.

She flipped her wrist at me. "Listen, it's final. It's not a case of maybe we should try again. That's for people who've been going together for six months, two years . . . We know every idea in each other's head, so we know that there's nothing there to go back for. We've used each other up. When you've loved each other for so long, you come to the point of exhaustion. It's like building a skyscraper. You build one story after another, each one is love. First floor is love, second floor is love, et cetera et cetera, hundredth floor is love—what do you have left? What's the antenna on top? The only thing you have left for the antenna is hate."

She plopped down cross-legged on a straw mat, as if resting after making an unassailable argument.

"Oy, Laurie," I said. I was shocked at my language. I didn't want to moralize at her, nor did I think I knew her feelings better than she did. I wanted to get my friends back together, but if she knew it was useless . . . To collect my thoughts, I started browsing through the private gallery on her walls.

"See, I have so much free time by myself, I've been doing art again. You like my new collages?"

I stepped closer to the pictures and said, "Hm," like a genuine art appreciator. Laurie was still doing spoofs of apartment interiors—a rather limited subject, I thought. One of the pictures showed a room dominated by an immense coffee table on which a plateful of raw vegetables, wearing swimsuits, were lining up to dive off a butter knife and into a bowl of dip. Some pieces of broccoli and scallion, wearing big sunglasses, were lounging under toothpick umbrellas on a beach composed of magazines. There was *Grab*, and its sister publication, *Take: The Magazine of Shameless Consumerism*. The issue of *Take* was open to an article, and I read it and my heart jumped.

" 'Consumer of the Month,' " I read aloud. " 'New York House-wife Sells World's Greatest Brush Collection for Two Million Dollars!' "

Under the headline was a black-and-white photo of Zipporah and Baruch Litovsky. They were standing in Zipporah's living room. The central bookcases had been removed, and the steel shelves along the walls were bare. Baruch was grinning enormously, and spreading his arms for the camera as if to measure the unbelievable clear space. Zipporah was smiling shyly, and holding up a brush in the shape of Elvis Presley, connected by a cord to a tiny brush in the shape of a microphone.

The caption said: " 'My wife is a woman of vision,' extols a proud and abashed helpmate, as the collector displays her most treasured possession."

I stood staring at the collage, moving my lips like an idiot while I read. The article said that the Litovskys had been estranged, but that when Zipporah had sold her collection for a record amount Baruch had finally accepted her right to be an independent career wom-an.

" 'As far as I'm concerned, she can keep seeing and being to her heart's content,' " he said. That's *being* and *watching*, I thought; but I was glad the magazine writer didn't stop to explain the cryptic phrase. I kept reading. Farther down the column Zipporah said, " 'I suddenly realized that with all those brushes in the apartment, I had no space to start my new collection of light bulbs. Of *course* I know who bought my brushes; but he wants to remain strictly anony-mous.' "

"Laurie, this is fantastic!" I said.

She said, "Thank you!"

She sprang up and stood beside me to share my vantage point. She look at the collage as if with new eyes. "You think it's really good?"

"I think *you're* really good," I said, and put my arm around her waist.

She shoved her elbow into my rib; and she was the one who yelped.

"Thanks." I straightened up and reinflated my lungs.

"You made me do it. You've made me mad at you; you've made me ask you to leave. See, now you're starting to make me blame you for things. If you stay around, you'll make me blame men for all the sufferings of women. Probably the next thing you'll want to do is apologize and act sweet, and I'm just not prepared to deal with that kind of male bullshit anymore. I've stopped even thinking about sex—" She stopped speaking, and pursed her lips.

"I see," I said.

"If I had an involuntary sexual thought just now, it was your fault for showing up. You're the one with sexual thoughts, and if you're gonna keep having them, you can't stay."

"Okay, no more sexual thoughts," I said, and turned around to look at her pictures again. But I felt her hands on my back—pushing me toward the door.

"I heard a sexual thought," she said.

"No, no, I wasn't thinking sexual thoughts, just friendly thoughts. I was thinking how nice it was to see you again. Please don't kick me out, don't send me back to the Elephant Hotel—"

"Sexual thoughts!" she cried out, like a sergeant in the Sexual Thought Police. She leaned forward to open the door, and her left leg brushed my left leg. . . .

"What is this, is every thought sexual to you or something?" I said.

She pushed me out into the hall. It was one of those factory hallways with glossy gray paint, an iron staircase with black bannister, and a red fire extinguisher hanging next to a freight elevator. From another floor came a metal, hammering sound.

"Tell Lawrence I'm perfectly happy without him," she said, and shut her door behind me. I heard the lock click into place. I pressed the elevator button and heard the pulley ropes start to whir.

• • •

I had good luck with the horses through the fall and winter—good enough, anyway, to pay my bills at the Elephant Hotel, and no better. I was getting to think of the hotel as home. I learned whose screams to investigate and whose to ignore; after I found a drillhole in my bathroom wall and taped it over, I felt a little more at ease on the toilet seat; on Christmas morning, the waitress at the coffee shop slipped me a free bicarbonate with my scrambled eggs. She was a dumpy blond in her thirties with a red lump under her nose, and yellow bowlegs showing under her white dress, and I think she had a crush on me. Maybe she thought I was her someone special; maybe she dreamed about me and waited anxiously for me to come to breakfast every morning. She sneaked looks at me when she was pouring my coffee. Or maybe it was that I was such a mystery. No one knew why I was staying at the Elephant Hotel. I kept mysteriously regular hours. I was suspiciously amiable. I was incongruously healthy. In fact, I wondered about it myself. I had every reason to hate the place, I was alone for the holidays, from my window I saw a pimp pull his girl's shoes off and dig out money from under the insole while she sobbed. I hadn't been meeting the class of people from among whom my true love might spring. I finished a can of beer and put it on the floor. A cockroach came up and sniffed it, then scooted toward the baseboard, and I threw a potato-chip crumb in his path. Uh-oh, I said to myself; I'm an innately humane and decent person. Is that like being retarded?

I went into the bathroom, keeping the light off so I could go with complete peace of mind, and the phone rang. It took me five rings to finish; I zipped up and raced out for the sixth ring; I snatched up the receiver.

"Rich, I want it," she said.

"What?"

"Please, you know what. I want it desperately."

"I thought you weren't having any sexual thoughts."

"This isn't a thought. It's a bodily sensation. I'm not responsible for it. I'm helpless in its grip; if you don't help me return to normal I'll be very mad at you. I've got to become a rational person again; then I can control my sexual thoughts. But if my body is overcoming my rationality . . . I'm practically rubbing the walls, I'm putting the telephone between my legs—hear? How can you do this to me? How can you sit by and laugh while I'm being reduced to an irresponsible state? Please, please, just this once and I'll never bother you again. . . ."

"It's no bother," I said.

215

Running down the cracked and buckling Elephant Stairs, I tried to think of myself as a fireman racing to the rescue of a woman on fire.

"Here I am," I called through Laurie's steel door, and she opened it halfway, jerked me inside with her bare arm, and pulled my pants down in the darkness while high-stepping to rub her legs against my thighs. She wrapped her legs tight around me while we were still standing, and we fell rather than sank to the floor. I thought it would be fun to roll over each other till we reached her bed—but she wasn't interested in fun. She was serious. She bear-hugged me to keep me aligned on top of her; she put one hand on my ass to shove me down in rhythm. Street light fell on us in window-shaped slabs, a car honked its horn, I smelled frying oil from a corner restaurant, Laurie was breathing like a marathon runner, her flesh squeaked sweatily on the cool floor planks, and my arm was getting cramped under her spine, but it was okay because her legs were climbing toward my shoulders as if she was trying to please me. . . .

"Okay, no more sexual thoughts," she said, after I rolled off her, and we were looking together at the invisible ceiling.

"Why no more?" I asked.

"Because it's uncivilized, undignified, embarrassing, and messy. Yuck," she added, to prove her point, and she wiped some cold wet gluey stuff from her thighs onto my belly. Hope, Constance, Grace . . .

"Yow, get that off me," I said.

"See? It's disgusting."

I took her hand in the darkness. I decided that by not saying anything, but merely being gentle and near, I would change her mind.

"Don't hold my hand," she said. "You're complicating our friendship."

"What?" But I let go of her hand.

"We better get dressed, we shouldn't see each other naked," she said.

"We've seen each other already, I believe." I stood up, then dipped down to pick up my pants from around my ankles.

"Beliefs can be deceiving," she said, "because actually what happened just now wasn't between you and me. It was between my genitalia and a convenient object, no offense. We were in a nonhuman, biological state of being. A disgusting state," she remembered to add. "It smells gross in here, open a window."

I sighed and shook my head, to show that I was so fond of her foolishness I'd be willing to make love with her again.

I opened the second window from the left, and stuck my head out to see if anyone passing by looked like my true love.

Laurie went to the bathroom and came back, turned on the TV, and plopped onto her bed with her legs straight in front of her. She was wearing jeans, a bra, and a three-button thermal undershirt that in the TV light turned out to be pale pink. Her short blond hair had been brushed, and, chin down, she was very seriously lifting spoonfuls from a carton of strawberry yogurt. The sight of her made all kinds of sentiments surge up in me, and I wanted to sit next to her, but I knew she would push me away.

"You *can* watch TV with me," she said. "After all, there's nothing wrong with two platonic friends watching the news together."

I shook my head and turned away, with my chin down even though I wasn't spooning yogurt. I wondered what was going on in the world, but I didn't want to watch the news. I stood up and looked out the window, looking down the street, looking at windows, looking up—

"Hey, there's the moon," I said. It was small, hard-looking and angrily white, in the blue-black sky between two rows of factory buildings. I looked at the halo around it, and the gray pits on its face. I knew that the moon was too silly a thing to call Laurie over to look at. But I resolved to look at it alone, and in fact I unbuttoned my shirt to catch the cold breeze. I hadn't taken off my shirt to make love, and it seemed like an omission I had to make up for right away. "The moon, it's hard to believe it still exists," I said. I knew what I meant. "In the old days, people used to talk about the moon all the time. It was in all the poems. It was the standard thing, to look up at the moon and feel a poetic emotion. People always looked at it, because they didn't have so many buildings and lights to look at. Nowadays, if you happen to look up from a street corner

217

or something, and you see the moon, it's a shock. 'My God, it's still there!' It's really there, it's really beautiful, people have stopped thinking about it, they don't even want to explore it, but once in a while, without anyone telling you, you look up from all this shit and you remember. That's why the moon is more beautiful now than when everyone was grinding out poems about it."

The cold air hurt my nipples and made my chest hair stand up; it went down my throat, and I shut my mouth, and breathed deep at the moon, and looked at its halo. I waited to hear Laurie's bedsprings. I waited to hear her voice. I didn't. Finally I held my breath, to take a mental photo of the moon; then I ducked inside and shut the window.

"The moon," I said.

"I heard you." The soles of her feet leaned toward me about an inch, then straightened upright. I could see the orange glow of her TV tubes, through the grille slats in back, and I heard the news-talk and the high-frequency hum that I'd been blocking out. "And here's Twinky McFloss with a story on a subject nice people didn't used to want to talk about. . . ."

"Rich, you'll just have to start getting interested in trivial matters, like buying decent clothes," Laurie said. "Not the meaning of celestial bodies. I mean, *I* respect you, but if you want new people to—"

"Okay, okay, forget I mentioned it," I said, and laughed at myself. Good old realistic Laurie, bringing me back to earth. Maybe I ought to sit next to her after all, in a brotherly way.

I did, and we didn't touch. She was on my blind side, and there was a wall of body heat between us. She was realism and I was folly, and folly tried to sit politely beside realism, asking, Don't I belong here, too? I looked at the TV and smiled, the way TV makes you do when you don't know what's on except alpha waves. We sat in the flickery light.

"There is, however, one group trying to bring the problem as much into the open as possible," Twinky McFloss said. "They call themselves Humans Against Herpes, and I spoke with two of their leaders. . . ."

Debs Goldfish came on the screen.

I scrambled to the front of the bed, and sat palming the edge as if

218

I was preparing to dive into the TV. Debs was sitting at a sidewalk table displaying leaflets outside City Hall Park. She wore a business suit, and a white silk blouse with a white silk ascot. Her eyes sparkled, her long black hair drifted over her cheekbones—and she had eyebrows! She looked great and proud. I looked back at Laurie, then at the screen. Debs was better-looking. My toes drummed the floor. Twinky McFloss asked Debs to tell us her personal story.

"Rhett and I both suffer from Herpes Nine," she said. And the camera panned to someone sitting beside her—an extremely mild-looking young man, bald and with horn-rimmed glasses, who kept wiggling his nose and looking at her like a sick rabbit looking at a prize lettuce. I was horrified. "There was a long time," Debs said, "when we were afraid to talk to anyone about it, or get romantically involved with anyone. I went through a period when the only men I'd get involved with were sordid creeps, to punish myself. There was one young punk, recently, who was little more than an animal—"

"Give me a break!" I shouted, and stood up.

"But now Rhett and I are planning to be married at HAH headquarters. . . ."

The camera showed a close-up of the table. On the table was Debs' hand, clasped in Rhett's.

"What kind of filthy news do they cover on this station?" I shouted, and changed the channel. I glared at Laurie. I blushed with anger. She looked at me inquisitively.

"This is what I call news," I said, for this station was covering the latest press conference of President-elect Jason A. Fleece. He stood under the canopied entrance of a Manhattan hotel, holding the reins of his palomino. The horse was chewing a potted plant, and was enclosed by panes of bulletproof glass, which Fleece walked around to speak to the press, to the consternation of his Secret Service men. His silver sideburns shone under his white cowboy hat, and a guitar was strapped around his neck. Every few seconds, he punctuated his words by strumming a chord, and I admired how one chord sounded decisive and presidential, while the next sounded simple and friendly—one sounded as if it had compassion for the needy, while the next sounded as if it wouldn't back down in a crisis.

"I welcome the chance to answer those questions," he said, with smile lines crinkling, "and let me say for, golly, it must be the millionth time, that at no time did Representative Slice tell me anything about any so-called secret training base or any Scenario Five. Representative Slice has assured me of his commitment to the idea of elected government, and I'm confident he'll be a fine Vice-President. Shucks, how can you blame a guy for trying his hardest to win? Now, if we can change to a lighter subject: yes, it's true, I've got a new guitar teacher, and I think he's helped, don't you?"

The newsmen laughed and applauded.

"We kept getting letters," Fleece said, "from a young man here in the East who kept saying my guitar was out of tune. I said to one of my staffers, Shucks, if he's got such a sensitive ear, maybe he can use it to help his country. We ran a routine check, and found that he'd been unable to find work for some time, just plumb ran out of opportunities. But I can report to you today that a fine young American, my friend Norm Goldfish, is now off the welfare rolls and onto the White House staff." Fleece strummed a rapid, triumphant chord; then his crinkly smile became a crinkly frown. "Wait a second." He bent his ear to the strings, and started adjusting one of the tuning pegs.

"Oh, no," I said, and flipped the channel.

But on the next channel there was also a videotape of Jason A. Fleece; it looked like he'd be unavoidable from now on. Well, I thought, let's hope Norm's influence is limited to the sphere of music. Although I recalled that Fleece's Secretary of State had started out as his barber . . .

I looked at the screen to see what our leader had done on this channel. He was walking out of a very expensive-looking Upper East Side brownstone, waving to the crowd with his cowboy hat, and swinging into the stirrups of his bulletproof horse. Then Wes McClean came on screen and said, "And so, in a way, this first foreign-policy mission of the President-elect takes place on American soil, where he spoke to the visiting El Presidente in an effort to ease tensions in the small but strategic nations of North-North-Central Eastern South America. The meeting was termed 'frank but not too frank' and 'forthcoming and possibly outspoken but giving no immediate cause for either optimism or gloom.' President-elect Fleece presented El Presidente with a pair of maracas and a set of flamenco guitar strings, to symbolize the U.S.'s deep concern about the national integrity of North-North-Central Eastern South America. In return, El Presidente presented President-elect Fleece with an autographed copy of his autobiography, *The Liberator of His People*, which, predictably, is the number-one best-seller in his homeland. In fact, it's required reading for the entire population. . . ."

I collapsed onto the bed. My forehead was all sweaty, I felt cold, the ceiling swirled.

Laurie crawled over to me and put her hand on my forehead. "What's wrong with you?"

"I'm famous," I babbled. "I'm famous, I'm a best-seller, Laurie, I'm famous, I'm required reading, Laurie. No. I'm not famous, they don't know it's my book. I wrote it, but they don't know I did. Laurie, what should I do? Well, what do I care about fame? Laurie, it's not fair! They don't know it's mine! They're all reading my book, isn't it wonderful?"

"Wes McClean, News Five," said the TV; and over Wes' shoulder, standing in front of the embassy stoop, in the crowd that had gathered on the sidewalk, was a stern, pencil-mustached, history-conscious face—

"Victor!" I called; and suddenly, although I was breathing fast, it seemed as if I couldn't possibly get enough air to fill my lungs. I kept breathing faster, and trying to get more air, but everything was getting pale, and it started to spin.

Falling backward onto the mattress seemed like the most glorious sensation in the universe. A few seconds later, waking up with Laurie's plump little hand slapping my face became the nicest sensation in the universe. Then she got a glass of water and trickled it all over my face, in patterns. It was very thoughtful of her.

I rubbed my face a lot, and felt alive again and got the water off. Soon my breathing was regular and I could sit up, though everything was still a little too bright, and objects tended to be surrounded by dance-choruses of light.

"Laurie, I wrote that book for the Flimes and now it's required reading. What should I do, what should I do?" I felt like asking that question forever, but of course I had to stop.

"I always wondered why you didn't try to write for real," she said.

Her comment sobered me instantly. I set my lips tight, and pressed my thumbs together.

"I can't invent stories," I said. I sighed in despair. "No, I'm a reader, not a writer. I'm okay with words, and I like books, but I'm lazy, and especially, I don't have that thing—that gift of invention. If I ever wrote a book, it would have to be ridiculously simple, just telling exactly what had happened to me with nothing made up—"

"So?" she asked.

I licked my lips and thought about it.

Then she pushed me off her bed.

"What are you doing?" I asked.

"Stop trying to look sexy. It's not gonna work again tonight."

"I wasn't; I was thinking. Cut it out, I'm not trying to assault your virtue."

But of course she was right; I was trying to get to her.

"Time to go home," she told me; and she ran ahead of me, opened the door, threw my shoes into the hall, and gave me an amiable kick in the back of the leg. I took the stairs to the street, and walked home under rows of fire escapes and black windows, in the cold, toward the moon. . . .

● ● ●

Four months later, I'm looking at a sunrise moon from my window at the Elephant Hotel. It's a dusty-white half moon in a pale-blue sky; bravely and shyly it hangs around where it no longer belongs, for the sake of us moon-lovers. The sunlight on the building across the street is expanding to the lower floors. The light is so strong on the tan bricks, the texture seems to jump out at you. The street lamp downstairs is flickering weak and pink when it should be off—it's got a broken photoelectric cell. A dark-green car drives away from its parking space and abandons the moon reflection that was in its windshield. I've been up all night, at Laurie's place, and when her alarm clock rang I came back here and made a cup of coffee on my hot plate and looked out the window to do a little work. I'm still being and watching, and since writing is only my hobby, I don't have to worry about it conflicting with my main job. Apparently my employers don't mind; I still win enough to pay my hotel bill. On the other hand, I'm not winning enough to live at the Pierre.

I didn't have much confidence at first. It had been so long since I'd taken a literature course that I felt I had no right to even put a sheet of paper into the typewriter. I had to get some credentials first, just to feel better about it. So I applied to one of those writers' conferences given by the Academy for Serioso Letters. But they turned me down, because my old mentor Professor Blatt wouldn't recommend me. When I sent him my request, he wrote back:

> DEAR MR. REDSTONE,
>   I remember all too distinctly a conversation I had with you, and I sincerely doubt whether a student who has expressed such violent contempt for the masters of modern fiction would wish to profit from the intellectually honest give-and-take of an advanced seminar. . . .

Profit? The goddamn seriosos were going to take two hundred a week in tuition; all I wanted was a few pointers on lofty narrative technique. I was heartbroken—I thought I'd never be able to even write a postcard again. Luckily, that same day I saw a magazine ad for a correspondence course given by the Funny Name School of Characterization. *They* accepted me. Maybe they didn't teach me much, but, on the other hand, I had the satisfaction of thinking I was ahead of them; and they gave me a six-by-nine-inch printed diploma that I taped to the wall, and that I look at on moonless days when I need confidence.

Last night I took the manuscript to Laurie for criticism. She had to read one of Larry's diary excerpts first, so I was surprised she could finish my script in one night; but she's dedicated to us. Besides, she confessed afterward that she skipped all the parts about her. She liked learning about my encounters with people like the Flimes, and *&?# and Jonathan Done and Skip Space and all the rest, and she had to admit not only that I had an interesting life, but that I sort of had the right to want to live this way. Then I asked her what she thought about the description of my search for Novella Swan.

"Oh, fine, fine." She nodded grimly. "I know you have to put that in, since you're writing about what really happened to you. If I can just point out a grammatical error here . . . some sloppy wording there . . . do you really need this phrase? . . ."

In my best interests, she didn't leave a word about Novella unscathed. She probably did improve it, too.

Laurie and I are good friends. We sleep together whenever we can't stand it anymore, but we know that neither of us is right for the other. We each have another, better love: she, the one she rejected, and I, the one I haven't found. In the meantime it's good to be able to trust someone so different from me. In true Laurie fashion, she's already making big plans for me:

"We should find some starving Ph.D.," she said, while we were sitting on one of her straw mats, "and have him write articles explicating your profound themes—"

"Oh, come on. I'm writing about my life. My book will have as much meaning as life does. If life has meaning, my book will have the same meaning. If life doesn't have meaning, why should I try to impose some artificial meaning on it? Actually, I'll tell you the meaning. I've written about trying to find Novella Swan. Maybe she'll read it, and recognize herself . . ."

Then I felt a fingernail running up and down my back, just to the left of my spine. "You can wait for her here," she said.